"Ma, you got any whiskey at your place?" I asked.

She squinted at the road while she thought about it.

"I might have some bourbon," she said.

I almost laughed in her face. She knew goddamn well exactly how much Jack was left in the bottle and how many tall boys of Bud were in the refrigerator. She used to keep tabs on me and Gary since we were in junior high, used to check her inventory every night before she went to work. That's why I started smoking pot. And, I guessed, why Gary did every other drug he could find.

"Maybe a couple of Buds in the refrigerator," she said.

I laughed—it popped right out of my mouth like a jack in the box. I leaned my head back on the seat and laughed like a clown while she looked at me, confused.

"What is it? What's so funny with you?" she kept saying over me, smiling her half-smile, like she was getting ready to laugh too.

"Nothing," I said, wiping my eyes with the heel of my hand. "Nothing, Mama, I'm just so glad to see you."

Also by Louisa Luna

Brave New Girl

CROOKED

LOUISA LUNA

POCKET BOOKS

New York   London   Toronto   Sydney   Singapore

This book is a work of fiction. Names, characters, places and incidents are products of the author's imagination or are used fictitiously. Any resemblance to actual events or locales or persons, living or dead, is entirely coincidental.

An *Original* Publication of MTV Books/Pocket Books

POCKET BOOKS, a division of Simon & Schuster, Inc.
1230 Avenue of the Americas, New York, NY 10020

Copyright © 2002 by Louisa Luna

MTV Music Television and all related titles, logos, and characters are trademarks of MTV Networks, a division of Viacom International Inc.

All rights reserved, including the right to reproduce this book or portions thereof in any form whatsoever. For information address Pocket Books, 1230 Avenue of the Americas, New York, NY 10020

ISBN 978-0-7434-3995-4

First MTV Books/Pocket Books trade paperback printing May 2002

10 9 8 7 6 5 4 3 2

POCKET and colophon are registered trademarks of Simon & Schuster, Inc.

For information regarding special discounts for bulk purchases, please contact Simon & Schuster Special Sales at 1-800-456-6798 or business@simonandschuster.com

Art direction by Lance Rusoff and Deklah Polansky
Design by Lance Rusoff
Illustrations by Evan Hecox

Printed in the U.S.A.

for Florence Buriloff Benedetti
and Mary Buriloff Treanor

ACKNOWLEDGMENTS

Many thanks to Clement Joseph; Stephanie Tade and Ruth Kagle; Greer Kessel Hendricks and Suzanne O'Neill; Ed Mullins III; Stuart Hanlon, Esq.; Mary Switzer; Matt Lamb, Marvin Resnikoff, and Lynn dela Merced; Detectives Patrick J. Early and George Dejesus; Officer Craig Boyer; and always, Norm and Sandra Luna.

CHAPTER

1

My mother picked me up in Holding and smelled like baby powder and Vaseline lotion when she hugged me. I could only hug her back with one arm because I had a plastic bag with my things under the other. She'd brought me the clothes I was wearing—jeans and a tank top, like what she had on except her tank top was tie-dyed, and her jeans were so tight I could see the skin of her stomach hanging over the rim.

She took my arm and asked if I was ready to go, and I looked back at Big Jim and Christian Haran from the P.B. Jeannie called him Christmas Hardon.

"Good-bye, Melody," he said seriously, like I was a kid leaving the principal's office.

I could imagine him saying that bit, too, saying, Life is about choices, kids. Do you know that smoking causes cancer? That's right, it can kill you. Do you know that it costs the school money to clean that spray paint off the wall? Money that could be spent for better books and greener lawns and food that doesn't taste like assholes.

I nodded at him. I didn't say anything to Big Jim, and he didn't say anything to me. He was trash, never helped me or anyone else unless something was in it for him and his dick. He stared right back, pretty smug, like he was saying, You can't touch me, little girl. I caught him looking at my mother's ass, too.

We were let out by two G's I didn't recognize, probably because they only worked back here. They looked right through me, didn't say anything when my mother said, "Thank you." One was Mexican and saw *juera* on my forearm, puffy and red, done with a razor the first week I was here. *You some tough white girl. You ain't shit in here, Mami.*

We walked down another hall with green walls and confetti linoleum, with wide windows where I could see the fence and part of the yard, but no one was out there now. My mother sped up, cowboy boots clacking along, swinging her hips. We got to the end, to the visitors' office, through a pea-green door with a tiny window in it, and we went up to another man behind a glass plate, like at the post office.

He slid her the clipboard through the tiny slat at the bottom. She leaned over, got as close as she could to the page without her nose touching it and popped her head back up again.

"What time is it now?" she said.

The man craned his head around to look at the clock and said, "11:28."

She scribbled 11:28 on the sheet and signed her name, big round bubbles like she was in the sixth grade: Sally Akers.

"You have a good day," she said, and then she winked at him.

He didn't know how to respond. He just smiled weirdly and looked at her like she was crazy. Then he looked at me.

"Do I have to sign out?" I asked.

He pulled the clipboard back, almost defensive, like he didn't want my greasy paws on his nice two-dollar clipboard and fancy computer sign-in sheet. He leaned forward and said through the hole in the glass, "No, they already know you're leaving today." He was smirking, too. Funny guy.

My mother tugged at my shirt and said softly, "Come on, baby." I let her pull me, turned around and followed her out, and another G held the door open for us in a polite way. He didn't look at me either, but straight out at the path. Just seeing it like that in the sun, you would almost think this was a nice place. Concrete and stone mix, polished and shiny, which wound and curved for a few yards with patches of grass on either side. We followed the path down, and then we were at the fence, and another G, the last, opened it for us. I didn't even look at him.

I stepped into the parking lot and heard the fence rattle closed behind me. That's what Jeannie said to listen for. All you wanna do is hear that shit close, Green, she said. I felt a warm breeze blow, and I could feel the heat from the asphalt floating up my jeans. They were too big. They used to fit pretty snug on me, but now they hung a little on my hips, and I had to roll up the cuffs at the bottom.

The sun was hot on my shoulders—I knew I'd burn soon if I didn't get in the car. I was always a pale thing and got pink after a couple of minutes out, red after an hour. Not like my mother, or my brother, Gary. Both of them tanned easy.

"What're you dragging your feet for?" my mother said, standing at her car, looking through her huge purse.

CROOKED

I caught up and stood at the door of her hatchback while she found her keys and unlocked the doors. The car smelled like leather and my mother's lotion, and it was stuffy. I rolled the window down.

"Roll that up. I'll put the a/c on soon as we get going," she said.

I rolled it back up and felt sweat forming on my forehead, and my shoulder started to sting from the sun coming in through the window. My mother tossed her purse in the back seat and put on her wide sunglasses, checked herself out in the mirror and touched her hair. I could see mealy white spots of deodorant on her underarm.

She turned to me and looked like a panda with those big glasses and said, "Let's get out of here, right?" She smiled her flirty half-smile, so I could only see a few teeth, specks of dark pink lipstick on the tips.

I smiled at her and then looked back as we pulled out of the parking lot at the fence, the squat towers. I watched it all shrink in the mirror, and my mother switched on the air-conditioning, and it blew out hot dusty air.

"It'll cool down in a second," she said.

I nodded and coughed; sweat dripped down my legs. We came to the security-lot booths, the dayman in blue pants and shirt, hat like a cop. My mother pulled her "V" card from the windshield and handed it to him.

"Thanks, hon," she said.

"Welcome," said the guard.

He flipped a switch, and the beam raised up. We turned onto the road and headed for the highway, and I wanted to stick my head out the window like a dog and let the air dry my teeth out, but the air-conditioning was starting to feel good so I didn't move. I leaned my head back, closed my eyes, and for the first time in three years, I fell asleep with no problem, holding everything I owned in a plastic bag on my lap.

We stopped in Newman to get gas and food. My mother suggested Lyon's, and I said I didn't care. I would've settled for three or four of those AM/PM bean burritos at that point.

I lagged behind while we made our way through the parking lot and looked up at all the big fast-food signs, high up so that people could see them from the road. I stared at the logos: McDonald's arches, the weird Carl's Jr. happy star face, the Kentucky Fried Chicken crazy old man. Bright colors, the kind you'd see in baby toys, big chunky plastic: yellow, red, purple.

I followed my mother into the Lyon's and looked around at the plastic plants hanging from the ceiling, wide shiny leaves. The hostess came up to us in a brown St. Pauli Girl get-up and asked how we were today. I looked at my mother.

"Just great, thanks," she said.

"Two for lunch?" the hostess asked, smiling big.

"Yes, ma'am," my mother said.

"Right this way."

She led us to a booth. I saw a family of four eating ice cream, the father holding the baby in his lap. The baby was covered in pink ice cream; it was smeared on his lips and fingers. Dougie loves strawberry, yes he does, the father said, like he was talking to a puppy. I heard waitresses taking orders, putting down checks. Thank you. Have a great day. Come back soon.

I slid in on the smooth brown leather, and the hostess handed us huge menus. My mother laid hers down in front of her, open, like it was a newspaper, so I did the same. There were at least eleven or twelve shiny plastic pages with big block writing, and so many categories: The Sandwich Board, The Salad Bin, The Bread Basket. I didn't know where to start.

"It's between a chef's salad and the turkey club for me," my mother said, closing her menu. Then she started fiddling with the bracelets on her arm. "I like to make the decision right on the spot when the waitress asks me, and then—whatever comes out of my mouth I figure is the one I wanted more." She winked at me. "There's some kind of psychological thing about it."

I must've looked confused because she leaned over and looked down at my menu, squinting.

"What's it between for you?" she asked.

I had no idea: hamburger, cheeseburger, bacon burger, turkey-bacon burger, Texas-style burger, Cali burger, veggie burger, roast beef on a roll, spicy chicken on a stick, taco salad, Cobb salad, crispy oriental-chicken salad, linguine with clam sauce, meatloaf, broiled scrod, foot-long hot dog, fruit plate, grilled cheese, western omelette, tomato surprise, tomato soup, tuna melt, Philly cheese steak, and lots of scrumptious sides to choose from. I hadn't even gotten to the page with the drinks on it.

"I don't know," I said. "There's so much stuff."

My mother patted my knee. "A lot more variety than you're used to."

She said it like I'd been at summer camp.

I knew I shouldn't order meat because I hadn't eaten any in two-and-a-half years. The meat in Staley was bricks of brown cow shit, chewy and thick enough to make you gag. I knew it was dumb to jump right in, that my stomach couldn't take it, but I could smell the burgers frying up in the kitchen every time someone pushed through the swinging door, and they smelled good as goddamn rain.

I ordered a hamburger, rare, and almost passed out thinking about it.

"Didn't you quit eating meat?" my mother asked.

She'd flipped out when I told her that. She said my hair would fall out and my teeth would chip off and I'd get horrible skin if I didn't eat meat. I told her I wasn't worried about those particular things just then.

"Yeah, the meat in Staley was shitty," I said.

"Right," she said. "You gotta build your strength back up," she said, squeezing my knee.

I nodded, even though I knew I was pretty physically strong. I'd been doing a lot of push-ups and sit-ups, but it was hard to build up any kind of real muscle for a long time because I didn't eat very much. Still, me and Jeannie and a couple of the other Reinas would try to see who could do the most. We'd do push-ups until our arms felt like applesauce.

Then came the food. My plate was thick and oval and covered with a pile of fries, wide like tongue depressors, and a burger heavy as clay. Why was everything so big here? Even my mother's salad was in a huge glass bowl filled to the top with square blocks of cheese and ham.

"What's wrong, baby?" she asked, starting in.

"Everything's so big," I said.

She nodded but didn't really get it.

"They give you healthy portions here," she said.

She sounded like a TV commercial. We give folks healthy portions here at Lyon's. I picked up my burger and took a bite, and it was perfect, so rare I could taste the juice in my throat. For a second, the meat felt fleshy in my mouth, like somebody's finger, but then I had it on my tongue, and it was thick and soft and just about the best thing I ever tasted. I felt my stomach turn a little bit, but I didn't care and couldn't stop.

"Well, you sure showed that who's boss," my mother said when I was done.

She'd only made a tiny dent in her salad. I could still taste the meat in my mouth and thought about ordering another one, but my stomach didn't feel well at all. It was gurgling like a baby.

"You all right?" my mother asked.

"Yeah, I'm fine. Can I get some cigarettes and meet you at the car?"

"Sure thing," she said, reaching into her purse.

She handed me a ten and said, "Get me a pack of Merits, right?"

I stood up and started to walk out.

"Hey, Mel," she said.

I turned around.

"Don't be shocked at the price. They're expensive as shit now," she said. And another wink.

"Okay," I said, and I gave her the thumbs up. If she was going to keep winking, I was going to start giving the thumbs up.

I walked outside and across to the Mobil Station, into the little store, and I started getting sharp pains in my gut. I put my hand on my belly and stood up straight as I could—sometimes that helped, but not now. I went up to the counter and stood behind a woman with her crying kid pulling at her shorts.

"You better quit it, y'hear?" she said.

I pinched the skin on my stomach under my tank top, my face starting to feel hot.

"You're not getting any Twix cookie bars unless you shut your mouth right now," the woman said.

She signed off on her gas card, and the kid kept screaming, his face red and drippy.

"All right, that's it, I've had it with you," she said, picking him up sideways like he was a suitcase. She carried him off, saying, "Your father lets you do every damn thing."

I stepped up and asked the counter guy for cigarettes. My stomach turned and flipped, and I stared at the wrinkly hot dogs turning on their metal rollers and felt my lunch start to come up. The kid behind the counter put the cigarettes down, and I slid him the ten, feeling like I was about to lose it.

"Bathroom," I said.

He handed me a key attached to a long plastic plank that said Twizzlers Make Mouths Happy and casually pointed outside. I grabbed the smokes and ran, covered my mouth, the kid behind the counter yelling something to me but I didn't catch it. I flipped the door open and ran around the corner, messed with the key for a second and got in there quick.

All it took was one whiff of the piss in that bathroom to send it up. I tossed my whole burger and felt it slam the back of my teeth. Then I flushed and sat down, leaned my head on the cool gray tiles and stared at the bowl. I rinsed my mouth out at the sink and put some water on my face and a little in my hair and walked back outside.

I brought the kid the key, and he said, "You forgot your change." He was helping someone else, a woman with a tight white jumpsuit. He didn't look at me when he spoke, slid the dollars and coins across the counter with two fingers like they were too heavy for him to pick up.

"Thanks," I said, and I wiped the change off the counter with my hand.

CROOKED

I left and crossed the gas station lot, packing both boxes against my palm. I stepped over the grassy divider into the Lyon's parking lot and found my mother's car. She was already in there, putting on lip gloss. She held the little wand between her thumb and forefinger and waved it at me.

I got in and handed her the cigarettes.

"Thanks, baby," she said.

"I already packed them," I said.

She reached into her purse and pulled out a small bottle of lotion, squeezed some out and rubbed her hands together hard and fast.

"You want?" she said, holding the bottle by the neck.

"No thanks."

"Right. You always had such great skin."

I looked down at my cut-up hands. There wasn't a lot of moisturizer at Staley, and it was so hot and dry most of the time. My cuticles were white and raw, nails bitten down, skin flaking off my fingertips like paint. I looked at the little dot scars on my left hand near my thumb, where I got stabbed with a fork. Hurt like a mother, and I sat straight-faced. The first time Jeannie thought I was okay.

"Yeah, Ma, I'll take some," I said.

She handed it to me and started up the car. I squeezed some lotion out, the bottle burping and spitting, and then it came out cool on my hands, and I rubbed them together, and it got sticky between my fingers in the tiny web parts. My mother cracked her window and pulled out one of her cigarettes. I unwrapped my pack, and my hands made the plastic greasy. I lit one.

"You smoking menthols now?" my mother asked.

"Yeah."

She shook her head. "Never knew how people could smoke those things," she said.

People, I thought. She's wondered this about hundreds and hundreds of people.

"They were all that were around at Staley," I said, flipping the box over in my hand.

She nodded, and we were quiet. I forgot about the puke taste in my mouth and just felt the prickly cold mint.

"Don't they burn?" she asked, touching her neck lightly.

"No, not really."

She nodded again, said quietly, "They always burned me. Always scratched my throat up."

I nodded and looked out the window. Big brown and yellow empty stretches between the towns. Huge sky, no clouds anywhere. Every once in a while a bunch of dust would blow through the vents.

"I think there's glass in them," my mother said after about five minutes.

"What? Glass in what?" I said.

"In those Newports. All menthol cigarettes, they have glass in them."

"Hey, Mom, you don't have to smoke them," I said, getting a little sick of this number.

"I know. I was just saying I don't care for them, right?"

"Fine. *I* do."

"Fine. No problem," she said, her voice high.

I balled my fist up and tapped it on my lap, thinking she would drive me to drink. Then I started thinking about drinks in general. I closed my eyes and thought about Irish whiskey on ice burning a hole in my tongue.

"Ma, you got any whiskey at your place?" I asked.

She squinted at the road while she thought about it.

"I might have some bourbon," she said.

I almost laughed in her face. She knew goddamn well exactly how much Jack was left in the bottle and how many tall boys of Bud were in the refrigerator. She used to keep tabs on me and Gary since we were in junior high, used to check her inventory every night before she went to work. That's why I started smoking pot. And, I guessed, why Gary did every other drug he could find.

"Maybe a couple of Buds in the refrigerator," she said.

I laughed—it popped right out of my mouth like a jack-in-the-box. I leaned my head back on the seat and laughed like a clown while she looked at me, confused.

"What is it? What's so funny with you?" she kept saying over me, smiling her half-smile, like she was getting ready to laugh, too.

"Nothing," I said, wiping my eyes with the heel of my hand. "Nothing, Mama, I'm just so glad to see you."

"Well, I'm glad to see you, too, darlin'," she said.

I smiled back at her, didn't want her to think I was having a joke on her. We were both quiet again and looking straight ahead. I threw my cashed cigarette out the window and watched it skip and tumble down the road in the side mirror.

My mother had moved to a new apartment since I'd been in Staley. The old one was in Marin City, but they'd pummeled the whole complex down to dirt and put up an outside mall, she told me. Her new place was in Mill Valley and looked like a Holiday Inn, the way you took an elevator up, and it let you out into a hallway but you were still outside.

"Here we are," she said when she pulled into the lot.

She took her glasses off and grabbed her bag, snatched up the plastic ribbon from her cigarettes, and mine, too.

"Do you have a nice view, Ma?" I asked, following her around the car.

"Hell no," she said, laughing. "I'm on the ground floor. You think I got rich?"

"Do you have windows?"

"Oh yeah, they just look out on the shrubs and underbrush out there. The light's not too bad, though."

We came to her door. 1D.

"It's a nice building," I said, thinking I should say something polite.

"Thanks, baby," she said, not really listening, opening the door.

I followed her into the living room, and everything was tan. Tan carpet, tan curtains, tan couch. I slid my shoes off and set my plastic bag on the kitchen counter, and I peeled off my socks, all wet at the tips and the heel from my sweaty feet, and I dug my toes into the rug.

My mother pulled back the curtains, and I could see a lot of low leafy shrubbery outside. It seemed like the ground apartments were built in a little bit because the rest of the building hung over like an awning and blocked out most of the light. There were also a couple of stout gray columns holding the building up. They made me nervous.

I sat on one of the tan bar chairs with a twisted wire back while my mother cleaned up. She took a rag from the handle of the refrigerator and started wiping down the coffee table in the living room.

"Come on, Ma, the place looks great," I said.

"I know, I know," she said, staring at the table. "I just wanted everything to look perfect for you."

CROOKED

The truth was, she wanted everything to look perfect for *her*, but I didn't care one way or the other—the carpet could've been covered with piss and it still would've been nicer than Staley.

The cabinets looked like the ones in our kitchen in Tacoma that we had growing up. For a second, I thought that might be why she took this apartment. They had black metal S's nailed on.

"I'm going to jump in the shower," my mother said, unbuttoning her jeans. "And I've got to get to work."

"Right."

She went into the bathroom and left the door open.

"Where do you work nights, again?" I said.

"This restaurant called The Barge. You'd like it. It's all seafood. Not one thing on the menu doesn't have seafood in it," she called.

I watched her take her tank top and bra off. Watched her examine her breasts and tug at the skin at the top to see what she'd look like with firmer tits. She'd been checking herself out in mirrors since I was a kid. Pulling at her eyes, sucking her stomach in, practicing smiles and kisses. There were always splintered lipstick smudges on the mirror in the bathroom. Now she let down her ratted hair and turned away.

I got off the stool and went into the little kitchen and opened the fridge. There was a pizza box, three cans of Bud, two bottles of Bud Light, pickles, and milk.

"When's the last time you went shopping, Ma?" I yelled.

"Huh?" she said. "Shopping? For food? I'm not sure. I've been on the Slim-Fast plan for a couple of weeks," she said. Then the shower blasted on.

She'd been on the Slim-Fast plan for a couple of weeks for as long as I could remember. I cracked a tall boy and went back into the living room and opened the tan wardrobe. There were clothes. I pulled out a pair of gray work pants and dropped them on the table, then a shirt, plain white, button down, short sleeves. It was too small to be a man's. There were jeans with a tear in the knee and a hole right under the ass, a yellow T-shirt that said, "Nacho Mama's," and black pants, and a small skirt. And a black dress with a long curvy neckline.

I sat on the couch and stared at all of it. The Nacho Mama's shirt was Gary's. He got it when we were sixteen, seventeen. I could see my hands through it, the threads were so thin, and it smelled like dust and clouded up my nostrils when I held it to my nose. I dropped it and coughed.

I sifted through some of the other things, put my hands in the pockets of the pants, sniffed at the collars like a dog. I pulled the work pants out and walked in front of the sliding glass doors. I held the pants in front of me and stared at the weird reflection. It made me look like a ghost.

My mother came out of the bathroom wearing a sundress cut low across her chest, and I stared at her freckled cleavage for a second. Her hair was wet and stringy, and she was brushing it out hard, ran the brush smooth near her roots and tore it through the tips.

"You found your stuff, huh?" she said.

"Yeah," I said, and I held the pants up. "I forgot all about these. I like them."

"I bought you some new underwear, too. They're in there," she said, pointing to the wardrobe drawers, and then she went back to the bathroom.

"Thanks," I said.

I opened the drawer and saw a few pairs of flowered bikini underwear and picked one up, rubbed it between my fingers. My hands still hurt; the skin was so dry and flaky, it made me think the underwear was the softest thing I ever felt. I unfolded them and stared at the little yellow bow on the front.

"I hope those fit okay," my mother said.

"They're great," I said. "They're so soft."

"What?"

"Nothing."

I grabbed my beer and went to stand in the doorway of the bathroom while she put on her makeup. Sweat gathered on her forehead from the steam, but she rubbed base right over it with a flat face pad. She dabbed her lips with a dark pink lipstick that matched the color of her heels and the rosebuds on her dress.

"You can order Chinese if you want," she said, blotting her lips on the pad.

"I'm not real hungry."

"Come on now," she said. "You haven't eaten since that hamburger."

"I know. My stomach's a little nervous."

She dipped a mascara wand in and out of its tube. Super-Lash, it read. She brushed it on dainty.

"Why don't you call Helen Healy?" she asked.

I sighed loudly and took a sip of beer.

"Well, sor-ry," she said.

"I haven't talked to her in years, Ma, not since before I went in," I said.

She opened a compact of eyeshadow, two columns of bright and dark powder, and she picked up the matted swab and rubbed brown on her lids.

"I just don't want you to be lonely your first night back," she said, reaching for the hair dryer.

"Don't worry, Ma."

Then she turned on the dryer, loud as a lawn mower, and I went back to the kitchen and opened up some cabinets and found some flour and a jar of olives and her Jack Daniel's. I grabbed the olive jar and opened it, pulled out one after another. They floated in warm pale juice and tasted slippery, swishing around in my mouth before they slid down my throat like little fish. I stuck two on my fingertips. Little English guards.

My mother came back out with her purse slung over her shoulder. She'd bunched and ratted up her hair again, piled it on her head, and it looked like straw.

"How do I look?" she said, holding her arms up.

I smiled and gave her the thumbs up.

She winked and opened her closet by the door, pushed clothes aside quickly, hangers scraping the bar.

"If you get lonely, you can go to the 3 A.M. Club; it's only a couple of blocks away, right?" she said.

"Right."

She pulled a sweater from the closet and hung it around her shoulders, walked over to me and pinched my forearm.

"All right, you," she said softly. "This is crap. You should go out, kick up your heels, baby," she said, lifting up her arms, snapping like a flamenco dancer.

I tried to smile.

"Your loss," she said.

"Yep," I said.

Then she headed for the door.

"Have a good night. I'll be home late—all the sheets and stuff are right next to the couch."

She stopped to stare at me and had this tender nice look in her eyes.

CROOKED

"Don't drink all my Jack," she said in a low voice.

I laughed and said, "I won't."

She left, and I finished my beer and the olives and started putting away the clothes I'd dumped out. I held the Nacho Mama's T-shirt again and thought about Gary. I used to think about him at Staley when I couldn't sleep, twisting around on the mat, listening to crazy Ria Diaz talk Spanish in her sleep. My mother said she always took an alternate route when she's near San Quentin and not visiting because it was too much for her to drive by it and see signs for it, knowing Gary's in there.

I flipped around on the TV awhile and got bored and tired so I shut it off and turned off the light. Pulled a sheet over me and couldn't sleep, stared at the red digital numbers on the clock radio on the coffee table. I turned on my side, and the couch gave, soft as Play-Doh, sank down wherever I moved to.

I tried not to think about anything, but that never worked for me. I thought about Jeannie saying, Too bad you can't be a real Reina, Green. I said it's okay. Thought about her and Ara and Lina and Ria Diaz sleeping hard on their racks.

And Gary, too—I saw him in my head with wet hair, leaning back on the pillow. Wearing the Nacho Mama's shirt under a ratty corduroy jacket. Cuffs and knees of his pants bloody.

I sat up and pushed the coffee table aside, wrapped myself in the sheet and settled on the floor. Curled up like a baby and brushed my toes on the bristly carpet. Took some deep breaths and dropped off, no problem.

CHAPTER

2

I took the bus to see my parole officer, all dolled up in the clothes my mother bought for me. I borrowed black nylons from her and didn't notice there was a big webby run on the inside of my thigh until I got to the bus stop.

I was supposed to meet him in the State building, which was near the civic center, where the trials were. I always thought the civic center would be good to live in; it was so big and round, and it had all these little circle windows like a cruise ship. The State building was down the block; it was short and looked like it was made entirely of cement.

I was carrying an old backpack that smelled like mildew. My mother found it in the closet that morning, slapped it like a prize pig and said, "Good as new." I knew it didn't look right with what I was wearing, even if I slung it over one shoulder casually, but I didn't have a purse to bring, and all of my mother's were too showy and big.

CROOKED

Parole was on the sixth floor. The waiting room looked like a dentist's office—little cubes for tables with wrinkly magazines on top. I sat across from a young black guy, around my age, wearing a pressed suit that looked a little too small for him. He held his hands in his lap and talked to himself, lips moving slowly, eyes closed.

There were a couple of other guys at the end of my row, looking at me, laughing. They kept at it for a few minutes—looking at me, at the guy across from me, and then they'd laugh. I held the backpack on my lap, sniffed at the stiff handle.

The receptionist called my name and pointed me down a hallway, and then I went into a room with twenty or thirty dark blue cubicles, all with thick laminated numbers taped to the sides. Looking over the tops, the cases all looked the same to me, all young, wearing cheap clothes, fake leather, polyester stretched out to look like silk. Taking notes, biting their nails, staring at the ceiling.

Bruce Gruder had close-cropped hair and buggy eyes and wore a collared short-sleeved shirt with a tie. I sat in the padded folding chair across from him while he looked through my file, eating a Croissan'wich. I stared at the bulletin board hanging over his desk. There was a beat-up sheet of paper that said, "Attitude is a little thing that makes a BIG difference."

"Melody Booth, Melody Booth," he said under his breath.

I rocked back and forth in my chair.

"How's the last week been for you?"

"Fine. You know, good."

"Getting used to things?" he said, writing something down.

"Yeah . . . yes."

He nodded and stuck his finger in his mouth, picking food out of his gums. Then he chewed it on the tips of his front teeth like a beaver.

"You're living with your mother?"

"Yeah, right now."

He looked up at me.

"I'll get my own place," I said. "When I get a job, save some money."

He nodded and turned loose pages in the folder.

"It's great that your mother took you in," he said. "Most people don't have a place to go."

He said it like I should feel lucky I could stay anywhere, like I was some dirty dog who'd shed and shit all over the place.

"She's a nice lady," I said.

He looked back at the file and wrote something else down. He coughed, and it sounded phlegmy. I leaned back, and he wiped his face with a napkin.

"Excuse me," he said quietly.

He started clicking the metal tip of his pen.

"You're a high school graduate," he said.

I nodded and thought about sitting between Helen Healy and my boyfriend, Sikes, at graduation. We passed a joint back and forth, and the smartest girl in school gave her speech, and I didn't remember one word after; her voice in the speakers sounded like she was speaking into a Styrofoam-cup telephone. Sikes's hand was moving under my robe, up my thigh.

"Yeah," I said.

"And you took some classes—" he said, trailing off.

"Yeah. At College of Marin."

"Would you be interested in going back to school at some point?"

I shrugged.

"I don't know. Maybe. It didn't do much for me, to tell you the truth," I said.

CROOKED

"Well, Melody," he said, coughed. "There's a lot more opportunities for you because you graduated high school."

He closed my file and dropped it on his desk. Then he picked up a clipboard and started scanning it.

"A lot of jobs. Help you get back on your feet quicker."

"I don't want to work in an office," I said.

"Why not?" he asked.

I shrugged. I'd temped before, and it almost got me physically sick. Offices made me lose my breath, all the carpeting, the white lights, the way coffee machines sounded like they were digesting. Staring at computer screens hurt my eyes, dried them out.

"I just can't do it. I'll do anything else," I said. "I mean it; whatever else you have, I'll do it."

"You're aware that nonoffice jobs pay a lot less."

"Yes, I am."

He cocked his head to the side, as if to say, It's your funeral. Goddamn right, I thought. He looked back down at his clipboard.

"Delivery person or cleaning person?"

"Either," I said.

"Pick one. It's your choice," he said, still clicking his pen, losing patience.

"Delivery person," I said.

"Are you in good physical condition?" he said.

"Yeah. I think so. What would I be delivering?"

"Port-o-Loo toilets," he said, making a note.

I laughed. "You mean, like, Porta Pottis?"

"Yes."

I didn't get how he couldn't find it funny, but he wasn't laughing at all, so I stopped short and turned it into a cough.

"Do I have to clean them?"

Gruder shrugged. "It just says delivery person here, but it's like any other thing—they might have you do whatever they need done."

I rolled my shoulders back and felt them crack.

"Sure. I'll do it," I said.

"Fine. You'll have an interview, which I will set up for you," he said, writing. "And here," he said, pulling a sheet of paper off the clipboard, "are your commandments."

He handed it to me, and I stared and squinted to see his thin scratchy writing.

"You and I meet every other week—don't ever miss a meeting. And don't get arrested. No drugs, no fights, no nothing," he said, then leaned forward. "No fuckups of any kind, Melody. You got off light," he said, stern.

I felt like I had a softball in my throat, and then I got pissed, letting this guy get to me with his creamed-corn bullshit lectures like he was God Jesus himself.

"And," he said, leaning back again. "You have an option to participate in an anger-management workshop." He handed me a brochure. "But it's not mandatory for you, because of your clean time in Staley."

I smiled at him. I had a rib fractured and got my face kicked in, got cut with a razor and saw girls get stabbed in the eye with pencils and open bobby pins, their fingers get snapped back and noses broken. Sounded like cracking open walnuts, or stepping on beetles. I looked at the brochure in my hands. "Work with Yourself," it said. It sounded dirty to me.

"So that's it," Gruder said, and he wrote something else down.

I could see it was a sheet of yellow legal paper, and my name was scrawled at the top in red pen, written over two or three times to look thicker. He signed his name and dated it.

"Questions?" he said.

"No."

He rubbed his chin.

"Do you have any interest in seeing your brother?" he asked.

"No."

He stared at me for a second and then leaned back. Shut my folder and pushed it to the bottom of the stack on his desk. He scratched at the back of his neck.

"Because I'd have to make a few calls, but I could probably get you in," he said. "Because you're immediate family."

I nodded.

"But I can't talk to people at Staley, right?" I said, and I already knew the answer.

He shrugged and stuck his pen behind his ear.

"It's possible, but there's a lot more red tape about it," he said. Then he squinted his eyes at me. "I wouldn't count on talking to any of them until they're out."

I sighed and thought, So long, Reinas. What did they think I was going to do—bake a cake with a file in it? I just wanted to see Jeannie through some goddamn bulletproof glass once in awhile.

Gruder stretched his arms over his head and yawned.

"Okay, Melody, I'll be coming to your mother's apartment in a couple of weeks," he said. "But I'll call you before then, about the interview."

He held his hand out, and I shook it. I stood up and picked up my backpack by the handle.

"Welcome back," he said, not looking up.

I made myself smile, and it felt like my mouth was full of ice, like pieces were breaking off, scratching up my gums.

*   *   *

I sat next to an old man on the bus. He wore thick shoes and had tight wet lips, and his hands were knotty and shaking in his lap. He laughed and mumbled nonsense every time the bus stopped, and he looked out the window the rest of the time, blinking hard. We watched the houses go by, yellow hills, dry grass. The bus stopped and picked up some kids and two young Mexican guys and more old people.

"*Mumf mumf mumf,*" said the old man, chuckling.

I smiled at him. He smiled back, didn't have any teeth.

I looked over at the kids, fourteen, fifteen, a boy and a girl. The girl was leaning against him and had on tight jean shorts. The boy had a shaved head. The girl kissed his neck, and he looked bored and stared at his hands. I stared at her pink lips.

It made me want to find a man to sleep with. I used to go crazy at Staley, used to twist a sheet up and pull it back and forth between my legs, bite the pillow so I wouldn't scream and wake up Ria. I didn't have someone's hands on me for three years, not counting fights and when I got fucked up by Lulu J. when I first got there.

I thought a lot about Sikes when I was in, how he used to bug me for sex all the time when we were in high school, and I just wanted to smoke pot and drink beer. But when I was all alone at Staley, yanking that sheet up like a choke chain, I thought about him on top of me, his skinny legs and knees pushing mine apart, hair in his face, bloodshot eyes.

We'd sit around and tell each other stories, get all heated up. Paulina always told us about her boyfriend, Carl. He had some big snake, she'd say, hold her hand to her chest like she was going to pass out. We laughed our asses off, coughed up smoke, got one on her later in the yard. Lina, your man got s*oooo*me snake, right? You laugh now, she said. You ain't never had it so big, she wagged her finger at Jeannie. Then she looked at me and said, I know *you* never had it so big.

The bus hit my stop. The old man chuckled. *"Gi gi,"* he said.

I winked at him, and he laughed in my direction, and I got off and started walking up the hill to my mother's place. There was a little breeze; the trees were shaking. I passed a big wooden house with flower boxes in front, wind chimes clinking, lacy curtains in the windows that blew back and forth. My feet started to hurt. My mother's shoes were too big for me; I had to curl my toes up to walk straight.

It was a nice day. Nice sun, nice air. I couldn't explain to Gruder that I didn't leave the house much. That I felt crazy and got confused really easily. At the supermarket, wandering through the cereal aisle, staring at all the boxes, watching people decide between Sugar Snap Pops and Wheatie O's. I didn't tell him I drank Nyquil and a couple of beers every night. That I woke up every morning and watched TV, kept the heavy drapes closed over the sliding door while I sat on the couch and smoked, taking deep breaths and staring at the ceiling.

At Staley, the nurse in Infirm told me she couldn't bind my ribs because it wasn't worth the risk of having them reform all crooked, on account of me slouching over all the time. She also told me to stand up straight so the fractured rib would place correctly and when I told her it hurt like hell, she told me to take deep breaths.

I would stand in the yard and lean, bend over a little from the waist even though I wasn't supposed to, but deep breaths weren't cutting it. Every time I took in air, it felt like I'd swallowed glass.

I was hunched against the wall in the yard, talking with Jeannie, about a week after she and Ara and Lina laid into me. Jeannie kept giving me Newports, and I was starting to like the taste of them. They were starting to feel like a cool drink to me.

"That's Rita," Jeannie said, pointing to a fat girl with sunglasses. "She helped her boyfriend rob a 7-Eleven store."

"Boyfriend, huh?" I said.

Jeannie laughed. "Yeah, I know, right? Like she ain't a big old dyke." Then she got serious again. "She hangs out with Renalda."

"Who's Renalda?"

"You know that girl who shaves her face—she got, like, a mustache?"

I shrugged.

Jeannie scanned the yard. "I don't see her. She's a big bitch, though, with a fuckin' mustache—you can't miss her. She and Rita run North Side."

Staley was a big cube. We were on the West Side.

Jeannie looked out at the yard again, squinting. "That's Audra," she said, nodding to a black girl with cornrows. "She broke some boy's neck. She stepped on it or something," Jeannie said, blowing out smoke. "She's from Richmond. She don't like white people—barely likes Mexicans. She's with Jolie and LaShawn and Toni. Toni and Audra knew each other outside. They just called '18,'—that's the street in Richmond they're from."

When Jeannie smoked, she held the cigarette in the middle of her mouth, just between her lips, not her teeth. Her lips were beautiful and round, full. She pointed to a girl with an Afro.

"Celine Montey," she said. "She's armed robbery, too. She's with Letta and Cindy—Aptos girls."

"What did the others do?" I asked.

Jeannie shook her head.

CROOKED

"Letta burned some shit down, I don't know. Cindy just stole a TV or something. You don't have to worry about them." Jeannie was quiet for a second and then said, "Who you got in your cell?"

"Janelle Roche."

Jeannie laughed. "You're lucky," she said. "You just got a crazy. They can't hurt nobody. Like Samma," she said, and she pointed to a Mexican sitting on a bench alone. She had long matty hair and was pulling at it, hard, strands coming out between her fingers.

"She pulls her hair until her head bleeds," said Jeannie. "It's some fucking sick shit. Hey, you know Addie Cloy?"

I shook my head.

"She's a white girl, she's real skinny, looks like she has cancer or something."

"Yeah, she doesn't smell too good, right?"

Jeannie nodded. "She doesn't shower, and she never changes her tampons—she leaves them in for like, six days. They got to send her to the nurse once a month so they'll take it out. She just screams and screams—she wants to keep it in."

I pictured her—pale thin girl who walked around like a ghost and talked to herself. She had almost no hair either, little tufts of blond fuzz on her head looking like tumbleweeds.

"How come nobody fucks with her?" I said suddenly.

Jeannie looked at me. "Someone like that, she's so crazy it's like nobody can fuck her up any more. White girl like you, you make a nice girlfriend or something, they use you for whatever they want, but them—Addie, Samma . . ." Jeannie nodded toward Samma pulling at her hair. "They don't have anything anybody wants, they just so far gone."

I felt sick to my stomach suddenly and closed my eyes. Pictures spun in front of me, a bright-colored cartoon version of Lulu J. over me. My rib started to ache, and I pressed my palm against it.

I opened my eyes, and Jeannie smiled. "I don't know, Green, fucking with someone so crazy like that—maybe it just takes the fun out of it."

I went to the Taqueria to get myself dinner, but nothing for my mother because she was still on her diet. Her boyfriend, Ken, was coming over for me to meet, it seemed like. I never liked any of her men. They were always around when Gary and me were young, walking around in their boxer shorts in the kitchen on Sunday morning like they owned it, giving me and Gary looks like, I just fucked your mama, kid.

I wanted the steak grande burrito, but I knew it wasn't a good idea, so I went with the chicken and rice. I'd had two more episodes like the one in the Newman gas-station bathroom, once with a Jack in the Box hamburger and then with hot dogs. I ordered a Corona while I was waiting because it was the only beer I liked at all. The rest of them were designer brands, and I hated all those; they tasted like cough medicine to me.

My lips burned from the lemon wedge that was stuck in the bottle, but the beer was plenty good. I'd been polishing off nearly a six-pack a day, drinking them down like soda pop, and I knew my mother was getting a little fed up with me not working yet. I tried not to drink so much, but it was the first thing I wanted in the morning. I had to sit on my hands not to have one before twelve noon.

I never liked that Corona was in a clear bottle—made it look too much like pee. It made me think of Nana. She was a farm worker when she was growing up, and she and her brothers and sisters used to piss on the hops. She could put away seven Black Russians in a row, used to call them Motor Oil cocktails, but she'd feel sick to her stomach if she even smelled beer.

I ordered another and pulled out my cigarettes.

"Excuse me," said the clean kid behind the bar.

I looked up.

"There's no smoking in here," he said, smiling stupid.

"I thought that was just in the restaurant area," I said.

"Not at the bar either. I'm sorry," he said, still smiling, looking like his whole face was going to burst open.

I put my cigarette back in the box.

"Sucks, doesn't it?" said a man sitting a couple of stools down.

"No shit."

"You won't be able to smoke on the sidewalk pretty soon," he said.

"Right."

"Can't even smoke in outdoor restaurants," he said.

I nodded again and turned to him. He was around my age, maybe a few years older, tan and skinny, shaggy blond hair. Squinting blue eyes, sleepy or stoned, or both, and there was a wide magazine open on the bar in front of him. He had on a T-shirt and corduroy pants and Birkenstocks. I didn't like it when men wore sandals—it looked girly and weird.

"I know what you mean," I said.

He smiled now, glad I said something. He had thick lips, and his skin was starting to crinkle up at his eyes, and his hair was pressed and sweaty like he just woke up.

The kid behind the bar brought me the burrito in a warm foil tube, and I paid him. The blond man looked back at his beer. I walked over to him, and he looked surprised.

"Can I sit here?" I said.

"Sure thing," he said.

He scooted over on his stool, and I sat.

"What's your name?" I asked.

He smiled and said, "Sam." Held out his hand.

I shook it. His fingertips were warm.

"I'm Mel."

He said it was nice to meet me.

"Yeah?" I said.

He nodded and looked down. "Yeah," he said. "How are you?" he asked.

"I'm fine," I said.

"What do you do?" he said.

I put the burrito in my lap, and it was warm against my legs.

"I'm between jobs right now," I told him.

I read that in a magazine once, that you should say you were between jobs instead of, I'm unemployed, or, I can't get a job. Or, I've been in prison for awhile.

"Ah," he said, nodded again.

"What—," I started, and then I stopped, it felt strange coming out of my mouth, like I was in a play or a soap opera. "What about you?"

"I teach science in junior high," he said.

"Oh yeah? What is that, dinosaurs, or what?" I asked.

He laughed a little bit.

"Mostly earth science," he said.

"Right, right . . . magma," I said quietly.

"Exactly," he said.

He smiled, put his beer down and drummed his fingers on the neck. I watched his hands; they were tan, light-blond hairs growing on top like wheat grass. Fingertips were wide and round, black under the nails. I thought about the kids on the bus, how the girl kissed that boy's neck.

His mouth was open a little, and it looked black inside, almost like he didn't have a tongue. I imagined saying to him, "Hey, can I ask you something?" And he'd say, "What's that?" And I'd say, "Can I go home with you?"

I drank down the rest of my beer and set it on the bar.

"Good talking to you," I said.

"Yeah, likewise."

I stood there for a second like I had something else to say, hovering over the bar. Sam went back to reading his magazine and leaned over it close, licked the tips of his fingers and turned the pages. I smashed my lips against each other and left.

I walked fast through the parking lot and fumbled with the keys in my pocket. I had a funny feeling in my throat, a little thin scratch, and I coughed a couple of times, but it didn't help. I got in the car and tossed the burrito on the seat next to me, pulled out of the lot and took off. The air felt full of dust to me; I thought I might've been allergic to some kind of pollen floating around. I rolled down the window, felt really thirsty and dry all over, still coughing, holding my hand in a tight fist in front of my mouth. I went up a couple of hills and saw a space in front of a nice-looking house and parked there, under a tree, heard a hundred of those little white blossom bulbs popping underneath the tires.

I turned off the car and sat there and looked at my lips in the rearview. I grabbed wads of my hair.

"Jesus."

I leaned my head against the window and knocked it a couple of times hard and smudged up the glass with the grease on my forehead. Then, I didn't know why, I started messing with myself. I moved my legs out to the sides, stretching out the thick plastic rain mat my mother put down. I slipped my hand down my pants, down inside my underwear. I thought about Sam, how he had a little bit of hair like peach fuzz poking through the top of his shirt, how that might feel on top of me. Then I made myself back up; I always jumped the gun, even during the real thing. Sikes used to say I didn't have any use for foreplay at all, and it was true.

So I backed up, maybe I got him to walk to my car, and then I ran my tongue along his upper lip, and then he kissed me hard on the mouth, and his stubble would scratch up my lips and the skin all around. Then we'd crawl in the back seat and only take off enough clothes to do it, and I'd still have my shirt and bra on, and we'd be cramped up and quiet, covering each other's mouths, and then maybe it was Sikes after all. Me and Sikes in his mother's house, the game room in the basement, under the stairs so no one would walk in on us. Sikes' and Sam's faces crashed into each other in my head, and then I couldn't remember what Sam really looked like at all.

I opened my eyes and stopped because I was dry and numb and not getting anywhere, and it was pissing me off. I didn't know why it was so easy at Staley. I thought, maybe I needed Ria in the next bed flopping around, and no daylight, no windows, no birds chirping. I punched the roof, and my fist bounced back in my lap, and I was thinking how it was goddamn easy for men. They could choke themselves off any place, anytime they wanted to. It was like everything had to be silent and pitch black just to get myself in any kind of mood.

I started the car and left, drove around for awhile, and almost went past where I went to high school but didn't want to risk seeing any teachers. Instead I went along the water and looked at the houseboats. There was a lot of green moss around the bottoms; it looked like mold, but the boats still looked like they'd be nice inside—small and warm.

I went to San Rafael for no good reason and looked at the apartment where we lived when me and Gary were in high school. It was situated on an incline, and it looked like it was leaning forward, the whole thing sliding down little by little. It was small, only had three floors, and it wasn't kept up nice. It looked like hell when we lived there, too, inside and out. The walls were all cracked, and everything in the bathroom and the kitchen leaked, and the pool in back was always full of this algae shit and dry leaves, dead bugs, and condoms.

I pulled into the carport and waited for someone to come in or out. Our neighbors used to change all the time. For a while, there was a young couple who lived next door, and they were always yelling or screwing. Gary said the woman had a black eye once, but I didn't believe him. Gary had a tendency to make things up.

I didn't know why I was sitting there. I didn't know what I was hoping to see, but I sat there until it started getting dark. The sky got dark blue, and I remembered my mother and Ken were waiting for me. I didn't actually forget; it was more like I just didn't care too much.

I lit a cigarette and took off and turned on the radio; my mother had it on some easy listening, and I felt too tired to flip around and look for something better. Say you, say me. There was a little bit of traffic, so I sat and stared out the window at all the dealerships with bright-colored flags on strings, swinging back and forth, cars laid out with orange block stickers on the windshields.

My whole body felt overheated so I opened the window more,

let it blow my hair around and fill up my ears. I looked out at the brown hills and thought they were pretty, even though they were surrounded with fast-food places and movie theaters, and the little patches of grass all went dry in the summer. They looked great to me, though, big hills of chocolate dust you could climb and squeeze through your fingers.

Then there was San Quentin. It seemed like it edged into the water, stadium lights around it shining white on the yellow walls, and it had a long red roof that looked like it had been dropped on at the last minute like the top of a Popsicle-stick house. Gary was in there, doing something, I thought. Eating trash in the hall, or lifting weights and doing push-ups. Picking a fight or banging his head against the wall or getting fucked in the shower by some sweaty big boy.

I got to my mother's building and parked, the lights above each door just turning on under the dirty glass cones. I tugged at my shirt to fan myself and wiped my nose. My sleeve smelled like the Taqueria, Mexican rice.

I opened the door to the apartment and heard baseball on the TV. My mother was sitting up, and Ken was leaning back on the couch, his feet in her lap. He straightened up when I came in. He had on a white shirt with a yellow stain on the collar and wrinkled pants, and he was pretty bald. There was a thin circle of hair around his head like a monk's. His face was round, soft, and white like dough, looked like if I pressed my thumb into his cheek it would stay that way.

"Long time, no see," said my mother, sounding edgy, and she blew smoke through her nose like a dragon.

"Sorry, Ma."

"So what happened to you?" she asked.

CROOKED

She was wearing a fake silk blouse with three round cloth buttons undone at the top. She raised her eyebrows at me, and I didn't know what to say. Ken touched his mustache and rubbed his chin. I couldn't tell her what I did for real, that I tried to get myself off but it didn't work so I sat in front of the old apartment for forty-five minutes.

"I ran into a girl from high school, and we had a few beers," I said. "I'm sorry."

"Don't get me worried no more, Mel," she said, rubbing her temple.

She looked tired. It had taken her a long time to get worried about me. It never kept her up nights when we were teenagers, and I was running around with Helen and Sikes, and Gary was out with Diamond Duke and Chicken Rodriguez, shoving everything up their noses that could fit. She never worried about our curfews back then, never made sure we were in bed tight. She still worked mostly bar jobs, out until three in the morning on weekends.

I looked at Ken, and he seemed tired and maybe a little drunk. He stood up and stuck out his hand.

"This is Melody," my mother said.

"Hi, Mel," said Ken.

His handshake was tight. I wasn't expecting it.

"Nice to meet you," I said.

Then we sat down, them on the couch, me in the Hawaii-Five-O wicker chair, army-green palm trees on the cushions.

"Who'd you run into, baby?" my mother asked me.

"Lisa Hecht."

My stomach growled, and it felt like something was scratching at me from the inside. I put my hand over it, pressed down and inhaled, and held my breath a second. Sometimes that worked to keep my stomach quiet. I used to do it when I was a kid and didn't want to feel hungry.

Ken leaned back on the couch and took a sip of beer and swished it around in his mouth like Listerine. My mother leaned against him, and he touched her hair, lightly, brushing it down with his fingers. She closed her eyes. I clenched my jaw.

"So, what do you do, Ken?" I asked.

"I'm in sales," he said.

Whenever anyone I knew said they were in sales, it meant they sold drugs. Ken did not. He sold hospital equipment—lots of things for babies: baby incubators, baby scales, baby respirators, baby IV stands. He told me about all of it while touching my mother—her hair, her shoulders, her leg. I tried to stare only at his eyes, which were small and close together on his face. My mother was dozing off, one side of her mouth dragging down. Her head drooped and then bobbed back up suddenly, and she opened her eyes and gazed at Ken and put her hand on his knee.

She had thin hands, long wrinkly fingers, and she wore at least five rings all the time. One was gold and belonged to Nana. The others were all costume: fake pearls, fake sapphires, and one long brown mood ring that looked like a slug. Her hands seemed too small to be carrying all that jewelry, like the fingers would snap right off at the knuckles if she tried to lift so much as a paper plate.

They used to look huge to me, though, those big spatula hands slapping my face when I was little. She used to be one mean-ass drunk, hauling through the kitchen at all hours, sweeping bottles and jars off counters, pulling at her hair while she cursed Daddy, even long after he left. Goddamn you and your mama, Jack Booth, goddamn you straight to hell.

She laid into us all the time back then, pressed a cigarette out

CROOKED

on my shoulder once, most of the time slapping us stupid, swinging those hands like windmills. I always ran and hid, and slipped under the bed with our rainboots and tennis shoes, buried my face in the rug while she screamed like a ghost. But Gary always stayed right in her face. From when we were seven or eight, he'd stand in front of her with his arms crossed like a smoke shop Indian. He didn't hardly cry either, would come back to our room with a bruise on him, maybe some blood in his ear. Then he'd start playing with his action figures.

My stomach growled again.

"Honey, don't starve yourself on our account," my mother said, yawning.

I peeled the foil off my burrito and started eating while they watched, felt sour cream dripping down my chin and didn't care, hot sauce in a tickly little line down my fingers and my hand. The chicken started burning the corners of my mouth, my lips, the back of my throat. My mother handed me a crumpled tissue. Hot sauce dribbled on my shirt.

"Sorry," I said, and I wiped my mouth up.

They went to bed soon after, and I opened a beer and poured a shot of Nyquil and lined them up on the coffee table. I flipped channels and left it on the news. A fire in the East Bay had burned up five square miles of grass and a few houses before it was put out. I drank the Nyquil and beer, sour and fizzy going down, and stared at the TV, waiting to get tired and watching the footage of the fire on the brush. I liked the look of it, how it ate up all that grass so quickly, burnt it all down to crispy little stubs in no time at all.

CHAPTER

3

Gary and I used to fight like crazy, used to have these knock-down biting kicking screaming fights. I bit him hard on the shoulder once and peeled off a small flap of skin like it was on a potato, and he screamed louder than I ever heard him and bit me on the arm to get back. One of his front teeth was crooked, folded over almost completely on top of the other and worked like one big tooth, and he just dug it right into me like a dog and pulled.

My mother couldn't afford braces for him. But then when we were twelve, Nana said she could pay for them. So they went and got Gary braces even though he should have started wearing them a couple years before. When they came home, Gary was red and sweaty, and his mouth was shut tight. My mother told me, "Your brother threw a little baby fit at the doctor's. Screamed just like a baby." I begged to see; I was jealous he got them and I didn't.

"C'mon, c'mon," I said in his face.

CROOKED

He stayed in his room for hours, and our mother went to work, and I fixed macaroni and cheese and knocked on his door and asked if he wanted any, and he didn't answer. Later I was watching TV, and I heard something crying; it sounded like the time a raccoon got its leg caught in a beer-can ring in our backyard.

Then I heard a clinking sound, fast, like someone dropping change on concrete, and a real scream, and then I knew it was Gary, so I ran to the bathroom and saw him with blood all over his mouth. He had pliers in his hand, and on the counter was a crimped wire string with about six square brackets, two teeth still connected.

Tears were coming out of his eyes, but it wasn't like he was crying because he looked at me and smiled, blood rushing, filling the spaces between his teeth. He stuck his head under the faucet and drank some water, rinsed and spit it out.

He couldn't speak very well, his gums bleeding and swollen, but I could still understand him.

"Fuck that shit, right?" he said to me, his hands shaking.

"Right," I said.

My new boss, Joe, told me exactly what I needed to know to do well here at Port-o-Loo while I chewed my nails and picked at my gums. He looked like a high-school gym teacher, tight slacks and white sneakers, hair cut short and blow-dried fluffy. I glanced around his office when he wasn't looking at me, black-mesh wire on the window, scratched-up tin file cabinets.

"Let's take a walk," he said.

We went into the main storage area, which was a one-floor warehouse, like a big gray barn with two loading entrances. There were rows and rows of sky-blue portable toilets, looked like the same blue plastic they made Frisbees out of. There were sixty or seventy of them here, the "units," Joe called them, but this was only one of the branches. There were also lots in the city and Oakland, but Joe was the big boss of this one, which he reminded me about four times during my first interview. Now he walked ahead of me with a clipboard.

"Eight-thirty," he said, and he stopped in front of a metal clock box. "You're here at eight-thirty every day. You take your card—" He picked up a card with M. Booth written on it. "And you punch it in." He slid it down and the clock bit it, and the box shook.

He turned to me.

"If you're sick, you call in. If you're late, you call in. If you can't come to work for *any* reason, you call in." He tapped the clipboard against his leg while he spoke. "Whatever you do, don't have someone else call in for you. You have someone else call in for you, don't bother coming to work the next day and take it up with the union. You in the union?"

I shook my head.

"Don't bother coming in then," he said.

He walked in front of a large room with a glass window.

"This is the staff room," Joe said, pointing to it with the clipboard. "This is where you take your break or your lunch if you're not on a job." He lowered the clipboard. "You'll usually be on a job."

The men in the staff room looked out at me through the window, and I stared back at one with tiny eyes and a few gold teeth.

"This is the sign-in sheet, and sign-out," he said, tapping two clipboards hanging from thick strings on the wall next to the staff-room door. "You log out the numbers of the units when you take them, and you log them in—" he said, staring, waiting for me to say something.

"When I bring them back," I said.

"Exactly," he said. "You have any phone calls to make, make them on the pay phone. No using the phone in my office or Wanda's," he said. "Ladies' room is back and to the right."

Then he opened the door to the staff room and stuck his head in. Two of the men looked his way and the other two didn't. Joe called to one of them, and a big Hispanic guy, belly hanging over his belt, stood up and came out. He smiled and had bright white teeth.

"This is Melody Booth," Joe said to him. "This is Angie."

"How're you doing?" said Angie, and he shook my hand.

"Good. Nice to meet you," I said, and I pulled my hand back quickly; I knew it was sweaty.

"You'll do drops and pickups with Angie," Joe said. "He knows everything about everything around here. Right, Angie?" he said, patting him on the back.

"Sure thing, boss," he said, laughing.

"Works harder than the rest of them," Joe said, nodding toward the staff room. "Get that pretty wife up here, right?" he said, and he winked.

"Right," Angie said, laughing still.

"He'll show you everything you need to know," Joe said. He chucked Angie on the shoulder with the clipboard.

Angie kept looking at Joe, and Joe chewed on his mustache with his bottom teeth and stared at the clipboard. Then he looked up.

"She's all yours," Joe said to him, like I was a Cadillac, and he turned toward his office.

There was a kid behind him pushing two flatbeds, scraping one against the cement wall, trying to pull it back but it kept grinding, wheels turning in like they were on a broken grocery cart.

"Move that fuckin' thing!" Joe yelled at him.

Angie smiled, only with half his mouth, and squinted at me, looked me up and down. I looked down, too, my work pants and sneakers.

"Boots are better," he said, looking at my feet. "You drop a unit, they crush your foot through those soft shoes—break every bone," he said.

I nodded and felt stupid.

"You like coffee?" he said.

"Sure."

I followed him into the staff room, and it smelled like coffee and sweat and feet. There were two vending machines, and a coffee keg, and a long brown table. Two of the men looked up at me. The one with gold teeth didn't.

"This is Melody Booth," said Angie.

My face flushed hot hearing my whole name. "Mel, it's Mel," I said quickly.

He introduced me to Tino, Rick, Tommy John. I shook their hands. Tino was short and wore an A's cap. He looked young and laughed out of the corner of his mouth when I shook his hand. Rick had and big arms and a scar that crossed his eyebrow; he barely touched my hand and jerked it back quick. He and Tino sat back down and started talking to Angie in Spanish.

Tommy John was the one with the gold teeth and had tattoos up and down his arms—barbwire, a wolf face, a cross with Jesus on it. He shook my hand slowly.

He said, "Parole put you here?"

The other three stopped talking and looked at me. I took my hand back and said, "Yeah."

"Where're you at?" he asked.

CROOKED

"Staley," I said.

Then he laughed with his mouth closed, through his nose. I stuck my hands in my pockets and pulled on a loose thread at the bottom. He sat back down, and the others started talking again, and I stood there alone for a second and then turned around and got some coffee. Spooned in powder creamer and sugar until it tasted like candy. I stared at the stuff in the vending machine and bought a pack of black licorice bites and sat down.

Tino was telling a story, and I watched him mime something, cross his eyes like a clown, stick his tongue out and wag it. Rick and Angie laughed. Tommy John wasn't listening or paying attention—it looked like he didn't understand or didn't care or both. He kept reading the paper, scratching at the cup with his thumbnail.

I drank my coffee, sweet and lukewarm with tiny flakes of wax swirling around on top. I chewed up the licorice bites, and they were tough and tasted like sugary rope. They started to make my mouth feel sore. I chewed hard on my nail and pressed it against my gums, between my teeth.

Angie said we had to go, and I said good-bye to Tino and Rick, and nodded to Tommy John, but he didn't look up. Angie and Tino had already loaded the truck while Joe was giving me the grand tour, so I stood next to the passenger's side while Angie looked over the assignment sheet. I ran my finger over the rust on the side mirror and scratched at it, trying to shave it off.

"Where are we going?" I asked.

He got into the truck and stared at me, then at the seat next to him. I got in quickly.

"Sonoma," he said, and then we took off, and he didn't say anything else for twenty minutes.

* * *

The air got hotter as we went further inland. We had the windows all the way down, and Angie was driving, eight units strapped down in the back. He was chewing gum, blowing bubbles, and cracking it loud. I tried making conversation, asked him a few questions, but he was mostly silent, mostly saying yes and no. I asked him about what Joe said, about his wife.

"She's coming up from Salvador," Angie said. "Joe thinks I'm from Mexico. He thinks they're the same place," he said.

We were quiet for a while, and then I tried getting him to talk again.

"Tino and all them seem like good guys," I said.

"Yeah," he said, staring straight ahead. Then he said, "Tommy John did five at Folsom for assault."

I nodded and wondered why he told me, but I could've guessed it anyway. There was something about some people that made it easy to guess. There was a gas-station attendant near my mother's house, and Tommy John, and the nervous black guy who sat across from me at the parole office, whispering to himself what he was going to say like he was about to take a test.

"How long were you at Staley?" Angie asked.

"Three years."

He nodded, straight-faced, kept looking ahead, and didn't say anything right away.

"Weird to be out," he said, and then he sighed, like he'd only thought it in his head.

I nodded. Weird to be out. Not "It's great to be out" or "You must be glad to be out," but it's just weird, weirder than shit to be out.

Lulu J. and her girls got me bad when I first got to Staley. They caught me in the rec room and pinned me to the floor, clamped

CROOKED

their bony hands down on my wrists. I looked up at three sets of crooked teeth, and Lulu J. had one screwed-up eye and black liner tattooed around her lips, tied black nylon over her hair. "Hey, white girl," she said, holding the blade up between her fingers. She leaned down in my face and whispered, "You ain't shit in here, Mami," and then she cut into me.

Shandra covered my mouth—her hand smelled like soap, and I tried to slip away but couldn't move at all, and I watched Lulu J. slash my forearm and split the skin. She held the blade in front of my face, the blood looked black on the tip and dripped on my chin, and then she kept going.

"You ain't shit," she said again, sounding far away. My eyes were clouding up, everything blurry, head filling up with fluid. I stopped watching and just stared past her at the yellow light on the ceiling, and then it looked like there were two lights, then three, then four—big yellow bulbs. My arm went numb, tears and snot running down my face.

Then she stopped, and stood up, and the rest let go and laughed and walked out, but Lulu J. stayed a second, hanging over me. "You're dead," she said. She left, and I didn't move, lied still, my head next to the cool metal bar of the Ping-Pong table, not sleeping, not crying, didn't move a muscle, just let the blood pour out of my arm like it was water. My fingers and toes and lips got cold, and I closed my eyes and pretended I was dead and thought I was until Jackson picked me up and took me to Infirm.

Turned out I didn't lose much blood at all, and it looked a lot worse than it was. I only needed a few stitches, not even over the whole word, which puffed out of my skin like a 3-D decal. I watched the nurse spray me with a split-stream faucet, like the one Inez and I used to wash the trays. Then she wrapped it quickly, wound the bandages and flipped my arm over, covered it in thick white gauze. No painkillers, no aspirin, no nothing, and then she sent me back in.

I made it almost another month. I was trying to lay low, and Lulu J. didn't like that no one else took a piece of me. I wasn't hardly sleeping, didn't talk to anyone, looked down all the time, looked at my shoes, at my food, at the trays, water spinning down the drain. I hadn't seen anyone's face in so long but I heard my name everywhere, thought everyone was talking about me. Heard voices wherever I went.

We were dropping the units off at a fairground in Sonoma, and they already had a few old ones, big metal things that looked like fallout shelters from the fifties. There were a couple of semis parked, guys unloading blocks of cheap painted iron passing for children's rides—six or seven red and yellow ladybugs with round human eyes and fuzzy black lines for smiles.

Angie got the orders from a skinny old man in a cowboy hat. We'd have to carry two across the fairgrounds, the rest we could leave at the entrance; they didn't know where they wanted them yet.

The ground was all tightly packed dirt that didn't give at all when we walked, and the toilets were harder to carry than I expected. They felt like they weighed twice as much as I did at least, and the edges and doorjamb were razory sharp plastic. I couldn't get a grip unless I used my whole hand, and I felt my palms getting sliced up. Angie wore thick white gloves.

We walked past the guys unloading booths and clear garbage bags full of stuffed animals. The guys wore cowboy boots and plaid shirts, and their radio played country. I felt them looking at us, at me. My hands began to throb, and I tightened them up around the edges. Angie spoke quietly, told me to move right or left.

"This way," he said, edging to the side.

We set it down next to two empty booths. My hands felt frozen, and I stretched them out, wiggled my fingers and heard them crack. I was sweating good now, and my mouth was dry, and I still had hard pieces of licorice stuck in my teeth.

"One more over there," said Angie.

We got back to the truck and slid another off, but when we started walking, my hands started to feel like deadweight, like two strips of wood. The toilet was too much suddenly, and I tried to lean into it, but it went the other way and slipped out of my hands. Angie wasn't expecting it and lost his grip, and the toilet slammed to the ground and rocked heavy back and forth, dust flying up in our faces.

The rednecks laughed behind us and shouted something I couldn't hear.

"Sorry," I said to Angie.

He nodded quickly without looking at me and wiped his brow with his forearm. Then he took my hand and turned it over. There were a few thin cuts, one a little bloody, and my fingers were red and stiff. Angie took his gloves off and shoved them in my hand.

"No, come on—" I started.

"We'll do it quicker if you put them on," he said.

I nodded and couldn't look him in the eye for a while. The gloves were hot and damp inside, and too big for me, an extra inch in each finger. Angie squatted down and put his bare hands on the side and the bottom of the unit. I took my side, and it hurt to bend my fingers at all, but it wasn't cutting into me anymore, and I wasn't going to complain. Angie didn't wince once, kept walking, jaw locked, sweat pouring down his face. I could feel the pull in my shoulders and my neck like wires were running through my whole body, through my arms, out the tips of my fingers.

"Set," said Angie.

We lowered it slowly. Angie shook his hands out hard and breathed in through his teeth like he was cold. I took the gloves off and handed them back to him.

"Keep them for now," he said, looking around. "I'm going to find a phone. You go, untie the rest. I'll be there in a second."

"Sure."

I headed toward the truck, and then he called out, "Wait if you have trouble."

I nodded to him and kept walking, wiggled the gloves back and forth in my hand, fingers blowing around in the wind. I went past the rednecks, and now they were leaning against their truck, smoking, watching me. They turned around and whispered and laughed.

"Hey, girl, you want some of this?" one of them said, pointing to his dick.

"No," I said.

They laughed again.

"Come on, hey, come on," he said, catching up with me.

I stepped onto the flatbed and tried to untie the next set. The cowboy stood under me.

"Hey, come on now, what's your name?" he said.

He had red hair and stubble, and his face was sunburned already and looked too big for the rest of his body, like it was swollen, and there was a wad of tobacco in his mouth, stuffed below his lip. He had on a baseball cap and squinted up at me.

"Jeannie," I said.

"Yeah? Jeannie what? What's your last name?"

CROOKED

I looked down at him and didn't answer, went back to working the knot. I tried to wedge my nails in it, but Angie had tied it twice over.

"Hey, I was just kidding back there," he said.

"Yeah? That was really funny."

"C'mon now, I'm sorry. But serious, Jeannie," he said, rubbing his chin. "You wanna go talk somewhere, just for five minutes, maybe get Pepe to let you have a break."

I could see his thick tongue tracing over his teeth. I had an urge to kick him in the chest, hear him cough and lose his wind, roll around on his back in the dirt like a bug.

"That sounds real pretty, but no thanks," I said.

He kept staring at me and leaned his head to the side and looked me over like I was wearing see-through clothes. I kept pulling at the knot, and the cowboy didn't move.

"You standing there all day?" I said to him.

I could feel the strain in my throat, my hands starting to shake, a little twist in my stomach and my temples.

He smiled dumbly again and was about to say something when Angie came up and stepped onto the flatbed next to me. He nodded and smiled at the cowboy.

"You're doing a great job, amigo," the cowboy said.

"Thanks," Angie said.

Then he walked away, and I didn't look up at all. Angie gently pushed my hands off the knot, and I watched him untie it, pulling one piece through another and another until the ropes dropped and sat like a pile of snakes at our feet.

It was Saturday, and my mother had worked the night before. She and Ken had come in late, stumbling drunk. She said loudly, "Don't wake her up," and she was slung around his neck, hanging off him like a purse.

I woke up early with dry mouth because I drank a six-pack the night before, watching the news as late as it went and then the weather. I found a channel where they did local, statewide, and national reports around the clock. I liked the national best, seeing how it was so hot in the South, humid back East, raining in Tacoma.

I took a quick shower and fixed it so the water was almost all cold. The water at Staley was always too hot, always felt a couple degrees away from burning the skin right off your body. I closed my eyes and let the water beat on my eyelids and drip into my ears, and I leaned my head against the wall and looked down and noticed the sides of my feet covered with dirt. I squatted down and felt it between my fingers, grainy. It was stuck under the nails and between the toes; I rubbed my feet with a washcloth and watched the dirt peel off like paint.

When I got out, I hunched over the sink and stared at my face in the mirror. I always thought I looked old. Since high school, I had crow's feet and laugh lines that made my face look split up in wooden pieces that would fall out if someone shook me too hard. My hair was cut right below my ears and used to be longer; it was longer my whole life, and then it made trouble for me at Staley, made me feel like people were looking at me, so I chopped it off and kept it short, held it back with a cutoff shirt sleeve or a bandanna.

I pulled on some clothes and went into the kitchen and got a bag of pretzels, dragged a stool to the small patch of concrete outside the sliding glass doors and sat down. The air was cool, fog blowing in from the Bay. If I strained my neck I could just see over the ivy bushes and spiky ice plants to downtown, people and cars passing.

CROOKED

My neck was still sore from work. My shoulders and back were stiff, too, but at least my hands were doing better. I'd bought my own gloves in the middle of the week, used the food money my mother gave me and went to a gardening-supplies store, got thick white ones with loose elastic in the wrists, just like Angie's.

I went inside to get water, and Ken was in the kitchen in his bare feet. I could hear them peeling off the vinyl floor every time he took a step, sounded like the plastic sheets in a photo album.

"Hi," I said.

His shoulders twitched, and he turned around.

"Good morning," he said. "You're up early."

He leaned back with a can of coffee in his hand and kept making a clicking noise with the plastic lid, couldn't get his fingernails under it. His lips tightened up, fingers turning white. He looked pale to me.

"I can't ever sleep too late," I said.

"Nothing wrong with that," he said, the lid popping off. He lifted his thumb to his lips. "You get more of the day that way," he said. "Do you drink coffee?"

"Sure."

He'd only slept over a few times since I got there, and he always took off early, slipping out the front door, thinking I was asleep. Whenever I saw him, he seemed out of it, tired or on cold medicine, something. He started rinsing out the coffee pot, the water on hard, spraying up in his face.

I went to my mother's room, tapped lightly on the door and opened it slowly. She was sleeping, her mouth open, and she was snoring, fuzzy mascara blotches settled right below her eyes. Her hair was everywhere, falling off her shoulders, spread on the pillow like a fan. I lied down next to her and pulled the tan comforter over me. I stared at her, touched her hair; it was stiff and webby. She had on lacy underwear.

I turned on my side and looked out the window at the tops of trees blowing. I thought about the old house in Tacoma, made of all those wooden slats, soaking up every bit of rain that fell. I used to stand at the glass door in the TV room before it became my room, and watch the grass in the backyard get matted down. It was all overgrown with weeds on one half, and there was concrete on the other, paved all the way up to the house. My earliest memory was us in the backyard when Daddy was still around. It must have been mine and Gary's birthday because we were all wearing pointy hats, and our parents were drinking bug juice out of Dixie cups. I ate a plate full of peanut brittle and taffy and had it in my hair and all over my clothes, and Daddy and my mother were leaning against each other and laughing, both old-man drunk, talking nonsense.

Ken came in holding two mugs and stopped in his tracks when he saw me there. For a second, his eyes got big and glassy, and his mouth went tense. I stared at him and put my hand on my mother's shoulder. She opened one eye.

"Mel?" she said.

"Hey, Ma."

Her shoulder was warm and smelled like pharmacy perfume.

"Hot coffee," Ken said, setting the cups down.

"Oh, thanks," she said, disoriented. She sat up and yawned loudly, rubbed her eyes. *"Uggh,"* she said, touching her temples like a TV psychic. "Honey, would you get me some aspirin?" she asked me. "My head's gonna pop right open."

Ken sat on the bed next to her, took a big sip of coffee, made a face. Blew on it to cool it off.

"Sure thing," I said.

CROOKED

My mother lit a cigarette and rose her arm up over her head quickly so the smoke wouldn't get in her eyes.

"Thanks, baby," she said.

I went to the bathroom and shook two aspirin out of the bottle. When I was little, she used to keep the bottle on her nightstand. She knew she would need it first thing.

"You little sonofabitch bastard, I'm not taking one more second of your dirty garbage mouth," she said to Gary once, yanked his arm so hard she could've snapped it, I thought. She'd already bruised him with a cookbook—I thought she was trying to slap him on the ass with it, but he got the corner instead, and it made a dark purple mark at the base of his spine. Now she didn't know what to do, so mad her whole body was shaking, her hands, her face. I thought her head was going to spin right off and blow up like a firecracker.

Gary wriggled away from her and jumped behind the kitchen counter. I ran to our room and jumped into bed and pulled the covers up. Then I heard her scream, glass breaking, and I peeked out and saw round pickle chips floating across the tile in front of our door. Gary ran in, slammed the door and locked it. She banged on it with her fist.

"You better goddamn stay in there, boy," she said, jiggling the doorknob.

He turned to me, his face red. "She can't even figure out how to open it," he said.

Then he climbed to the top bunk, and we heard her go into her room and slam the door. I could hear Gary breathing loudly, like his nose was stuffed up. I stared up at the wire metal frame, and then it got darker outside. I had to pee but didn't get up, just went on myself right there and didn't hardly sleep, my bed wet, listening to Gary punch his pillow all night.

CHAPTER

4

Gruder came over later on, after Ken went back to his place. My mother put on makeup and a string of fake pearls and sprayed her hair in place. She offered him a seat on the couch next to me, and I felt the cushions sink down when he took it. He said it was a lovely apartment, and she said thank you. She asked where he lived, and he said Tiburon. They talked about how nice it was there, and how nice it was here in Mill Valley. She offered him coffee, and he said okay.

He turned to me and asked, "How's work?"

"It's good," I said.

"Any problems?" he asked, quieter, tucking his chin in.

I leaned over to him and whispered, slower, "It's. Good."

My mother brought him coffee, and showed him around while I stayed in the living room and smoked. I heard him saying that it was really something that she took me in like this. She said, "Family's family." They kept talking—weather, traffic, what she did for a living. I finished one cigarette and lit another, and they came back in and sat at the counter.

"You must meet a lot of people working in a doctor's office," Gruder said.

"Oh, yeah," my mother said, leaning on one leg, still on the floor. "That's where I met my companion, matter of fact."

I laughed out loud. They looked at me.

"What's so funny with you?" my mother said.

I shrugged and shook my head.

"Spill it," she said.

"You sound like you're gay. 'Companion' is what gay people say, Ma," I said.

She waved her hand, shooing me, and turned back to Gruder.

"I don't like saying 'boyfriend,' it makes me sound like a teenager," she said.

He smiled at her and drank the coffee down, and he was starting to sweat. He pulled a tissue from his pocket and wiped his forehead and then coughed into it. I lit another cigarette.

"Excuse me," he said.

He pulled out a legal pad and made some notes, coughed some more, and shifted on the stool from side to side. My mother lit a cigarette and pressed her finger down flat on the counter, picking up stray ash.

"Well, I'm sorry, I've got to get going, then," he said to my mother.

"So soon?" she said, smiling, flashing her teeth like a movie star.

"I have another appointment," he said. "Nice to meet you, ma'am," he said, and he shook her hand.

"Very nice to meet you," she said, winked at him.

I looked in my lap and smiled, thought, For chrissake, Ma, why don't you just straddle him?

"I'll see you the week after next, Melody," he said, nodding at me. His double chin looked like a puffy collar.

"Sure thing."

He headed for the door, and my mother stood up to follow him.

"Oh, hey there, can I ask you something?" she said.

"Yes, ma'am?"

"Could I take Mel to see her brother? Is that a violation?" she asked.

Gruder looked at me, confused. I felt like the top of my head was coming off.

"Ma," I said.

"What?"

"I told her before," Gruder said slowly, "that shouldn't be a problem."

"Oh yeah?" she said, looking back at me. "Thanks so much then. You have a good day," she said to him.

He left, and she leaned against the counter.

"He told you that already?" she said.

"Yeah, he did."

"And what'd you say?"

She put out her cigarette in three quick stamps and wiped her hands.

"I said I didn't want to see him," I said, scratching at the edge of the coffee table.

She squinted her eyes at me like I was far away.

"Why'd you say that?"

I put out my cigarette quickly and grabbed the army surplus

jacket next to me. I used to wear it in high school, stole it from Sikes's dad.

My mother put her hands on her hips and stood in front of me.

"Why'd you tell him you don't want to see Gary?" she said again, getting mad.

"Because I don't."

Her hands dropped to her sides, and she opened her mouth, and it looked like she was going to laugh but she gasped instead.

"Why the hell not?"

I stood up and fumbled with my jacket.

"I don't want to talk about it."

"You don't want to see your brother, and that's just fine and normal to you?"

"I don't have anything to say to him, Ma," I said, getting louder.

"Well la-de-da for you," she said, laughing. "You can't take an afternoon out of your busy schedule to see your goddamn brother, living in the hell he is."

"Hey, Ma, I did some time, too, you know what I'm saying?" I said, and my hands started to shake.

"You know what, Mel, it just about makes his day when I go to see him. It just near makes his whole damn week, right?" she shouted.

I knew he told her to come only once every few weeks because she always cried when she went. She never cried when she came to see me, but I thought that was probably because I was getting out, and Gary wasn't.

"I don't think he cares, Ma," I said, rubbing my eyes.

"That's a bunch of horseshit," she said, pointing at me. "He talks about you all the damn time. Last time I was there, he says, 'Mel's getting out right around the corner, right?'"

I sat back down and ran my hands through my hair. It was still wet and clumpy from the shower.

"You're plain nuts you think he doesn't care," she said.

I looked at my hands. Dirt under the nails, still cut and sore. Still hurt to bend them.

"I'm going in a couple weeks. You could come with me."

"No."

"Just like that—no," she said, louder.

"Just like that."

"Well that's just *great,*" she shouted, standing up. "Just because you don't feel like it, you're not going."

"Yes."

"I think you're acting like a little spoiled brat," she said.

"You're gonna have to call me something a hell of a lot worse, Ma," I said, standing up again. "I've heard a lot of shit, you better come up with something fucking meaner than that to make me do this."

She stared at me.

"And then I'm not doing it anyway," I said.

She didn't say anything back to me, and then after a minute, not looking at me, not even looking in my direction, she said, "Fine."

She went into the bathroom, walked past me with her chin so far up I could see all the thick lines in her neck. A few minutes later, she came back out and got some cleaning products from the kitchen and went back into the bathroom. I followed her and stood in the doorway, watched while she sprinkled blue powder in the sink. She shook it back and forth fast and sloppy; it fell on the counter in little piles. She finally spoke.

"You going to stand there like an oil painting or make yourself useful?" she said, pulling the yellow gloves down tighter on her hand, bracelets clanking on her wrist.

I shrugged.

"You can take the kitchen," she said, and she turned on the water.

I left, went into the kitchen and poured some Mr. Clean on a thin pink sponge that was brown at the edges and smelled like the inside of a pipe. I started scrubbing the counter and heard my mother push the shower curtain back. I circled the sponge over the Formica and pushed a glass around on the counter for fun, watched it glide and do a little spin like a top. I brushed coffee grounds into my hand, and the sponge felt doughy on my fingers.

I filled a small plastic tub with Mr. Clean and hot water, and then I mopped the tan and brown vinyl, which was laid down in one sheet but was supposed to look like separated tiles. The mop squeaked, handle loose in my hand; my brain was out to lunch.

I washed trays and cups, scrubbed hot pots and pans my whole time at Staley. Shifts of two and three hours, the skin nearly coming off my hands from the water, my nails almost mush. Inez worked with me most of the time, and her hands were so dry and cracked they looked like claws. Sometimes me and her would talk, but most of the time we had the water on loud, my back so stiff and hands so numb I felt like I was just about to go nuts. So I tried thinking about other things, usually about holding Big Jim's football head under the snake faucet, watching his skin bubble up and all the blood vessels in his face burst open. He'd squirm, water would fill his mouth and throat, and he'd choke.

The floor was as shiny as it was going to get. There was still a little dirt, wet and lumpy in the corners where the linoleum met the counter, but I wasn't going to worry about it.

I brought the tub and the mop to my mother, and she was on her knees next to the bathtub, scrubbing hard with a toughie sponge in one spot.

"You done in there already?" she said.

"I've got to do the sink."

She nodded.

I grabbed the cleanser, went back into the kitchen and shook some out on the sink, but it wasn't too dirty because she never cooked. There were some macaroni noodles that I'd made a couple of nights before, stuck under the drain, mealy and wet, and I picked them out and threw them in the trash. Let the blue powder set.

At Staley, me and Inez would scrape all the uneaten tray food into a big blue garbage can—wet potatoes, gristle edges of pepper steak, canned peas, and green-bean pulp, enough to make you gag.

The first time I met Inez, she was spraying dishes. She was short, fat, had a crew cut like a man. Lomey walked me in and pointed to her.

"Inez'll tell you," he said.

She was older, around forty, and a big dyke, which was one of the first things she told me, along with "Don't fuck up" and "Keep going." She showed me how to load the washer, two levels, twenty in a row. When they came out, they were hot as wax.

The first few days I thought I'd die from the steam, sweat was dripping into my eyes, down my back. I felt like I had a fever all the time, and I couldn't piss. The second week, after Lulu J. cut into my arm, I was scraping trays, and my forearm felt like it was burnt to a crisp, and I was so new, and so fucking tired and hot; it felt like I was sweating out blood, and I started to cry. I tried to anyway.

CROOKED

I was shuddering, my shoulders were hunching up and shaking back and forth like they were wings, but my eyes were dried up, nothing coming out.

Inez noticed and said to me, "The fuck long you got?"

I held up three fingers, and she shook her head.

"Shit, girl," she said. "There's only one way you can go, you know what I'm saying?"

I nodded, but I didn't know what she meant. I didn't know shit about shit, as she'd say. Not for a long time either.

CHAPTER 5

There was one night when Gary and I were in the eighth grade, and our mother was working, and I was doing homework in the living room and eating bread and butter. For about two years, all I ate was bread and butter. Gary was in his room with his girlfriend, Jen, and the door was closed. The door was always closed when she was over, unless our mother was home because she made Gary keep it open.

Our mother didn't like Jen because everyone knew Jen was a little bit of a slut. It seemed like a whole pot-calling-the-kettle-black kind of thing, though, our mother not liking Jen when she herself brought home a new guy every couple of weeks.

At some point, Gary came out of his room suddenly and went into the bathroom and shut the door. He stayed in there for about five seconds, and I heard the toilet flush, and then Gary came out and went back to his room and slammed the door hard behind him.

A few minutes later I went to the bathroom, and the tank was making a rattling sound, the seat cover down. I lifted the cover up, and there was a limp condom swirling around in the bowl. I stared at it, thinking, Gary had sex. Gary had sex with Jen.

For some reason, I was a little pissed off. At her because I heard she did it with everyone. At Gary, too, because I guess I was jealous. I hadn't done it with anyone yet, but it wasn't like I was dying to—it just pissed me off that he did it first. And I was thinking he was stupid and easy to do it with Jen.

I flushed the toilet again, and it made more creaky noises and sucked the condom down.

In the living room, I kept watching TV but turned it down low, trying to hear Gary and Jen, but I couldn't. I stared at my tired little piece of wheat bread with cold heavy chunks of butter on top, ripping at the center, and I wasn't hungry anymore. I picked up my algebra book and tried to focus on some numbers.

Then Gary's door opened, and only Jen came out. She had sprayed blond bangs and was wearing a jean jacket, and she walked really quickly to the front door. She didn't look at me, exactly, just tilted her head in my direction and said, "Bye, Mel."

Her voice sounded shaky.

"See you, Jen," I said.

She closed the door quietly, and soon after Gary came out in his bare feet. I tried hard not to look at him, stared at *The Facts of Life*.

He walked to the kitchen and pulled orange juice out of the refrigerator and drank it down from the carton.

"That's fucking sick," I said to him.

He smiled at me and burped. Then he dropped the carton into the sink.

He came into the living room and stood in front of the TV for a second, then walked to the couch and stood next to it. I ignored him and felt him staring at me.

He sat down on the couch next to me and inched closer so our legs were touching. Then he pressed his leg against mine and breathed on me, practically on my lap.

"Quit it," I said, shoving him.

He leaned back lengthwise and rested his head on the arm of the couch, feet in my lap.

"What's wrong with you?" he said.

I kept staring at the TV. I could smell his dirty feet.

"Nothing."

"Right," he said.

He started curling his toes on my thighs, pinching me like he was a cat.

"Cut it out," I said.

"No."

I let him keep going for a couple of minutes, trying to drive him crazy by not letting it drive me crazy, but I always lost this kind of game with Gary. He always drove me crazy first. I pushed his feet off my lap hard and onto the ground, the bottom half of his body shifting like a turnstile.

"She's done it with everyone, you know," I said to him.

Gary sniffed.

"That's not true," he said, matter-of-fact. "She's done a lot of fucking around, but she's only done *it* a couple of times."

I rolled my eyes.

"Sure," I said.

"No, really," said Gary, sitting up. "She's real fucked-up in the head about it."

"What do you mean?" I said.

CROOKED

Gary looked at the television screen. "Her Dad used to mess around with her when she was a kid."

"Ugh," I said, and I buried my face in my hands. "That's so fucking sick."

"Yep," Gary said. "I'm telling you, it's really hard for her to actually do it."

He sniffed again, and I raised my head back up.

"Why'd she do it with you, then?" I said.

He shrugged.

"I'm nice to her," he said.

"Oh yeah, I'm so sure. Why'd she, like, take off crying then?"

"Be-cause," he said, rocking his head from side to side. "She wanted to. I told her to sleep over but she was upset, you know, because she was remembering about her Dad I think, and I asked her if she wanted to talk about it and she said, 'No,' and I asked if she just wanted to cry for a second and she said, 'Yeah, for a second', and so she did, and then she said she wanted to go, so she left."

He said it all in one breath, still watching TV. I felt my heart beating hard.

"I wasn't going to, like, make her stay," he said.

I nodded and pictures flew into my head of men, men like my mother dated, all hands all over me, and it made me want to throw up. I slapped my hands over my eyes.

"You're thinking about it, aren't you?" Gary said.

"Yeah," I said, and I knew he knew. Men—dirty drunk men touching me everywhere.

Gary started poking me in the thigh with his toes, over and over.

"Stop," I said.

"Stop," he said, making fun. Then he actually did stop and said, "Hey, Mel, you wanna go for a ride?"

"Now?"

"Yeah, now."

I turned my head and looked out the front window. The street was quiet and dark.

"Yeah, okay," I said.

I grabbed a sweatshirt and put on shoes and Gary slid his feet into his beat-up Adidas with no laces and shuffled toward the back door, swinging his house keys around his finger.

We went into our tiny backyard and found our bikes in the corner. Two boy Huffys with soft black wheels, the foam around the handles on Gary's worn down in the mold of his fingers. They were exactly the same, except mine looked newer because I didn't ride it as much. Gary kicked my back tire lightly.

"You're a little low," he said.

"I know," I said. "It doesn't matter."

I didn't feel like going to the gas station for the pump. There were always drunk high-school kids hanging out, and they made me nervous. They didn't make Gary nervous. Nothing made Gary nervous.

Gary pulled his bike up by the right handle and stepped on, flipped the pedals backward and listened to them spin. I picked mine up and straddled the seat. Nana had bought them for us when we were in the fifth grade—the same make. She knew I wouldn't want a girl's. The only dirt bikes made for girls came in pink and white and had plastic tassels stuck in the handles.

Gary swung the fence open that led to the driveway and leaned down to roll his pants up a little. It was a warm night.

"Let's go," he said to me, and he smiled with only half of his mouth.

CROOKED

He closed the fence behind us, and I started out slow. He buzzed ahead of me quickly and stood straight up, standing on the pedals. It scared me, the way he rode, high above the seat, sometimes with his hands at his sides and always so goddamn fast. I could never ride like he did. I was always afraid of crashing a curb and falling and smashing my face into the concrete, my teeth breaking into bits.

"Catch up," Gary yelled back to me.

I went faster, wheels spinning, warm wind blowing my hair back and in my eyes and nostrils, but I still couldn't quite catch up to him. I got my front wheel kissing his back, and he turned his head and howled.

"Ow—ow—owww," he called like he was a dog.

I laughed and stood above my seat, just a little.

Then Gary slowed down and said, "Check it, Mel." He nodded toward a house with rusty green aluminum siding. "That's Ramer's house."

Freddy Ramer was a kid a couple years older than us who thought he was too cool for school from day one, and he would still come around the junior high even though he was in high school. He was dating a goddamn seventh grader named Cherisse Wyland, and he would pick her up in his dad's truck. Still acting like he was God's gift, laughing at everyone like he had something on us.

"Come on!" Gary yelled, and he sailed in front of me.

He leaned toward Freddy Ramer's house, right next to the curb, next to the garbage cans. Three green and one blue. Gary didn't stop, just stuck his leg out as he went past and kicked a green one, and it tipped and landed hard, and the bag inside broke, thick dark liquid dripping out.

"Do it, Mel," he shouted, breathless, peeling away.

I lingered for a second and didn't move, started thinking about if Freddy Ramer's dad was a drunk or had a temper or something, if he would come out and kick the shit out of me.

"Come on, girl," yelled Gary from down the block. "Show it who's boss!"

I sped up and flew past the cans and stood up the way Gary did. I wobbled above the seat, hovering and losing my balance quick. I stuck my leg out and felt my whole body leaning to the right, almost ready to topple over, and then I kicked the blue can, not hard, but it rocked back and forth for a second and then fell like a bowling pin.

"Whooo!" Gary yelled.

I rode fast to catch up to him, my heart beating hard and my face red, and he turned at the next corner. When I turned, I saw him, standing above the seat again, holding his arms out like he was on a roller coaster. I got scared, thought he would fall, couldn't understand how he didn't.

Then his bike started to sway, and I could see his legs shake, and he plopped back down on the seat and grabbed the handles. He slowed down, then, and I caught up to him and rode alongside. He looked relaxed, like he was ready to go to sleep, eyes narrow and calm.

"Hey, Gare," I said quietly.

"Yeah?"

I looked up at the sky, all dark blue and gray.

"How was it?" I said.

"How was what?"

"You know what," I said. "Jen."

He smiled and said, "Cool." Then he shrugged. "You know, what's it like with Ray?"

"I haven't done it with Ray," I said, defensive.

Raymond LaCroix was my sort-of boyfriend. We didn't really talk at school, just stuck our tongues in each other's mouths at parties.

"It's different for girls, anyway," I said.

Gary nodded but looked spacey and far away. He stared straight ahead.

"So what was it like?" I said.

"Huh?"

"What was it like?"

"Shit, Mel," he said, shaking his head, looking about twenty-five years old. "You know—cool."

I drove into the city a few nights after me and my mother fought about Gary. She wasn't saying much lately and spent most of her time cleaning, talking to Ken on the phone, drinking her thin drippy diet shakes or light beer, sometimes both. She said she didn't need the car so I took it and went across the bridge. I hadn't been to San Francisco since I got out.

I paid the toll and took 19th Avenue, thinking about how I left the apartment. I just couldn't sit around anymore; it was beginning to get me crazy, and I felt like I couldn't take a clean breath in there to save my life. There was always the 3 A.M. Club, which used to be a dive but got all cleaned up somewhere along the way. Now there was no good beer on tap, prices were higher, no more regulars. My mother said it wasn't the place to drink your shit off anymore.

I rolled down the windows and smelled the trees and saw groups of Asian kids at the bus stops, beers inside their windbreakers, hair up in black spikes. The fog was coming in, and I could feel it on my face. It smelled like water, and it made me think of Sikes. I spent more and more time in the city during our senior year. Sikes's dad lived in the Haight and used to disappear for a few weeks sometimes; he'd just leave Sikes and his brother a few twenties and a twelve pack of Snickers bars. Me and Sikes and Helen used to get drunk in a bar on Haight that would serve us when we were in high school. We really liked screwdrivers back then, spent all night drinking screwdrivers and then went back to Sikes's and scraped up change for a beer.

I headed along Market, toward the Mission. Gary and all his friends used to hang out there because a lot of them lived close by, and there was a pool club they went to. I liked the way all the buildings were low and old. A lot of them made it through the big earthquake.

I parked on a small street and started walking, not remembering streets by name exactly, but everything looked familiar. There seemed to be cafés and stores everywhere, which was not the way I remembered it. There were a lot of people out, tough kids, girls like Jeannie, wearing small jeans, hair pulled back slick with a few strands hanging down in a tight curl. There were also a lot of fashionable people, club people, rich kids, beepers on their belts.

I stopped at a corner store and bought a couple of beers, asked for separate bags and twisted the bag around one like a peppermint stick. The old man behind the counter asked if I wanted to buy a lottery ticket. I said no, and he shook his head like there was no hope for me at all. I noticed there was something wrong with his eye; it sagged low, the skin below it looked like wax paper. It rolled up to look at me.

"Don't get in trouble with that," he said, nodding at my beer.

I smiled at him and left and cracked the first one outside. I

CROOKED

sipped the head off it and sat on some steps. My ass was getting cold; the work pants weren't thick and were almost see-through in the seat, and I didn't have much padding down there anyway. Jeannie said to me once, "You have no ass, Green—I don't know how you don't slide right off the fucking chair." I laughed to myself, and people passed me, looked down for a second and kept going. I drank my beer quick, in three big sips, and tapped the empty can against my shoe and smoked four cigarettes, one after another, lighting one head off the one before.

I thought about where I could go, about finding Manny's Pool Club, Gary's old place, but I couldn't remember exactly where it was; I'd only been there when I was drunk. We used to drive into the city together and go our separate ways, and then I'd go meet him or he'd come meet me, and we'd go home together. We'd take turns driving home, both of us drunk, one of us shotgun, slumped against the side, the other driving, smoking, hunched over the wheel, staring at the white line.

Gary and his friends would always go to Manny's, set up in back and take over a few tables, all fucked up on crank and meth like nuts, Gary's eyes wide, biting his cigarette tight between his teeth. He drank club soda with lots of lemon because he didn't like booze when he was all raced out. Him and his boys and their skinny burnt girlfriends would play cards and shoot pool, look for fights.

I drank down the last of my beer and burped. A young guy with a tank top and leather pants stared at me.

"Can I help you?" I said.

He kept walking.

"Hey, hey, wait," I said, standing.

He turned his head halfway.

"Hey, do you know where Manny's Pool is?" I said.

"Two blocks," he said, lifting up his arm and pointing right. "Near Dolores," he said, not looking at me.

"Right . . . thanks."

I stared at the ground and walked along the lines in the pavement. Twice I thought I heard someone behind me, two or three sets of feet, hushed Spanish, but when I turned around, I didn't see anyone.

Manny's looked the same, except the sign had changed to neon from plain black print, and inside they'd changed the fluorescent lights to stained-glass lamps. There were kids everywhere, smoking, wearing bulky shirts, looking like they weren't old enough to drive, shooting games, drinking at the bar. I eyed some guys at one of the tables who looked like they might have known Gary, dressed shabby like he did, worn-down cords and dirty shirts, but I didn't know them.

I sat at the end of the bar next to a man drinking bourbon and soda. He looked like he hadn't showered for a while. His hands were almost black at the tips, like he'd been digging in hard dirt. He took big sips of his drink and chewed the ice with his mouth open. It made my teeth hurt.

I didn't recognize the bartender—young with chunky sideburns and built big, arms bursting out of his shirt. He nodded at me.

"How much is a Heineken?" I said.

He held up four fingers. I pulled my wallet out and looked inside. Two.

"What's the cheapest drink you have?" I asked.

"Cans of Old Milwaukee for a buck."

"Good," I said, and I put the money on the bar.

The man next to me kept chomping on his ice. It sounded like glass to me and made the hair on my arms stand up. I swiveled around on the chair so he wouldn't be right in my ear and looked around.

I remembered coming there to find Gary one time when I was drunk as hell; his boys were shooting a game, Gary sitting on the stool in the corner with some girl all over him. She was older, in her thirties; she had on a short leather skirt. I said hi to the guys and then walked straight up to Gary, looked at the girl on his lap and said, "Nice hooker."

There was a hand on my arm, on the other side of me, and I yanked it away, elbowed the man next to me in the shoulder. He said, "Hey." I turned around quick and stood up, and the guy held his hands up like I had a gun on him, and he grinned at me. He had an almost shaved head, smooth brownish skin with freckles on his nose, wore tinted amber sunglasses. His lips curled up at the ends like a clown.

"Goddamn last time I say hello nicey-nicey to you," he said.

I smiled.

"Hey, Chick," I said.

He held his arms out, said, "Hey, girl."

I walked to him, put my arms tight around his neck and stuck there for a second. His neck was slippery and warm, and he was lean, strong, squeezed me hard around the waist and almost cracked my back. Then he held my face in his hands, and they were cold.

"Look at you. *Look at you,*" he said.

He stood back and took off his glasses, and looked me up and down, and I felt it in my throat. Me and him always had a little thing for each other but never did anything because it would've pissed the shit out of Gary. He and Gary used to pick fights with each other for fun, just to pass the time, and I didn't ever want to get in the middle of that. It never mattered much; I was still mess-ing around with Sikes, and Chick always had some girl anyway.

"How long you been out?" he said.

"About a month."

"Yeah, feels good, huh?" he said.

"Yeah."

"You fucking some shit up?" he said, tugging my sleeve.

"Oh yeah," I said, laughing. "Same as you, right? Same as always."

He laughed through his teeth.

"Yeah—I got two nights in the tank to show."

"What for?"

"Fucking holding pucks. Searched me for no reason, man," he said, holding his arms out.

I smirked and thought, no reason my ass. He looked a little offended so I straightened up.

"The tank's not messing around," I said.

"No shit, girl, I learned some fucking *shit.*"

He laughed quick and sharp, rubbed his nose and the back of his neck. He kept touching his eyebrows, pulling on his lips, ear-lobes, his upper lip sweating. He said we should go outside and have a cigarette.

It was getting cooler, still wet, and I could feel it, little drops lining my throat, in my nose. Chick lit our cigarettes and scratched at the back of his neck lightly with his fingertips, and it sounded like he was brushing them against a washboard. We sat on the curb like kids.

"What've you been doing?" he asked.

"Not much. Working. What about you?"

"Oh yeah, you know, I'm between jobs," he said, grinning again.

CROOKED

He looked down into the street and pulled at a small thread hanging off the cuff of his jeans.

Then he winced and said, "Shit, man, three years, fucking three years you guys've been gone." His shoulders shook. "It must just goddamn blow your head to be out."

He wrapped the thread around his finger tight, unwound it and wound it again so the tip turned red. He pressed it with his fingernail.

"Yeah, it's something," I said.

"Did you get messed up?" he said, and he held his cigarette to the thread. It started to smoke, got brown and shriveled up, broke in two.

"Hard not to."

"Yeah? People fuck with you?"

"Everybody fucked with me."

He laughed and leaned back for a second like he was going to stretch but then snapped back up, hunched forward again.

"Fucking three years," he said. "I saw you sitting over there, and I'm thinking, that can't be her, but then I was like—" He mimed counting on his fingers. One, two, three. "Yeah, it was you. It is you. Mel Booth, back from the dead," he said, getting louder, and he smacked his palm against the pavement.

I laughed.

"You look great. You look . . . great," he said.

"Thanks."

We sat and smoked and talked about nothing. Then I saw him staring at my hand, and he took my wrist and pulled it to him.

"What happened?" he said.

I told him I cut myself, about my new job and the first couple of weeks, about how I got gloves, about how nobody said a word to me.

He held onto the bottoms of his shoes and rocked back and forth.

"You're doing okay then," he said.

"Okay enough."

"Hey," he said. "Hey, you been to see Gary? I went a couple of months ago," he said, starting to talk faster. "He looks tough—all he does is work out, you know? He is one tough motherfucker, duke it out like he does, but he doesn't fight no more, which is weird to me, you know—you get out there yet?" he said suddenly.

"Not yet."

"We should go. Me and you should go."

"I don't want to go."

Chick stopped rocking and looked at me in the eyes and got still.

"You don't want to tell me about that," he said.

"Right."

We were quiet. We lit more cigarettes and looked around and watched people go by across the street.

"Hey, how's Duke?" I asked him.

He perked up, lifted his head and breathed in deep like he was about to go underwater.

"Same shit with that guy, he's such a fuckup. Living with his uncle still, fixing shit—TVs, stereos, I don't know—lamps, but he's never on time, and he's always coming in hungover and still drunk and falling asleep and shit, and his uncle wants to fire his ass but he can't because he owes it to his old man."

He rubbed his cigarette out on the bottom of his shoe. Then he giggled and said, "I fucking wouldn't hire Duke as a goddamn dog-catcher."

"Hey, Little Chicken, you should talk, seeing you don't even have a fucking job," I said.

CROOKED

"Oh, *there it is,*" he shouted.

The kids in the doorway stared at us.

"There's the fuckin' Mel I know *and* slash *or* love," he yelled, laughing, pointing.

I laughed, too. He stood up in the street and paced back and forth in front of me like a shooting-gallery duck.

"I remember that shit," he said. "I remember 'Nice hooker, Gare.' Almost pissed my panties I was laughing so hard. . . . Gary looked like he was gonna kick your ass, remember?"

"I was too wrecked."

"You could just see him barely holding his shit in," Chick said, not listening to me. He clenched his fists in front of him like he was Gary and scrunched his face up. Then he let it go and pinched his nose, held his breath.

Gary used to hold his breath all the time. He'd been doing it for as long as I could remember, and it got to the point where you'd be talking to him and his face would start to get red, his eyes bulge out a little, but he'd still be nodding, listening to you, drinking beer. You could see the veins in his hands and forehead start to come out, and then he'd start tapping his fingers slowly, counting. He stopped timing himself after he made it to four minutes.

Chick let it out and held his hands up like he was about to bow.

One of the kids at the door said loudly, "Fuckin' junkie."

Chick rolled his shoulders back, and his eyes went crazy, and he started walking over.

"Hey, you little faggot, you wanna fuck with me?" he said, going for him. "Huh?"

"Fuck you, dude," said one of the kid's friends.

I jumped up and followed him, stood behind him and put my hands on his shoulders and pulled at him gently. The kids were all skinny and young, and me and Chick together probably could have taken them, maybe even Chick alone, but I didn't see any reason to get it started.

"Come on, Chick," I said.

His shoulders felt knobby like doll parts that could pop in and out.

The kid looked up at him and brushed the blond hair out of his face. He had acne all over his chin and a ring in his lip, and I thought about how it would slice open his gums if someone hit him there. He couldn't have been more than fifteen but was puffing up his chest, sticking his chin out like a tough guy. His friends crowded behind him.

"Come on, Chick," I said.

I pulled him harder now, grabbed his hand, yanked it, and he gave a little and walked away with me, still facing the kids. I touched his arm, and he jerked it away fast, and then he finally turned around and faced forward.

"I fucking hate kids," he shouted over his shoulder. Then he yelled, "Fuck!" and punched the air in front of him.

"Why you want to hang out with that trash?" my mother asked.

We were both getting ready for work. She was fastening big pearl clip-ons to her ears. I was dressed, sitting on the couch, gloves in my lap.

"He's not trash, Ma. He's a friend of Gary's, for a long time."

"Chick Rodriguez was always in trouble, always on drugs," she said, pulling on her white leather jacket.

I felt my neck get stiff.

"Ma. Gary did more drugs than Chick'll ever do," I said.

She turned around, her mouth open a little, and put her hand on her hip.

"Why you need to say something like that to me for?" she said. "You know that rubs me the wrong way, right; why you need to go and say it?"

I rubbed my eyes fast and felt them start to burn in the corners.

"Chick's not a bad guy is all," I said. "That's all."

"Yeah, that's fine," she said. "That's just so fine. That Chick's a great fella."

"Forget it, forget it," I said quietly.

"I forgot it already, sweet pea," she said. "You want a ride, better move your ass off that couch."

Angie kept falling asleep at the wheel, so I told him to let me drive. He looked like a giant baby, head drooping down over his double chin. He almost protested when I wanted to take over but gave up pretty quickly and dropped off for a few minutes and leaned his head against the window. He was snoring quietly, and I watched his belly move back and forth over his belt. It was big but firm, looked like it was stuffed with mattress filling.

My neck and shoulders still hurt, so I lolled my head around, tried to stretch and get something to crack. I woke up most mornings with my chin pressed to my chest, my legs sore.

I hadn't talked to Chick since the night I ran into him, but I thought about him a lot and had a dream about him where he pushed me against a wall, pressed his body on me. He was holding my face in his hands and saying some kind of gibberish, and I could feel his breath. I woke up feeling like I was in a hot tub, all warm wet skin.

Angie shook awake suddenly.

"Ay," he said, and he held onto the door handle.

He yawned.

"How long've I been sleeping?"

"Ten, fifteen minutes," I said. "Why're you so tired today?"

"I was up late," he said, looking out the window. Then he said quietly, "I boxed."

"You boxed?" I asked. He looked at me sideways. "Do you do that a lot?"

"You know, here and there."

"Who do you fight?"

He opened the window a crack and stuck his hand out, held onto the top of the cab.

"There's a group—we have a league, amateur league."

"Do people ever come to watch?"

"There's a few people, not a crowd, not like Vegas," he said.

I laughed.

"Could I come watch?" I asked.

He shrugged.

"Why do you want to see that?" he said.

I hunched my shoulders up and let them drop.

"I don't know," I said. "It sounds good to me."

He was quiet.

"You know, if it's not cool, forget it. No big deal," I said under my breath.

We didn't say anything for a few minutes. I stared ahead, didn't want to look over.

Then he said, "No, it's cool. You can come. I'll let you know."

"All right," I said.

He went back to sleep soon after. We weren't going far, only to San Anselmo where there'd been an outdoor wedding, and we were supposed to pick up three units. I shook Angie awake when I pulled in. He stretched and yawned again and put his gloves on.

We got out, and it was hot and smoky, like there was a fire somewhere near. The inn where we were picking the units up was a fake Victorian, not like the ones in San Francisco, which were old and detailed down to the stroke. This one was painted bright purple with gold trim and looked like a birthday cake. I put my hand to my forehead to block the sun from my eyes and told Angie I'd find out what's what.

I rang the doorbell and an older lady wearing a long flowy dress opened it. She was tan and wrinkled and had her hair pulled back with a thick orange headband. The skin at the top of her head was stretched tight, looked like water would slide right off it.

"We're from Port-o-Loo," I said.

She looked at me blankly. I pointed to the truck, and she snapped her fingers.

"Right, right, right-o," she said. "They're in back."

I stood in front of her, waiting for her to move out of the way, and she looked down at my dirty sneakers, and then over at Angie with pit stains on his shirt, the right side of his face creased from sleeping so hard.

"I'll, uh, meet you back there. The fence is open," she said.

I gave her the thumbs-up, and she shut the door.

"She said the fence is unlocked," I said to Angie, jumping off the porch. "We're too dirty to walk on her shiny carpets apparently."

"She say that?"

"Nah, I'm just kidding."

We pushed the fence open and walked into the garden, and it smelled fresh. There was a patch of flowers so bright it looked fake, like all the petals were drawn on.

The tan lady came out of the house through a screen door and stood on the deck.

"You know, we only needed two," she said. "The man on the phone said we'd need three for two hundred people."

"Sorry about that," Angie said, so genuine, so sweet it made me want to scream.

"I think I should get some kind of discount or credit, don't you?" she said, like we were children.

"Oh yeah," Angie said. "Sure. No problem—you have to call Joe, though. We don't do the billing, only delivery," he said, headed to the units.

The lady looked impatient and sighed like she'd been waiting for hours.

"Can't you just tell him? You work for him," she said.

I felt my throat get dry, heard my pulse in my head and took a deep breath, pulled my gloves on tight. I clapped my hands together a couple of times just to do something with them.

Angie smiled wide, all teeth. He looked like an alligator.

"Sure thing, miss. No problem," he said.

She went back inside, and her shoes sounded like hooves. I shook my head and breathed hard through my nose.

"What an asshole," I whispered, and me and Angie bent down to grab the unit at the base.

Angie shook his head.

"She's not bad," he said. "She thinks she's been cheated."

We lifted it up, and the smell wafted up through the vents and made my eyes water. It was so much heavier now; I had to lean back as I walked, staring at the sticker on the side that said, "Do Not Handle. Vessel Contains Human Waste." I could hear the piss and shit sloshing around like waves. Waves of shit. I coughed so I wouldn't gag.

The worst thing I ever smelled was the garbage pit at Staley. Usually there were other girls to bring it down, but a few times me and Inez had to go after kitchen duty, haul all the shit we scraped into the cans and throw it in the huge orange Dumpster filled to the top with four or five days' worth of old food, rotten meat and wet vegetables and mold, dead air and no circulation.

The shit me and Angie were carrying was worse, but at least we were outside. I still felt an inch away from puking.

"Hold your breath," said Angie.

I took a deep breath in through my mouth and held it until I saw stars.

Joe was pissed off about something when we got back to the shop.

"Sometimes he has a chip on his shoulder for no reason," Angie told me.

We pulled up at the drop-off doors, and Joe came out of the dock waving his clipboard, yelling as he got closer.

"Were you planning to unload these without signing them in?" he shouted.

Angie nodded and smiled again.

"Oh yeah. Sorry," he said cheerfully.

Joe pointed at him with his pen and said, "You better be sorry. Don't fuck with the process."

My head started to thump again; it felt like a big fist was knocking around between my ears. I thought my nose would start bleeding, and I shook my head quickly. Joe looked at me.

"You haven't been here long enough to give me attitude, Booth, all right?" he said.

My heart rapped against my chest, and I grabbed the edge of my seat.

"Right," I said.

He stared back at me and narrowed his eyes, chewed on his mustache. Then he slapped his clipboard on the hood.

"Get this outta here until you sign them in."

"Sure thing, boss," Angie said.

He backed the truck up and headed for the main entrance. I leaned my head back and felt my heart slow down.

"I thought it didn't matter when you signed them in," I said.

Angie shrugged.

"Sometimes Joe likes to do it exactly by the rules, sometimes he don't."

He stopped, and I got out, went around back and wrote the numbers down on the small pad he kept in the glove.

"Meet me at drop-off," Angie said, and left.

I went in and grabbed the sign-in sheet and started writing the numbers in. Tommy John was on the pay phone a few feet away. He leaned against the wall, his back to me.

"Sure, baby," he said. "No big thing."

He was talking all low and husky, like he was in bed with someone.

"Yeah, don't you worry. All right, later," he said and hung up.

He turned and saw me there and smiled. I could see his two gold teeth on either side of his mouth.

"You hear that?" he said to me, still quiet.

"Yeah," I said, smirking. "It was *hot.*"

He stopped smiling and walked up to me.

CROOKED

"You shouldn't listen to other people's phone conversations," he said, and I could feel his breath on my neck. "It's an invasion of privacy."

"You should make sure no one's around if it's so goddamn private," I said.

I wrote the last number and let the board drop against the wall. Tommy John looked me over.

"So tell me, Staley," he said, "what'd you do time for?"

A lot of times lately I felt like something was going to come up out of my mouth and choke me to death. A thick wet worm—I could feel it twisting up my throat while I stood there and stared at Tommy John and he stared back, all smug.

"None of your fucking business, Folsom," I said, out of breath.

He smiled. I didn't.

"Hey, Booth!" Joe shouted at the other end of the dock.

He waved his arms and looked like a pelican.

"You have enough time to write a goddamn number down? Huh?"

"Yeah," I yelled back, and I turned away from Tommy John.

"Quit pissing around," he called.

He headed back, yelling at Tino on the way.

"Sir, yes SIR," Tommy John whispered behind me.

I chewed on my lip so I wouldn't smile and started walking away. I heard Tommy John laughing low, and then he called, "Hey, Staley—"

I turned around without thinking about it.

He pointed his finger at me like it was a gun and said, "I bet you killed someone."

CHAPTER

6

Chick didn't have an answering machine, and I wasn't surprised. I called three days in a row but could never get him so I kept staring at the matchbook he gave me, thinking maybe the 9 was an 0, the 5 was a 6, and then I gave up. And then he called.

"What's going on with you?" he said.

"Nothing. Where've you been, though? I've been trying to call you."

"Yeah? Oh well, yeah, I don't know, I'm usually around, I usually never leave. What time about?" he said, sniffling.

"I don't know, six, seven."

"Oh, yeah, not then. I'm not really home then," he said. "Sorry."

"Get a machine, man. Don't waste my time like that," I said, smiling.

"Right, right, you're a busy lady, right," he mumbled. "Hey, I saw Duke," he said, excited, "He wants to see you—I always thought he had a little thing for you, you know, he got dopey when you were around."

"Yeah? That bug you?" I said.

He giggled like he was nervous, and cleared his throat.

"Nah, man, free country."

We were quiet. I sat on a stool and rubbed the balls of my feet against the carpet until they burned. I imagined him on the other end, his mouth close to the receiver. I breathed in deep through my nose like I could smell him.

"So what else you been doing, Mel?" he said.

"I don't know," I said, looking out the sliding glass doors at the shrubs. "Not so much, just working."

"Yeah? What else?" he said.

"Shit, man, I don't know," I said, my eyes wandering to the kitchen. "I did the dishes yesterday."

Chick laughed.

"Yeah, girl, that's what I'm talking about. What *do* you do with yourself, Mel? What else you do yesterday?"

I wound the phone cord around my finger.

"Uh," I said. "I had a bowl of Froot Loops."

He laughed again, high and quick, like a little boy.

"Which ones are your favorite? What color?" he said.

"Uh," I said, trying to think about it, trying to picture all the different colors.

"No, quick, tell me, don't think about it too much."

I could hear him catch his breath on the other end, getting excited. It made me excited, hearing him like that.

"Yellow," I said.

"Yellow," he said quietly. "What is that, like, lemon-flavored, or what?"

"I think so," I said. "They all taste kind of the same, though."

"So what'd you do last night?" he said quickly, excited again, like he didn't hear what I had said.

"I watched TV."

"What you watch?"

"Weather."

"What else, what else?" he said fast.

I bent my leg up on the stool and sniffed at the knee of my jeans. It smelled like smoke.

"That's it," I said. "Just weather."

"That's it? No infomercials or anything?"

"No—hey, enough, okay, why are you asking me all this shit?" I said.

I didn't have to laugh but I forced one out anyway because I didn't want to make him uncomfortable.

He was quiet. I heard him breathing through his mouth. I closed my eyes and listened.

"Shit, Mel, I don't know," he said. "I just, I like to picture you doing different things."

I froze up; the back of my head got tingly, like I'd bumped it.

"You watching TV, the weather or whatever, or smoking, or doing the dishes, which I bet just pisses you off, having to do shit like that," he said.

I laughed for real now and covered my mouth. He laughed, too, and trailed off.

Then loudly, suddenly, he said, "Do you have any cigarettes?"

"What? Now?"

"Yeah, now. Do you have any?"

"Yeah," I said. "Why?"

"We should have a smoke, okay?" he said. "I know I'm probably not getting you out here tonight, at least have a smoke with me."

"Over the phone?"

"Yeah, over the phone," he said.

"Okay," I said. I grabbed my cigarettes from the counter and lit one. "You light yet?" I said.

"Hold on," he said, and I could tell he had the cigarette between his teeth. Then I heard a Zippo snap open and close. He exhaled. "There we go," he said, relaxed.

"So what did you do yesterday?" I said.

"I don't know—nothing."

I coughed up smoke. "Oh, come on, man, you make me tell you what fucking cereal I eat and you're like, 'I don't know'?"

He laughed skittishly. "Well, let's see here," he said. "I went to the corner. Wait, first I woke up, and I counted all the dimes and nickels on my dresser, and then I went looking in all the ashtrays for half-smokes, and Colin was up and he was like, you want to smoke a bowl, and I said, yeah."

Then he was quiet.

"Wow," I said. "That's a great story, Chick."

He laughed like crazy. He laughed so hard he had to pull the receiver away from his mouth.

Then he calmed down for a second and said, "Come on, Mel, come over."

It was sexy, the way he said it—drove me nuts thinking of him lying on his bed, maybe with his shirt off.

"No, baby, I can't, not now," I said quietly.

"Baby" just came out, just floated liquid past my lips, and I couldn't control it. I heard him catch his breath.

"All right, Mel," he said, growly. "You're not getting away from me this weekend, though, right?"

"Right," I said, pulling my lip, trying to turn the smile down.

"Can't you come now?" he said again. "Just, like, for an hour?"

"I have work tomorrow," I said.

"What happened to you? So straight," he sighed.

"Right," I said, spacey, staring at the black tin plates on the cupboard handles below the sink.

The drunkest I ever got was on the fourth of July, the one before I went to Staley. I was with Helen, and me and her met Gary and Chick and Duke at Duke's uncle's place in San Rafael. Me and Helen were drinking Bushmills and RC, and then we ran out of RC so we drank it on ice, and then we ran out of ice so we drank it mixed with a little tap water and then just straight. I remembered being hot as hell, and that the CD player was broken and I kept messing with it.

Gary was wearing a wrinkled white shirt that looked yellow, and he and Chick were hopped on meth and getting into arguments about nothing. Chick was on the phone a lot with some girl, but I didn't care because I was still messed up about Sikes even though we weren't speaking.

We all climbed up to the roof to watch the fireworks, but we could only see the very tips, little sparks of red and blue, and I cut my shin on the drainpipe going back down. Helen sat between Gary's legs and later I caught them kissing in the bathroom.

Then there was no more whiskey so we started drinking beer, and Duke took his clothes off because we asked him to, and I laughed, and his dick was really long and floppy.

Gary told me later that we went for a walk, that I drove us to the supermarket, that I sniffed up some of their shit off the ten-of-hearts card that Gary kept in his wallet, and that I pissed in some-

CROOKED

body's driveway. Gary told me this the next afternoon when I woke up on the couch with dried blood on my upper lip. He hadn't been to sleep yet, and Chick was out on the floor.

Gary was rocking back and forth, sweating clear through all of his clothes, smoking. He had bad dandruff, greasy hair, never took showers, but he never really smelled bad, only salty. He started to gnaw at his nails, chewed at the skin around them, nibbling like a mouse, and he was pale, lighter than his shirt; his eyes bounced back and forth like tennis balls. He looked real sick to me. I remembered thinking, Gary never feels well.

When I got off the phone with Chick, I started drinking my mother's Jack. There was no ice, so I scraped the frost out from the bottom of the trays into my mug, and it stuck to the side like magnets. The whiskey was a little hard to take; I had to cough after the first sip.

I flipped on the TV and turned the sound off and left it on the weather channel. I watched the weatherman point to the map of California. His hair didn't move, and he only had two gestures, the point, and the frame, when he held both his hands out, explaining things. There were fat cartoon drops on their way down, and a storm coming in from the Pacific, looked like a big Brillo pad.

I turned off the TV and kept drinking and lit a smoke. I hummed to myself. Thought about when Chick said, "Nah, free country," and I laughed out loud. "Screw you, big boy," I said to the air.

I poured a refill and went to my mother's room and sat on the bed. It squeaked and sank in toward the middle. There was a coffee-colored ashtray on the nightstand with ash pressed into the side like wax, and one butt with lipstick on the pinched end. There was a framed picture of her and Ken—they were drunk, laughing; he was pointing at the camera; his forehead looked greasy. They were at a restaurant; there were big fried tortilla shells on plates in front of them that looked like giant clams.

I went to the dresser and saw a picture of me and Gary, probably five or six, standing in the backyard of the house in Tacoma. We're both squinting, sun in our eyes. We looked skinny, partially because we were just bony kids, but mostly because we were underfed. I was wearing a yellow sundress. I was surprised how much Gary and me actually looked like real live twins when we were little. We had the same color hair, and I hadn't gone pale yet. We were a little bit Ohlone on our mother's side; Nana's grandma was full, and Gary looked it but I never did. Sometime soon after the picture was taken, I started burning like crazy in the sun, started looking pink all the time; my hair got lighter, and my eyes, too, from what I could tell but I wasn't ever sure. No one seemed to be able to remember too much from around then, and there weren't a lot of pictures. I just remembered being hungry most of the time.

I went to the bathroom and stared at my face for a while, pinched my cheeks and the skin on my chin hard, my forehead, my neck. I watched it turn pink and snap back like a rubber suit. I stared at myself and imagined talking to Chick, imagined telling a funny story. Hey, Chick, you remember when me and Helen got wrecked on the fourth of July? Remember when I drove you and Gary around?

"I was *so* shitty," I said aloud, drawing it out like a movie star on a talk show.

I went for another refill and sat back on the couch and looked at the ceiling, at the plaster that looked like it was never smoothed out, dried into little icicles. I crossed my legs and swung one back and forth and imagined I was talking to Gary. Hey, Gare, I thought in my head. Remember how we never ate when we were kids? Remember how we looked alike?

"Do you?" I said.

I laughed with my mouth wide open, and it sounded nutty, like an old lady, like an old witch.

Then my mother and Ken came home. I heard the door open and saw them kissing out of the corner of my eye, heard them smacking their lips on each other like they were eating chicken wings.

"Hey, there," my mother said, surprised.

She pulled Ken into the living room, one finger hooked in his. His mouth was stained pink with her lipstick. She put her purse down on the counter and straightened her dress out, and I looked down at her calves; the skin of her ankles spilled out over the straps of her chunky straw heels.

"Hi, Ma," I sighed.

"Well, hey," she said, tired, looking down at the table. "Drank all my Jack, huh?"

She sounded disappointed.

"Yeah, I'm sorry about that. I got carried away," I said. "Howdy, Ken."

"Evening," said Ken quietly, and he sat straight up on a stool by the counter.

My mother got two beers and slid one to him.

"How was your dinner?" I asked.

She took a swig of her beer, and the bracelets on her wrists clinked.

"It was real good, you know, I always get the same thing—the Mu Shu pork. I love that sauce, the plum sauce," she said. "Ken, he always gets something new—he's brave that way," she said, winked at him and pinched his elbow. He smiled and tried to wink back but blinked both of his eyes instead, and it looked like he had a facial tic.

"He got this thing tonight, what's it called, baby, what you got?"

"What's that?" Ken said.

"What'd you get tonight, the dish?"

"General Ti-so's chicken."

"That's it," she said. "It was spicy as hell. What about you? What've you been doing?"

"Nothing much. Watched TV."

"Yeah? Anything good on?" she said, looking down at her hand.

I didn't think she was listening. She came around and sat on the Hawaiian chair, started untying her sandals.

"Weather," I said.

It came out sounding slow. My lips were numb, my fingers, too, but my ears were hot, and my palms felt like they were being steamed. I looked at Ken, propping himself on the counter with his arms. He looked at me and stared blankly, like he was looking at something behind me.

"Weather? All night you watched weather?" she asked.

"I like it," I said, getting edgy.

She laughed. "I like to know if it's going to rain tomorrow, too, but how much else can they tell you, right?" she said, looking over at Ken.

He nodded and laughed. They were having a joke on me.

"I also hung out in your room," I said. "I was looking at that picture of me and Gary."

She stopped messing with her shoes and looked at me.

When I was a kid, I wasn't supposed to go in her room when she wasn't home, and I was always supposed to knock. It was usually because she had a man in there, and she didn't want us to see them doing it, even though we could hear everything. When I was older, I thought she might have been into drugs, but I never knew for sure either way. She wasn't going to get into it with me now, though; maybe she didn't care anymore.

"That's a sweet picture," she said, like it was someone else's kids. Then she smiled at Ken and said, "My two babies."

She looked back at me and winked. She sipped her beer. Ken was nodding out on the stool. They were both so calm, and it made me feel crazy. It was so easy to be calm.

"What's so sweet about it?" I said.

She looked at me, confused.

"Excuse me," she said.

"It's real sweet," I said, standing. "It's sweet as anything, Ken, you have no idea."

His mouth hung open a little, like a trout.

"What's *so* sweet about it is we were starving all the time," I announced.

"Mel," my mother said low.

"We had chicken broth and peppermint candies," I said, swinging my glass around.

"Mel," she said, angrier.

"Sometimes, you know, she'd be so busy out there *providing* for us she'd forget to come home for a couple of days sometimes."

"Melody," she said, and she was pissed now.

"What?" I said. "You tell him anything, Ma? Anything that's the truth at all? He know Gary's in jail, even?"

"Okay!" she shouted, and she sliced her hand in front of her like she was yelling *cut.*

Her eyes were starting to get filmy but not quite. I couldn't ever make her cry. Gary could, but not me.

"That's enough now," she said.

"Does he know anything?" I said. "About you?"

"Mel, I'm not talking to you when you're like this."

"Like what?" I said, tough, walking up to her.

I could smell the beer, the cabbage in her teeth, soy sauce on her breath like smoke.

"Ugly drunk like you are. Go to bed," she said, looking disgusted, shaking her head at me.

She turned around and bent down to pick up her sandals by the straps, walked to her room and slammed the door. Ken stood up.

"Why've you got to say those things?" he said, almost sadly.

"Good night, *Ken.*"

I lied down on the couch and shut my eyes, and I heard him go to my mother's room. I punched the air in front of me and then got on the floor and started doing push-ups. Around thirty I felt the strain in my chest like strings pulling and stretching, and my arms felt soft. I kept going and counted off, my voice getting quieter and quieter as I got out of breath: "57, 58, 59." I kept going, whispering, until it felt like I didn't have any more air in my chest at all, and then I dropped to the carpet and just stayed there, buried my face in the threads.

I wet a rag from a water fountain and squeezed it on the back of my neck, and lukewarm drops fell down my shirt. I leaned my head down to the faucet, and the water tasted like rust, but I lapped it up anyway.

I looked up and didn't see Angie. The sky was gray and overcast, and the wind was starting up even though it was still warm. It whipped my hair around my face and felt good. We were a few miles east of Antioch where everything was flat. All the buildings were one-story, brown cement with big red letters—Target, Kmart, Denny's.

Angie turned the corner, said something to the man with the 49ers hat, who nodded and shook his hand. Angie walked toward me, waddled a little bit, like a nesting doll rocking back and forth. He waved to me.

"What do they need?" I called.

"No more," Angie said. "They're all set."

I barely heard him; the wind was starting to suck everything up.

"I thought they needed eight," I said.

"Just five," he said. "You got a fever?" he asked, pointed to the rag.

"I'm just hot."

He smiled wide. He was kidding; he knew I didn't have a fever. I laughed, too late.

"You want to eat?" he said.

"Yeah. I do."

We started walking, and the block reminded me of L.A.—all cars and no people. Cars went past us, pulled in and out of lots. We went into a Burger King and made tracks with our shoes on the white tile.

"What do you want?" Angie asked.

"Get me a chicken sandwich," I said, and I reached for my wallet.

"Later, later," he said, and he waved me away.

I sat at a booth next to the window and ran my palms along the table. At the next table there was a mother with her children, and one of them was crying. She held the other one in her lap and kept feeding it French fries. She stared into the parking lot. Angie came back and pushed a drink across the table to me.

"They bring it to you now," he said.

He placed a small plastic card that read "17" on the edge of our table.

"First class," I said.

"Better not want a tip," he said.

The Coke chilled my teeth. Angie stretched his arms over him and yawned, rolled his neck around and cracked it. I wanted to tell him about things all of a sudden.

Then our food came, and we ate it and didn't speak. I looked at Angie's Whopper, the meat hanging out of the bun, and I wanted to lean over and bite it off. My chicken tasted chewy and dry. The breading was too thin, not enough mayonnaise.

"You want a taste?" Angie said, holding the burger out.

"No, no thanks. Sorry," I said quietly.

I stared out the window for a minute and then said, "I had a fight with my mother last night."

Angie raised his eyebrows.

"Oh, yeah?" he said. "What's it about?"

"I think she's been lying to her boyfriend."

Angie nodded.

"She have other boyfriends?"

"No, I don't think so."

"Then what she lie about?"

My fingers felt cold from the air-conditioning. I sat on my hands.

"Herself. Things in her life," I said.

Angie nodded again.

"Me. My brother," I said.

He looked thoughtful and peered out the window at the shrubs blowing around.

"Why do you care?" he said.

CROOKED

"I don't know."

"Why do you make yourself feel bad, you don't care?" he said, and he rolled his napkin into a ball. "You tell the truth all the time?"

I laughed.

"No."

"Me neither," he said. "Leave Mami alone."

I laughed again, and then he leaned across the table, like he was telling me a secret, and said, "Everybody lies, Booth."

It was still raining when I got over to see Chick. I took the bus because my mother said she needed the car, and I didn't make a stink about it. We weren't talking much.

Chick was living off Clement Street way up in the avenues, in a flat with a guy I didn't know. I rang the bell on the metal gate and got buzzed in, walked up the confetti concrete stairs and knocked on the glass door. The blinds shook behind it.

Chick opened it and barely looked me in the eye, nervous.

"Hey, what's going on," he said.

He hugged me quickly, put his hands on my back for only a second and then pulled them away fast like they were getting burned. I stepped into the living room after him and saw a dirty futon slouching to one side on broken wooden boards, and a few crates full of clothes next to it. There was a blue plastic table that looked like part of a lawn set; it was covered with beer cans, water bottles, a couple of ashtrays.

"Colin sleeps out here," Chick said. "Motherfucker doesn't know how to keep house."

He shook his head sadly, and it made me laugh. Then he clapped his hands together.

"There is a very special guest here tonight," he said.

"Oh, boy."

Then he said, "Wait here," and went into the other room.

I sat on the high end of the futon, and it sank. My legs slid out in front of me until I stopped them with my feet.

Chick came out pushing a tall guy with hunched-over shoulders and a kerchief on his head.

"Duke?" I said, not really believing it.

I jumped up and ran to hug him, didn't realize I even missed him until that second, and I just fell right to pieces. I got overwhelmed by it, felt like I was choking a little. He was so big, too big, always hunched over like he felt bad about being tall, always wearing his big owl glasses, long arms and legs like a Daddy spider. I hooked my arms around his neck, and he lifted me up.

"What's up, Mel?" he said, and he swung me lightly back and forth.

He smelled like he hadn't showered or washed his shirt for a while, but I didn't care. I put my face in his shoulder and just hung on for a second, and my feet dangled.

"Nothing at all," I said, and he put me down. "How the fuck *are* you, man?" I said, giddy, punching at him.

"Good."

I took his hands and pulled him to the futon, sat us both down. Chick noticed and looked away.

"Fucking Diamond Duke," I said, looking him over.

"Yeah . . . that's me," he said, grinning, looking shy. He always looked shy, always seemed like he was embarrassed about something.

Chick got us some beers, and I took my shoes off. Duke took his bandanna off and rubbed his hand over what there was of his hair, and my mouth fell open.

"Shit, you lost *a lot* of hair," I said.

Chick laughed like a maniac, held his stomach and almost spit up.

"Thanks, Mel. I can always count on you," Duke said, getting pink.

"I'm sorry, it's just . . . shocking."

He started to smile, but Chick wouldn't shut up, still laughing like crazy, jaw hanging open like a puppet.

"It's not that fucking funny," Duke said.

"Oh yeah," Chick said, nodding, "Fuckin' Mel, right? 'Nice hooker.'"

Now they both laughed, and I started, too, but not about Duke's bald head, or the time I said, "Nice hooker." I just really couldn't believe I was right there shooting the shit with Chick and Duke, like I was Gary, like it was a long time ago, and soon we'd be talking about caps and pucks and where to go and what to drink. Then my stomach turned over, and I got nervous, like I was a big fake and they were going to find out.

Soon we started drinking seriously, though, and I didn't think about it anymore. Chick brought out some whiskey, and we talked about nothing, but I was laughing so hard at everything and wasn't even drunk yet. I slid off the futon and sat propped up against it, wiped my eyes with my sleeves.

"Wow," said Duke, looking at my arm, at *juera.*

"Isn't that fucking tough?" said Chick. "Some *chula* cut that into you—that's so *tough.* "

Duke pulled my wrist to him to get a better look, and I let it go limp.

Suddenly Chick said, "Oh yeah, hey, Duke, don't feel bad, Mel hasn't seen Gary either."

I craned my head up to look at Duke, and he didn't look back. Chick rooted around on the floor next to his chair, kept lifting up magazines and papers.

"Where are my fucking smokes, dude?" he said.

Duke ran his finger around the rim of his glass and looked like he was about to say something.

"It's okay," I said.

I hugged my knees to my chest. I felt like he was going to touch me, lay his palm on the back of my head or my neck. I closed my eyes.

Chick sat up on his chair again and lit a cigarette, stuck his tongue out at us. It was long and pointed at the tip.

"I haven't had a chance to make it out there," Duke said quietly.

"It's okay," I said.

"What's okay?" said Chick.

"Nothing."

Chick nodded and said like he was a high school teacher, "That is so true, Miss Booth." Then he giggled and nodded to Duke. "Hey, man, tell her about what we did at Sammy's."

"No, come on," said Duke. He took his glasses off and rubbed his nose.

"Yeah, yeah," Chick shouted at him, and then he turned to me and almost fell off his chair. "Duke hit this guy, this fucking punk," Chick told me, excited like a little kid. "Mouthing off to him, come on, what he say, Duke, what he say, like—" Chick took on a fake Southern accent, "'You and yer skinhead boyfriend better go,' or some fuckin' thing."

Duke shifted his legs around. I leaned forward.

"And Duke says," Chick said, standing up to demonstrate.

CROOKED

He hunched his shoulders over like he was Duke and kept talking. Duke looked down and started turning red again.

"Duke says, 'All right, man, no problem,' and then he"—Chick said, snapping a right fast—"BOOM!" Then he mimed the other guy, looking dazed, holding his nose, stumbling backward and falling into his chair like a bum in a cartoon.

The second time it was in the rec room again and Shandra sat on me to keep me from kicking. It was just her and Lulu J., and I'd seen Lomey a second before and could hear him whistling down the hall. Jeannie told me later Lulu was giving it to him and it didn't shock me.

My arm still throbbed first thing when I woke up every morning, but I didn't need the bandage anymore and I started screaming when she pulled the razor blade out of her pocket, thinking they were going for my arm again, and Shandra covered my mouth and I bit her.

"Fuck you, bitch," she said, and she grabbed my hair and knocked my head against the floor.

I saw stars and felt nauseous, right about to puke. She held both my arms down over my head, and I tried to make fists but just grabbed soft at nothing. My legs felt like there were no bones in them, and my mouth was full of spit; I could feel it running down my chin.

"She's drooling," Shandra said to Lulu J., laughing.

"Shut up," Lulu J. said to her.

I was dizzy, ready to pass out, and didn't get it when she pulled my pants down around my ankles. I thought she was going to write something else, on my thigh, my hip. And then her hand went up, I felt her short ropey fingers in my pussy, jabbing in and out, scraping the skin. My thighs clamped up, like a reflex, like I was a virgin. I thought about the guy I lost it to when I was thirteen, his face swam around in my head, we didn't know what we were doing; I tried to say his name, Raymond, Raymond LaCroix.

"Shut the fuck up," Shandra said.

She put her hand over my mouth, and then Lulu J. stopped fingering me and stuck in the blade. Later I couldn't remember screaming, but I did remember Shandra grabbing my hair in a wad above my forehead, saying, Shut up bitch, shut your fuckin' mouth. Lulu J. cut me up, three four five times, thin lines; I felt the blood well up like water and start to spill out.

I couldn't breathe anymore, couldn't hear right. It was like I was being held down in a swimming pool. There was puke rising in my throat, and I coughed but nothing came up, and she kept going until I couldn't feel it at all, and there was just nothing, a black screen in front of my face and voices saying, You're dead, in English and Spanish, and I passed out.

Chick popped a couple of chalky newlyweds, one white, one blue, and gave Duke a white, rolled his eyes when I said no. He mashed his face up and pointed his finger at me.

"No, Dad, I learned it from watching you!" he shouted.

Duke laughed, and I did, too, but didn't know what he was talking about. Chick sat up and picked at his eyebrows, scratched his arms. It made my elbows itch watching him. I scratched at them, and they felt like tree bark.

Chick wiped his forehead with his hand and smelled it. Leaned back, leaned forward, his leg going up and down like a sewing machine. He looked at me and smiled, pupils big as quarters.

We were almost done with the whiskey, and my shoulders and

neck were starting to feel warm. Chick turned on the TV and flipped channels and stood holding the remote and wouldn't sit back down, smoking, pacing.

"What are we watching?" I said.

"I don't know," Duke whispered.

Chick left it on a home-shopping channel. There was a lady modeling a thick gold bracelet. Her forearm took up the whole screen and looked smooth and white.

"She has really nice nails," Duke said.

"Yeah," I said.

We watched the lady turn her forearm toward the camera and away again, three or four times. I looked down at my hands, and they were dry and felt cold suddenly; the tip of my nose did, too.

Duke stood up and said, "I have to use the facilities."

I laughed at him and Chick said, "Don't fucking take anything."

Duke said, "Ha, ha," and left. Chick raised his eyebrows at me, and the bracelet lady kept at it on TV, kept twisting her arm around while another lady talked about how beautiful the bracelet was. Chick sat down next to me.

"Gimme your hand," he said.

"Why?"

"I want to hold it."

His eyes were huge in his face, big and shoe-polish brown. I stuck out my hand, and he took it and started petting it, concentrating, touching each of my fingers.

Duke came back in and looked at us, a little surprised, and then he sat down on the other side of me. He smelled like deodorant and B.O., and Chick smelled like cigarettes and mint. My nose started to run, and my toes were cold inside my shoes.

"Hey," I said to Chick.

He shook, like I'd woken him up; his hand twitched out of mine.

"Sorry," I said.

He shook his head.

"Forget it."

"Hey, though, do you have a jacket or something. I'm fucking cold."

"Yeah, yeah, in my room, past the bathroom, take whatever."

I got up and took my beer and went to the bathroom first. It was filthy, and I liked it in a way. The bathroom at my mother's apartment was too clean; she scraped the sink and the tub so hard there were thin ridges carved in by the cleanser.

I peed and washed my hands and saw that Chick's sink was brown around the rim and the faucets, and the drain was covered with dried-up toothpaste. I noticed two ants walking near the soap shelf and pressed down on them with the tip of my finger. They felt like sand.

I went into Chick's room and flipped on the light, and it was cold, the window open with the blinds half up, the other half pinched together. There was a single bed with a metal frame, looked like a hospital bed, with a green wool blanket on it and a meat-colored mattress underneath. Clothes and magazines, cereal boxes, newspapers everywhere.

I opened some drawers, saw two pairs of white sports socks and a few T-shirts. I picked up a napkin from the top of the dresser, and it had a fuzzy phone number on it and a name I couldn't read.

"Nosy, nosy," I said at myself in the mirror.

I went into the closet and saw some clothes thrown over the wooden bar, sinking low in the middle, and I pulled a pair of pants off, and they all came down, piled on the floor.

CROOKED

"Shit."

I knelt down and sifted through—jeans, jacket, shorts. I pulled a blue hooded sweatshirt out and put it on, and it smelled like the dirt in a potted plant. I tried to balance on my haunches but was too drunk, tipped forward and fell on my face, pushed over a shoe-box, and then a gun fell out. I held it between two fingers, and it was heavy and cold. I put it back in the box.

Nana had three guns and taught me and Gary how to load and hold and shoot when we were ten. She and a bunch of her friends, the nicest little old ladies you could meet, used to go to a range and practice, packed pieces in their patent-leather handbags. Hold it here, honey, she said, put my tiny hand around the other. Don't let anyone tell you you can't handle an autoload just because you're a girl. Hold it tight, now.

I stayed in the closet for a minute, on my knees, my big drunk head moving slow and sloppy, and I shut my eyes, thought, God-damn you, Chick.

He watched me when I came back. He was rubbing his thumb and finger together, like there was something between them he was trying to keep warm. I looked at him and smiled. He smiled back, baring teeth, sweating bullets.

CHAPTER

7

Out of all of them, there were two of my mother's men who were a lot worse than the others, who stayed in my head for years afterward. The first was Denny. The second was Cal.

My mother started dating Denny when Gary and I'd just turned thirteen. She'd picked him up at the bar people called the Mill because it was right down from the big paper mill, where Denny worked. He was football-player wide and had a blocky forehead that stuck out over his eyes, and Gary called him The Caveman. He had blue tattoos on his forearms you could see when he rolled his flannel shirts up. At first I liked him a little; at least I could see what my mother liked about him, the way he was so strong, the way his arms and legs were so thick. But Gary said there wasn't anything different about him. He's just another asshole who does her when she's drunk, Gary said.

There was this one time when Gary and I saw Evan Trambleau

get hit by a car, heard his head crack on the pavement and watched his whole body roll, and saw the blood drip into the gutter. Someone called for an ambulance, and there was a crowd gathering, and Evan's big sister sat cross-legged on the ground with his head in her lap, his arms stuck out like a scarecrow. She rocked him back and forth, and whispered something to him we couldn't hear.

He was one of Gary's best friends. Gary stood there and didn't say anything, smoked about a pack of cigarettes and made a big show about it, lighting them by thumbing the match and blowing rings. He knew adults wouldn't give him shit about smoking when there was this dead kid a few yards away.

I didn't want to see Evan get lifted away, all smashed to pieces, arms and legs hanging off him everywhere, so I took off, ran home, busted in through the back door and went straight to my mother's room. I tapped on her door and said, "Mama." I knew she was in there, sleeping.

I opened the door slowly and saw her asleep on her stomach, her ears stuffed with cotton balls, and Denny was lying next to her, and a sheet was tucked over his private parts. He smiled at me slow, and it made me feel sick in my stomach. I was sweaty and flushed and felt like I didn't have any air to breathe at all. My mother's back rose and fell, and she snored, face down in the pillow, wearing just her underwear and a lacy red top.

I didn't want to look at Denny anymore, but I felt like I couldn't leave. He nodded at me and beckoned with his hand. Come closer. I didn't. Then he reached down, under his jacket in a heap on the floor, and pulled a gun out, and pointed it at me.

He was still smiling, nodding, like he was excited; I thought he was going to start laughing. Then it looked like he had an idea, like he was surprised and pleased at himself, and he swung his arm over slow and held the gun at my mother's head. I thought I would piss my pants, and I opened my mouth to scream but I didn't. He still stared at me, smiling, almost laughing, looking at me like I was in on the joke, like this was all for me, to make me laugh.

Then we heard the back door open and slam, and I knew it was Gary. Denny took the gun away from my mother's head and tucked it back under his jacket, and I backed up slowly, like there were landmines underneath the floorboards.

I didn't tell anyone about it and was almost glad when Nana got sick soon after and my mother picked up and moved us to California.

For about a month when Nana was really bad, it was all hospital rooms and garage sales. It seemed like every day Gary and I would get home from school, and another thing would be gone—the couch, the kitchen table and chairs, pictures of fruit off the walls. Our mother would set them all down in the driveway when we were at school, having taped paper signs to telephone poles which read, "GARAGE SALE EVERY DAY."

Only the TV was left in the living room after a while, and I'd sit in front of it on the brown carpet. Our mother'd told us we could take one piece of furniture from our rooms in the tiny U-haul she would rent; the rest would be sold.

Gary and I were in the hospital room when Nana died. So was our mother, for that matter, but she'd been drinking heavily for a week straight, since Nana had gone into some kind of coma. A week before, our mother had driven us, ugly drunk, to the hospital and then stumbled through the parking lot with Gary and me trailing behind, Gary making faces at her behind her back.

When we arrived in Nana's room, she was still awake but doped up on all kinds of drugs; her eyes were glassy and clear. At first she smiled when she saw Gary and me, but then her face turned down, her mouth pinched like a prune, and she said to my mother, "Girly, why in hell'd you bring the babies for?"

Now she was all shut down, not moving, barely breathing. Her mouth was open, her face chalky. Her hair was white and fuzzy and sparse; usually, she sprayed it and had colored highlights put in, but not now. They had her hooked up to oxygen; there was a plastic hood over her nose and mouth. Her breath sounded deep and hollow, like it had an echo.

Our mother was slumped in a chair next to Nana's bed, sleeping, snoring. Gary and I were sitting at the foot of the bed, wide awake. Gary had lifted his foot to his lap and was drawing on the white strip of his Adidas sole with a ballpoint pen that had been left behind by a doctor or a nurse.

He was drawing eyes. Rows and rows. Some were round and bubbly and looked like they belonged on fish, and some had long thin lashes and were obviously female eyes.

I watched Nana's chest go up and down and thought about how quickly she'd gotten sick, how in one month she became weak and skinny and coughed up red and green and black, but how she still smoked two packs a day almost right up until she was in the coma. When I'd leaned down to kiss her face a week before, I could still smell the smoke on her lips and skin.

There was a blackened pad of gum on the bottom of Gary's shoe, and he stuck the tip of his pen into it, then pierced it with his fingernail.

"That's gross," I whispered to him.

He shrugged.

The room was cool, cold almost, and smelled like cleanser and lotion. Our mother had rubbed Nana's hands slick and shiny with moisturizing lotion for some reason.

"Why did she put lotion on her hands?" I said, thinking out loud.

Gary said, "What?"

"Why did she," I said, nodding to our mother, "put lotion on Nana's hands?"

Gary glanced at Nana's hands and then at our mother and squinted.

"She's drunk," he said.

I ignored him.

"Does she think Nana's going to wake up or something?" I said.

Gary stretched his arms back, behind his head.

"Probably," he said. Then he laughed quietly. "Jesus Christ knows she's gonna be worried about her goddamn dry hands when she wakes up."

I pictured Nana's eyes popping open, lids rolling up like window shades and yelling at our mother, "Why in hell'd you let my hands get so goddamn dry?" I wanted to laugh, thinking about it, really let one out, but when I opened my mouth, Gary put his hand over my lips and said, "Shh." His fingers were grubby but I didn't mind so much, just squeaked into his hand and felt my tongue brush against his sweaty palm.

He mouthed, "Shut up," but he was smiling too—his face was so thin that it seemed to stretch all the skin when he smiled, down his cheekbones, across his chin.

Then I stopped laughing but Gary kept his hand over my mouth until I gently clasped my fingers around his wrist and guided it down.

We sat for a while quietly, listening to Nana's empty breath. Gary went back to drawing eyes, and then it got quiet. Completely quiet. I looked up and saw Nana's shiny hands stretch like they were grabbing hold of something—a rope in a tug-of-war.

CROOKED

"Gare," I said.

He looked up then, too, and we both watched Nana crane her neck like she was trying to see over a person in front of her. Then she stopped.

I couldn't move. Gary stood up, his hands at his sides, and walked to the bed. He was moving silently; it was like he was gliding, like his feet weren't touching the ground. He leaned down to Nana, his face over hers. I opened my mouth to gasp or cry but nothing came out.

Gary hovered above Nana for what seemed like a long time but was probably only a few seconds, and then he slowly let his head dip down further. He closed his eyes and pressed his face to hers, right up on her skin, his nose against her cold plastic mask.

Then he lifted his head and backed up, just as slowly and smoothly as he had walked over, stepping backward until he was next to me, standing.

I looked up at him and wanted to talk to him suddenly, about what had just happened, and what was going to happen, about what had happened with Denny, about how I was scared to go to California and about how sometimes I wished I would die but more often wished our mother would die, about all of it.

I reached my hand up to take Gary's, and I took his hand so we were palm to palm and squeezed his fingers. For a second, he let me; for a second, he even started to curl his dirty fingers around mine, but it didn't last. He jerked his hand away and dropped mine like it was on fire.

I got carsick on the way back from Point Reyes where me and Angie had a drop. He was swinging the truck around the curves, and I tried to close my eyes and smell the ocean air, but the coffee came up in my throat, and I waved my hand hard at Angie and pointed to the side of the road.

I got out on the shoulder and puked into a patch of dry grass and listened to the cars buzzing around the bend like mosquitoes. I spit and wiped my mouth, let the wind blow on my face. It was cool and felt good on the back of my neck, too, and I could smell the water stronger out here. I could even see tiny surfers in the ocean on bright little boards.

"You okay?" Angie called.

I walked back to the truck.

"You want to rest?" he asked.

I climbed in and put my head between my knees. The floor of the cab smelled like shoe leather and gum.

"I'm good," I said.

"You want me to go slow?"

"Nah," I said. "I think that'll make it worse. Just go normal."

We took off again, and I felt a little better, mostly because I didn't have anything left in my stomach. I shook my shoes off and scrunched up my toes. I'd woken up too late and missed a shower, and I could feel the dirt packed in between my toes and under the nails. I pulled my socks off and wiggled my toes around. Angie looked at me.

"Sorry," I said, wrapping my hands around my feet. "Do they smell?"

"No, they don't smell," he said. "You ever wash them, though?"

I started laughing like crazy; it just tickled me, and him, too. Both of us laughed like a couple of nuts.

"No, I don't. It's against my religion," I said, and that kept us going.

We died down, and Angie stopped at 7-Eleven, and I got some

crackers and a soda to settle myself. Angie bought two hot dogs, and we left.

We were on the road for a couple of minutes when Angie said, "Look at that."

It was some kind of tiny street fair, with tables set up along the side of the road. I could see jewelry and scarves and incense and candles.

"You want to stop?" Angie said.

I shrugged.

"Only rushing home to Joe," he said, smiling.

We stopped and walked around a little bit. The candles were homemade beeswax and smelled like honey, and that made me want to take a bite out of them. There was a table covered with crystals, some pink, some blue, some clear. The woman behind the table had one hanging around her neck from a leather strap.

"Small ones are three dollars," she said.

I felt like saying, That's just all I need, lady, to get into this tarot Ren fair crap, start wearing capes and hoods.

"No thanks," I said nicely.

I moved to the next table and picked up a strand of wooden beads and smelled them. They smelled like the forest. I hadn't been camping in so long; me and Gary and our friends in junior high would camp out in Grant Woods, look up at the sky and sleep in a warm bag, and the first thing you'd see when you'd wake up was all the trees.

"Booth," Angie said.

He was standing in front of a card table with a scarf on it, and there was a woman with a puffy vest and feathered hair sitting on the other side.

"She'll read your palm," Angie said, holding his out. "Five

bucks, and she's good. She knows my wife's in Salvador," he whispered to me.

"No, that's okay," I said.

"Can't beat the deal," the lady said.

"I'll pay," Angie said.

"No, I don't believe in that stuff."

"It's just for fun," he said.

Nana used to believe in all that jazz, too. She threw out the Ouija board game we had and told me and Gary we should pray to our guardian angels for forgiveness. She believed in ghosts and bad luck, and she was convinced we had both hanging around our house.

Angie tugged on my sleeve, and I pulled my arm away.

"I really don't like that kind of stuff," I said.

He shrugged.

"Whatever you say," he said. "Now you won't know about the million dollars you're gonna get."

"Yeah, well, it'll just be a nice surprise, then."

We walked past a table with turquoise jewelry laid out, and then there were all these wild animals carved out of wood—giraffe, monkey, lion. I looked back at the palm reader; she was rubbing her lips with a Chap Stick.

"Do it, Booth," Angie said, nodding over to her.

I looked at all the little animals again, frozen in their positions, leaning down and grazing, chewing on a branch, one paw out in front.

"All right, sure," I said, and Angie smiled.

I walked over to the card table, and it shook when I put my hands on it.

"You're back," she said.

"Yeah," I said, and I sat down.

CROOKED

"Your right hand," she said.

Her hand was cold and soft; it felt like tissue paper. I could see a blue wad of gum rolling around in her mouth. She held my hand at an angle away from her, like she needed to see it in the light.

"Long lifeline," she said.

I rolled my eyes.

"But branched," she said. "You'll probably encounter some sort of illness."

She looked up at me, and I thought she was looking for clues so I kept my face straight. No nods, no smiles. She leaned my palm to one side and then the other and said, "You are going to be doing a lot of traveling, a lot of exploring."

"Uh-huh."

My palm began to sweat, and I wanted to clench up my fist or wipe it on my shirt, but I didn't want to look nervous so I sat still.

"You have many family-related problems," she said.

"Is that right?" I asked, sounding cocky.

She didn't seem to be paying attention to me. She looked to the side, spacy, like there was a TV next to us.

"Yes," she said. She had beady black eyes like the dots on a pair of dice. "It is."

I went to see Chick later that afternoon. He'd sounded surprised and happy on the phone when I called and told him I was taking the bus over after work. It also sounded like he'd just woken up.

When he let me in, he looked just about the same as he'd sounded, eyes bleary and confused, and his shirt was wrinkled up.

"Hey, Mel," he said, his voice scratchy.

He hugged me, and I put my head in his neck, and I wanted so badly to stick my tongue out and swipe it against his brown skin, lick him like an ice cream.

I felt his hands on my back, and I got nervous all of a sudden and pulled away, but not completely. We stood a few inches apart from each other, his hands on my shoulders, and he smiled.

He cupped my face in his hand, and it felt like something was caught in my throat.

"You want some coffee?" he said.

I let my breath out and said, "Sure."

I followed him into the kitchen. He scratched his lower back, the crevice right above the waist of his pants.

"I fell back asleep after I talked to you," he said.

"Yeah?"

"Yeah," he said, yawning, pouring coffee. "I only have sugar," he said.

"That's okay."

"How much you want?"

"Two spoons."

He dumped in sugar from a glass restaurant dispenser and stirred the coffee with a knife, tapped it on the rim when he was done.

"Here," he said, handing me the mug. His fingertip touched my thumb.

The mug had a bumblebee on the side, and the words, "Groom to Bee," were written across the top. I didn't really get it.

"Thanks," I said. "You tired?"

"Yeah," he said, rubbing his eyes. "Haven't had my Wheaties yet."

I followed him back into the living room, and he headed for the bathroom.

"How's the fucking MUNI?" he said on the way.

"It's a pain in the ass," I said.

He closed the door, and there was a pause. I saw a *CLUB* magazine on the plastic table.

"Shit, you know, if I still had my fuckin' car I totally could've come get you on Lombard," he said from inside.

"Yeah," I said.

I picked up the *CLUB* and flipped through it. A lot of shaved pussy.

"Wait, what happened to your car?" I said.

"It broke . . . it just went to shit," he said.

Then water in the bathroom sink went on, and Chick stopped talking. I stared at a picture of two girls in baseball caps kissing, at their long shiny nails. The water in the bathroom kept going.

"Chick?" I called.

There was no answer. I stood up and walked to the bathroom and lingered by the door. I could hear Chick shifting around inside. There was a tapping noise, plastic or metal against tile.

I put my ear up to the door, and the water in the sink sounded like rapids. I heard Chick sniffing loud and fast, and I stood back, listening to him snorting. I banged my head against the wall behind me and shut my eyes.

The water finally stopped, and Chick opened the door, his face wet. He jumped when he saw me.

"Shit, girl, you scared me," he said. His eyes were open wide, and he blinked hard. "You gotta go?" he said, pointing into the bathroom.

"Yeah."

He nodded and then blew air out and flapped his lips, gave it a humming noise. He slid past me; I could smell the sweat on him. I rested my hand on his shoulder, and he jumped again.

"Sorry, sorry," he said under his breath.

I peed and washed my hands and looked at myself in the yellow light in the mirror. I thought I looked sick.

When I went back to the living room, Chick was lighting two cigarettes in his mouth. He handed me one of them.

"How's Sally?" he said quickly.

I shrugged.

"She drives me crazy," I said, staring at the tip of the cigarette. "I drive her crazy, too. I think she hates me right now."

Chick nodded and bit his thumbnail, snapped at it and winced. I didn't think he was listening.

"Are you listening to me?" I said gently.

He turned to me, his eyes beady, and he started laughing again. Then he quickly put his face in his hands and rubbed his eyes and forehead.

"Shit—sorry, Mel," he said. "Coffee's got me jumpy."

"Yeah," I said. "Coffee."

Now he laughed loudly, open-mouthed cackling, and I looked into the blackness of his mouth and throat, at the ripples in his tongue. I laughed, too.

He placed his hand on my knee while he calmed down. I stared at his fingers and felt them making my skin hot.

"No, no," he said, shaking his head, still giggling. "No, we're talking about Sally, right? Right?"

"Right."

"Right, right," he whispered. Then he was quiet. "What're we saying about Sally?"

I smiled. "Forget about it. Hey, though, I never even asked you—how're your folks?"

CROOKED

"I don't know," he said, cracking his neck, head wobbling side to side. "You know, all my mom talks about, she's like bitching to me about Sara and Jimmy—"

"How old are they now?"

He thought about it, looked up at the ceiling.

"Jimmy's thirteen, and Sara must be fifteen." He paused. "I still look at them like they're babies, you know, like they're still pissing the bed."

He stared straight ahead and smoked.

"What's I saying?" he said.

"All your mom talks about . . ."

"Right, right—she's like, bitching to me about how they're smoking pot in the backyard and shit, and it's like, Moms, you're barking up the wrong fucking tree, you want some sympathy."

"What about Papi?" I asked.

Chick went as pale as he could go and looked down, tapped his leg with his thumb. The only thing I remembered about Chick's father was that he threw a beer bottle at Chick's head when Chick was twelve, and Chick had to go to the hospital to get stitched up. I could see the white fuzzy scar above his ear.

"What about him?" he said.

Then he forced himself to smile. His whole face seemed to sink; all that smooth brown skin folded up in the corners of his mouth, at the top of his nose. He stared into his lap and leaned forward a bit, and his shirt hiked up again, the pants having slid down on his thin frame, leaving most of his hip exposed.

I touched it—his hip, his skin, reached my hand out and placed it gently on his side. He didn't look, didn't say anything, just put his hand over mine and didn't move, and we sat like that until we finished our cigarettes and for some time after.

CHAPTER

8

When I woke up, it was still dark outside, and the living room was cold. I was lying on top of the blankets, shivering, my teeth knocking like I was a skeleton in a fun house. I grabbed a blanket and pulled it over me. It was wool and made my nose itch, made it run.

There was a pain in my foot; it felt like something was pinching it, like I had a splinter. I sat up and reached for it, and it stung. Something was in it deep, a piece of glass or wood.

I yanked my foot up to my face and saw some blood trickling out of a cut, and what looked like a piece of glass stuck in the bottom. I hoisted myself up on one leg, held onto the couch and hobbled to the bathroom, walking on one heel, leaning against the wall like a blind person.

I flipped on the light and sat on the toilet, and blinked the crud out of my eyes. I held my foot up again to get a better look, and it was dirty, black on the bottom like I'd stepped in wet newspapers, and there was a tiny piece of green glass sticking out of the arch, slid under the skin sideways. I tapped the glass with my fingertip and it sent a little slice through my foot, pins and needles, worse than hitting your funny bone. I flexed my foot and gasped, and rested my heel on the floor.

The blood rushed to it, and my toes started to feel cold. I lifted the foot back up and set it on the end of my knee and tried to think about when I could have stepped on glass. It must have been in the rug, in the threads, broken from a beer bottle maybe. I pinched my fingers around it and pulled, tried to anyway, but my hands were shaking, and I was shivering all over.

I didn't like the early morning. From four until the sun came up was bad news. For Gary, those hours were always his crash time until he kept pushing crash time later and later until it was only a couple of hours in the late afternoon. For me, it was just unnerving when I wasn't asleep. I remembered being awake early in the morning, whether it was in bed with Sikes, or with my mother in the next room, or alone in the apartment I had for a few months, or listening to Ria Diaz swearing *"Chingate* motherfucker" in her sleep—wherever it was, when you're alone awake at that time of the morning it feels like you're a mutant, like you're the last living thing stumbling around after the big mushroom cloud hits.

My mother appeared in the doorway, and I jumped. She had on her thin blue bathrobe that looked like a bedspread, pulled tight around her body, and her eyes were dim and almost shut. Her face looked blank without makeup, like a white sheet, no features. She scrunched up her nose at me.

"What's going on with you? You sick?" she said, curling her toes up on the tile.

"Nah, I got something in my foot," I said. "Did I wake you up?"

She shrugged and came in, glanced at herself in the mirror.

"Uggh," she said, holding her hand in front of her face. "I look like shit."

"No, you don't."

She got closer and looked at my foot.

"What'd you do?"

"I don't know. There's a piece of glass in it."

"How'd you do that?"

"Ma, I *don't know,"* I said again. "It must've been in the carpet."

She looked at me, offended.

"The hell it was," she said, kneeling.

"Well, I think I would've noticed a big piece of glass in my foot before I went to bed."

She put her hand on my foot gently, and I jerked it away.

"Sorry, sorry," she said, holding her hands up. "Come on now, let me have a look."

I set my heel down in her palm, and she cupped her hands around it. I could feel her breath on my toes.

"Would you relax?" she said.

"It really hurts, Ma."

"Well, I'm trying to take care of that," she said. "Don't move."

It hurt too much to let it go limp so I arched it up again.

"How much you drink last night?" she asked me, touching the bottom of my foot lightly.

"I don't know."

"It won't hurt if you quit moving," she said. "Don't look at it—that'll make it worse. Close your eyes."

I leaned back against the tank. As soon as she touched the glass, it stung bad, and then she yanked the glass, and I yelped.

CROOKED

"Is it out?" I asked.

My mother held the glass up between her fingers and smiled. Blood dripped off it and onto the floor, ran between the tiles.

"Stay there," she said.

She stood up and put a towel under warm water, and then she kneeled back down and wiped the bottom of my foot. It tickled when she brushed the towel against my toes.

"Christ Jesus, baby, your feet are filthy," she said.

She laughed, and I did, too.

"Some job I got down here," she said.

"Yeah, I don't know how they get that way. They're always like that, though."

"I know how," she said. "Because you're a dirtybird. Had to goddamn wrestle to get you into the tub, you and your brother both."

She started wiping off my other foot.

"You don't have to do that, Ma."

"Oh yeah, I do. You're not walking on the carpet with these paws," she said, pinching my big toe.

I laughed again. She finished with my foot and swept the towel over the tiles. The blood smeared and looked like fingerpaints, and then she scrubbed harder, moving her hand in circles, wiped the floor clean.

"You want coffee?" she said.

She hadn't asked me if I wanted coffee for a while. We hadn't been talking much.

"Sure."

She stood up and left, and I followed her into the living room and folded up my blankets.

"No sense going back to sleep," she said. "We'd be up in a half hour anyway."

I limped to the couch and sat down, and took my cigarettes off the table.

"Hey, what's that story—isn't it a fairy tale where a lion gets something in his foot and a mouse pulls it out," she said, dreamy, staring into the coffee can.

"I thought it was an elephant," I said.

"Huh?"

"I thought an elephant gets a thorn in its foot, and the mouse pulls it out."

My mother shook her head and scooped out grounds. They sounded like gravel.

"No, I really think it's a lion, and then he grants the mouse some wishes," she said.

I blew smoke out fast.

"Wishes don't come into it, Ma," I said.

"They do so," she said. "They're the whole point of the story."

"Maybe the elephant grants the mouse wishes."

She shook her head.

"That just doesn't make any sense. The lion's the goddamn king of the jungle," she said.

"So what? That doesn't make him a magician."

"My point is, if anyone, any kind of wildlife creature's giving out wishes, it's gonna be the lion, right?" she said.

The coffee started to hum. She took her cigarettes out of her robe and lit one.

"Right?" she said again, more urgent.

"Right," I said, and I gave her the thumbs-up.

I did not want to fight with her about this.

The living room was getting brighter, but the rest of the apartment stayed fairly dark. She stood in the harsh kitchen light, and the smoke puffed around her face, framing her like a mane, and for once she didn't move her arm right away.

Then she said, "So how much you have to drink last night?"

"Ma, I don't know," I said. "Not that much, though. Not enough to hurt myself and not feel it."

She stared at me and played with her bottom lip.

"Mm-hmm," she said.

"I swear. A couple of beers."

She came around to the living room and looked down at the carpet.

"Oh, you see here," she said, squatting. "You got dirt on my rug."

She said it sadly, and I felt bad for a second and then just laughed.

"Chrissake, you can barely see it," I said.

She rubbed two fingers over the pale dust.

"I'll clean it up when I get home," I said quietly. "I promise."

She nodded but still looked pouty, and she stood up and walked to the closet by the door, about to open it but something caught her eye.

"Dammit, Mel," she said.

She leaned over and turned the double bolt on the door, locking it.

"You can't forget to bolt it," she said. "Even if you're three sheets."

"I didn't lock it?"

"Nope," she said. "I know I don't have anything too fancy in here, but that doesn't mean I want to lose it."

"I'm sorry."

"You leave your door unlocked, you're practically inviting someone in," she muttered.

I touched the cut on my foot lightly.

"You might as well leave it wide open," she said.

"Okay, Ma, okay, I'm sorry. Jesus."

She lifted her hands next to her face like she was about to fan herself.

"I know, I know," she said. "Just try to remember, please."

I put my hands over my face and tried to breathe slowly.

"Do you hear?" she said.

"Yes," I said. "I hear."

I was a couple of minutes late that day because traffic was all clogged up on account of the rain the night before. It was still Indian-summer hot, but bad storms were starting up again. The rain had been bad out here during the winters when I was at Staley, apparently. My mother said she had to put bags of flour against the glass door to stop the water from leaking in. This morning it was just coming down in sprinkles when my mother dropped me off, but it had come down hard most of the night, and there had been some trouble—mudslides and accidents.

It didn't end up making much difference, though, because Angie was sick. Joe told me to go with Tommy John.

"Just me and you, Staley," he said.

I ignored him, and he looked me up and down, and his eyes stopped at my stomach.

"Are you limping?" he said.

"I hurt my foot," I said, getting into the cab.

"How?"

"I don't know."

He got in and unhooked the keys from a ring on his belt.

"You don't know? Were you fucked up?" he said.

CROOKED

"No. I don't know," I said. "Where are we going?"

"Ross, Kentfield, San Rafael."

"How many in Ross?"

"Just one," he said. "What do you mean, you don't know? You twist your ankle?"

I sighed.

"I got glass in my foot."

"Glass, huh?" he said. "That must smart."

I laughed when he said that. I only heard people say that in cartoons. He rolled his window down and took out cigarettes, and he held them out to me. I shook my head.

"Too early?" he said.

"No, no," I said. "I already had about four."

It sounded bad as soon as I said it, like I was trying to impress him. Tommy John laughed.

"Right. Tough girl, right? Tough—what's that say now, *'juera'?*" he said, glancing at my arm. "What's that mean?"

"It's, you know, white girl," I said. "White mare, actually. Literally."

"Mare," he said quietly. "Tough *juera.*"

I looked down at my arm and my hands and thought about Jeannie's for a second. She showed me a picture once of her and her two kids, and she was holding her little boy on her lap, and her nails were long and red and shiny. She said the first place she was going when she got out was the beauty shop to get her nails done and polished because everyone's hands and nails were always shot to shit in Staley. But I liked the way her skin felt. It was dry and cracking like mine, but it always felt warm to me. I took her hand once when she was standing above me and I was on the floor, holding my ribs and stomach, feeling like they would fall right out of my body if I let go, and she said, "You can be, like, a little Reina, Green."

I looked out the window. Ross wasn't far from where we lived when me and Gary were in high school, but we never made it out there much. It was woodsy, but not for real. It was fake woodsy, made for rich people, a lot of cheese and coffee places, and slick earth-colored cars, brown and blue and green.

Tommy John sneezed, and I didn't say anything. I stared at the tattoo of Jesus on his shoulder. It was done in green ink and looked like smeared ballpoint pen. He saw me looking.

"You religious?" I said.

He shrugged.

"My old man was," he said. "He held me down and my uncle inked it. When I was a kid."

We stopped at a light, and Tommy John leaned his head out the window to spit. He leaned back and looked tired.

"Poor Folsom," I said.

He didn't seem to hear me. The light turned, and we went, and he still didn't say anything, which never happened. He always talked to me when I talked to him; he always had to put in his two cents. I stared at his profile. He had a small mouth and pockmarks on his cheeks. His hands were big and scraped-up, and his cut-off shirt and jeans were tight, looked like they were almost a size too small.

I stared out the window at the Halloween decorations on the stores. There was a big crepe-paper ghost on top of Trader Joe's. Me and Tommy John didn't talk.

We got to the address, and I got out and knocked on the front door. It was a big ranch-style house, and it was supposed to look like a cabin, but I knew it wasn't anything like that inside. All designer furniture and creamy off-white walls. The Mexican maid opened the door, and she was old and short and chubby; there seemed to be a lot of extra skin on her elbows. She had on a blue dress that looked more like a uniform.

"Yes?" she said.

"Hi, I'm picking up the toilets . . . from Port-o-Loo."

No matter how many times I said where I was from or what I was doing there, it never sounded right. It felt like I was playacting.

"In the garage," she said. She had an accent. "I open it for you. Wait in front, okay?" she said, and she closed the door in my face.

"Okay," I said to myself.

I walked down the brick steps and back to Tommy John, and he was leaning against the cab.

"Where they at?" he said.

I pointed to the garage. The maid came out, shuffling on her thick rubber shoes, and she sneered at Tommy John. He winked at her, and she put her hand to her chest. Then she motioned to me to follow her.

We stood in front of the long garage door; it was beige with planks of wood sanded over the whole thing to make it look like someone built it with their own two hands. The maid stared at the remote in her hand and back up at the door like it was the TV and she didn't know what channel was on. She pressed a button, and the door heaved up, and I smelled shit.

The maid covered her nose.

"In there," she said.

She left, and I held my breath. Me and Tommy John went in and saw the unit in a corner.

"What'd they need them for?" I said.

"A party," Tommy John said.

He wrinkled his nose and blinked hard and walked around the unit. I reached for my gloves in my back pocket, and he leaned down and started lifting his side.

"Can you give me a second?" I said. I yanked the gloves on.

"Hurry up, Staley. Quit fucking around."

"Fuck off," I said, and I squatted down.

He smiled, and I felt my breathing speed up. I couldn't look at him; I felt just barely there, like my whole body was connected by a very little string about to snap. Tommy John started to lift his side and hoist it up quick, not slow and easy like Angie. He was taller than Angie, too, a lot taller than me, and it screwed our balance up. I leaned back, and the unit started to tip, started to crush my chest and neck. Tommy John didn't notice.

"Give a little," I said.

"What?" he said, not listening.

"You've got to bend a little," I said. "I can't carry it up here," I said, nudging my chest with my chin; it felt like the air was being pushed out of me.

He let the unit down a bit, and I watched his arms, watched the Jesus on his shoulder move; it looked like it was underwater. He raised his eyebrows at me.

"That good?" he said softly.

"Yeah."

We walked out, and I could hear the piss sloshing around, but it wasn't getting to me as much. Tommy John still stared at me, but blankly; he looked a little out to lunch. I noticed before that he got that way sometimes, when he was reading the paper in the staff room or smoking or drinking coffee. Sometimes he'd stare straight ahead at nothing, too, leaning next to the pay phone, not waiting for a call, just staring. You could stand right in front of him, and he wouldn't see you. It was like he was sleepwalking.

We got to the truck and started to set the unit down, and Tommy John let his side go too soon, and it slipped from my hands and slammed down.

"Goddammit," I said. "What the hell was that?"

"We're right here," he said, nodding at the truck.

"I'm short, you know," I said, getting loud. "You have to tell me when you're setting—I can't hold that shit alone."

"Hey," he said. "Relax, all right? It's not the end of the world."

He stepped on the bed of the truck, and I stood below him, and he slid the plywood ramp down and handed me the rubber heel we used for a stop. I shoved it under the wood, and he jumped back down.

"Well, get up there, Staley, 'cause you sure as hell can't push it up," he said.

I chewed my bottom lip and stomped up to the bed and made a real nice racket doing it.

"Are you ready, now?" he said.

"Yeah."

He straddled the plywood and rocked the unit over and then heaved it up. I held tight to the jamb and pulled. We stared at each other, his mouth was tense and angry, eyebrows bunched up. I thought, You are some piece of work, man. We inched the unit up the plywood, scraping the bottom, and my arms started feeling like rubber, and then, keeping his hands on it, he stepped on the bed next to me, and we pulled it over the edge.

He wiped his forehead with his arm and shook his head quick like he was a dog drying off. Both of us breathed heavy for a second.

"Can you tie it up all by yourself?" he said.

"Yeah, I think I got it."

He jumped down, and I picked up the ropes and started lacing them around like Angie showed me. The ropes worked easy between my fingers now; Angie had told me how to wedge my fingertips in just right and loosen them up. I watched Tommy John walk toward the front door of the house, to use the bathroom or the phone, I thought. I wound the ropes around the unit and pulled them tight, so tight it hurt my hands under the gloves, but I didn't mind it much.

I watched Tommy John talking to the maid. She looked up at him because she was so tiny and he was so big, and she covered her eyes with her hand. He said something to her, and she nodded and smiled shyly. Then she went inside, and he started to follow her, but first he turned around and looked back at me, winked and smiled evil, like he knew I was watching the whole time. It just about burned me up.

It started pouring when I was waiting at the bus stop to see Gruder. I lifted my jacket over my head but it didn't help. The water seeped through to my hair, dripped into my ears. The shirt I was wearing was thin and white and was getting soaked, too. You could see the outline of my bra.

There were some kids waiting and an old woman who was standing under a skinny tree that was tied to a long thin stick so it wouldn't fall over. She was making noises like the rain was painful to her. *"Ah . . . umph,"* she said.

Cars drove by, windows fogged up, and water splashed up from all the tires. I could feel my feet through my sneakers getting cold and wet, and my shins, and the cuffs of my cords.

The bus finally came and made noises like a whale. The old

woman and the kids crowded near the curb, and I stood behind them. The bus lurched up a good three yards ahead of where we were and then a few people stepped off and opened their umbrellas before they got out of the stairwell.

The bus driver looked bored, and the bus was crowded, and the floors were sticky and wet. By now, I was soaked all over, down to my bra and underwear and socks. There were no seats, and everyone looked out the window or down in their laps. The old woman stood crunched up by the entrance and held onto a pole with both hands.

I moved as far back as I could and ended up pressed against a young guy who was sitting in an aisle seat. He was scratching the top of his hand hard, and the skin was flaking off, splitting into tiny red cracks on his knuckles. His elbow jabbed into my stomach.

I bit the inside of my cheek and held onto the pole above my head. My stomach was starting to turn a little bit. It felt like there was a pile of rope in my gut, the kind me and Angie used to tie down the units, and it was unraveling, inching up my throat; I couldn't swallow.

The bus sat still in traffic for a few minutes. I looked out the window at the sky, already dark, at the beads of water sitting on the glass like ladybugs, sliding down, making little trails. The windows were steamed up at the bottom so I could only see if the cars outside were light or dark, no specific colors, wipers snapping back and forth, everything blurry.

The bus started moving, and I jerked forward, and the hand-scratcher's elbow went into my ribs. He glared at me. I could see up his nose.

"Sorry," I said.

He didn't say anything and faced forward again. He'd stopped scratching his hand, but now he started in on his leg. His fingers were long and thin and moved fast, and they reminded me of insects. I looked down at his head and saw dandruff on his neck and shoulders, buried in his hair like bug eggs.

The bus pulled into my stop, and I got out in front of the civic center. It was cold, and when I stepped down on the concrete I felt the water in my shoe surging up, soaking my toes again. I walked quickly to the State building, pushed through the revolving doors.

I dragged wet tracks on the marble, and the ladies behind the counter stared at me like I was homeless. When I got to the sixth floor, I told the receptionist who I was and she buzzed Gruder and told me to go in. It felt like my feet were sinking into the carpet every time I took a step.

Gruder was on the phone when I got to his cubicle, and he waved me in, and I sat down and dropped my wet jacket on the floor. Gruder looked at it sideways.

"No, he had two . . . no, he did two, he's got two more here. . . . Yeah."

He held a pen between two fingers and twirled it around like a baton but not fast at all; it looked hard for him to coordinate. Then he said good-bye and hung up.

"Sorry about that," he said.

"That's all right."

"Raining out?" he said.

I stared at him, still felt water dripping off my chin.

"Yeah. A little."

"Mm-hm," he said, not listening.

Then he wrote something down on a pad, maybe that I came here like a wet dog and dropped my jacket on his nice diarrhea-colored carpet.

"How are things?" he asked.

"You know, good."

"Do you have enough money?" he said, like he was my dad and I wanted to go to the movies.

"I guess so," I said.

"I mean, are you making ends meet?" he said slowly.

"Oh yeah," I said. "I don't have many expenses."

"Are you paying your mother any rent?" he asked.

"Yeah, I give her a chunk when I get paid."

"How much?"

"How much," I said, staring at the ceiling. "You know, I don't know, a couple hundred bucks."

He grabbed a calculator from his desk.

"Does that cover your portion of the rent?" he said.

"I really don't know," I said. "She doesn't, you know, *bill* me."

My stomach started twisting up again.

"Apartments in that location can't be cheap," he said.

He sat there, fat and dumb, like a teacher, like Joe at work, thinking he had something to teach me, like I wasn't a full-grown person. I dug my nails into my knee and leaned forward.

"Hey, I don't think you should worry about it," I said quietly.

"See, Melody, I need to worry about it," he said, leaning forward on his chair, too. I could smell his breath. "Why don't you ask your mother what she feels is appropriate?"

I wanted to kick him right in the nuts, is what I would have preferred to do just then. Say, What the fuck you know about it, you fucking fat-ass cocksucker? You probably get paid for teabagging cops on the weekend, and you're telling me how to live? My life isn't any of your business. Your only business is when I fuck up.

I looked down at my lap, and closed my eyes and tried to shake it off.

"Fine," I said.

"All right then," Gruder said, looking at my file again. "Joe says you're doing well," he said. "He says you're a hard worker but you have a little bit of an attitude."

I laughed and let my head drop down. Gruder ignored me.

"Is that true?" he said.

"He's an asshole."

"What was that, now?"

I lifted my head back up.

"He's an asshole," I said, louder. "He's a large asshole. He treats people like shit."

Gruder looked stone-faced. He crinkled his lips.

"That may be, but he still runs the place, and he says you can have an attitude sometimes."

"Yeah, well, he doesn't have the best attitude himself, that's all," I said.

I tapped the end of his desk with my nail, and it made a quiet tinny sound.

"Fine," said Gruder. "I don't want to know about it is all I'm saying."

Then he sighed and rolled his pen around in his hand and stared at me.

"You haven't been out here since you were nineteen, and now you're an adult all of a sudden," he said.

"I already got the whole 'What's happening to my body' thing if that's where you're going," I said.

"That's funny," he said, not smiling. Then he went on like I hadn't said anything. "I know, in Staley, there's nothing behind the surface, right? What you see is what you get," he said, nodding at me, waiting for me to answer.

CROOKED

"Sure," I said, even though I didn't know what he was getting at.

"But it's not like that out here. Everything looks different than it is, yes?"

He spoke slowly and quietly, and it was making me a little bit confused. I tilted my head down and stared at him, trying to make both of us think I knew what in hell he was talking about. So everything is different than it looks, can't judge a book by its cover, I thought. You can lead a horse to water, grass is always greener.

I shrugged and knew I better say yes.

"Yeah," I said.

Gruder leaned back again, and his face relaxed, and he went back to his file. I was thinking just then I'd rather listen to Jeannie and Aracelia sing their tone-deaf religious songs, or to my mother bitch and scream about Daddy, or to Gary's rolling cigarettes and talking nonsense under his breath than listen to Gruder tell me all his big ideas about life outside.

CHAPTER

9

Wednesday night it was spaghetti that looked like it had been torn from one big sheet of wet toilet paper. Red sauce that was just dyed water, soft green beans and a small bread roll, which I always ate first. It was the only thing that tasted decent, and I'd start to salivate staring at it while I found a seat, two streams down the insides of my cheeks.

I wasn't sleeping. I'd fall asleep for five minutes and wake up for five. It was before Ria Diaz got there; then it was Janelle Roche who poured a pot of boiling water on her two-year-old. She was fairly crazy as well, used to rock back and forth on the edge of her bed most of the time, mumbling. She didn't look at me, talk to me, didn't notice when I spent a night in Infirm.

I'd had about five hours' sleep in seven or eight days since I got cut up. I wasn't seeing so well either; my eyes would well up but I didn't cry. Water seemed to leak from them sometimes, though, drip down like on a bottle of beer on a hot day. If I closed my eyes I saw Sikes or Helen, my mother, or Gary, Daddy, Cal Trimmer, Raymond LaCroix, the skinny public defender, all outlined in yellow, and then they would fall apart and turn into flowers.

I stared at the spaghetti sauce running down the sides, and I heard voices, getting loud, English and Spanish. I closed my eyes again and felt my head drop down, almost hit the table, and then I opened them, leaned on one hand and pinched the skin underneath the lids. My head rocked back, and I stared at the white ceiling, made of long cinderblocks, like in a high school or a hospital.

A girl with a big Afro was sitting at the end of the table, shifting around on her stool, and I could feel it under my ass because all the stools were connected to the table. I watched her break her roll apart and pop pieces into her mouth, and then she got up suddenly and spilled her drink. Water ran down the table in a line with a bullet head, like it was going to the top of a thermometer. It reached my elbow and went through my shirt, and I looked up and saw Lulu J. standing there with her tray.

She set it down hard on the table, dropped it a couple of inches, and green beans rolled out. I saw little white flashes in front of my eyes like glitter paint. I gripped my fork tight and turned to her, looked at her wide hips and remembered Inez said she had a kid, a little girl. Most of the women at Staley did, and I usually couldn't imagine it. But then for some reason, I thought about Lulu J. and her daughter, breastfeeding her, washing her hair, cooking dinner, slapping her around with her woodblock hands.

"Hey, *Gaba,*" she said, sitting down. "How's your *coño?*"

I didn't say anything and held my breath. I wasn't going to tell her that it burned every time I took a piss. Again, not too much blood, no stitches; the nurse padded me full of tissue until it stopped bleeding, and then she shrugged. They asked me who did it, the nurse and Jackson and the other guy in charge, the one with the big eyebrows, and I didn't say anything and stared straight ahead. I knew they didn't care all too much because they sent me right back in.

Lulu J. drank her water down.

"Come on, girl, don't you speak English?" she said. "I never hear you say anything. Maybe you can't speak nothing," she said, then she laughed. "Maybe you're a retard."

I thought about Gary yanking the braces and teeth right out of his mouth, holding a lighter to his palm, stepping out cigarettes with his bare foot. I could hear him saying, Just take it, it's just skin, ain't nothing. He'd talk trash and pound it out best he could; even when he was getting his ass kicked, he wouldn't stay down until he wasn't conscious.

"What're you gonna do?" I said, and it didn't sound like me. My voice cracked. Lulu J. looked surprised and laughed again.

"You're some crazy bitch," she said. "I'll fuck you up again good."

I smiled at her. Just skin.

"What're you gonna do, you goddamn dyke? You gonna fuck me again? You might have a mustache but you don't have a dick down there, right, just your dirty little *criqua,*" I said, spit the words out quick.

I watched her face go shocked, her eyes get wide. She shook her head.

"Oh shit, man, you are dead, white girl; you ain't gonna make it one day."

I heard Gary in my head again like when we were young, Don't go for the easy kill, for the fat kids, or pimples; you've got to get deep quick, go for family, anything you know, daddy's in jail, mama's a drunk.

"Bring it on," I said. "Somebody's gonna have to tell your little girl her mama's a bulldyke who can't speak English," I said, the words coming out fast like I was a tape recorder, and I heard some girls at the next table turn around. "She's got a lot to look forward to, maybe someday she'll be in jail just like her mama, she can cut up *gringa* pussy and give her ass away to butt-ugly G's." I didn't know then that she was fucking Lomey, it was only a guess, but I figured I was right because she held onto her fork like it was a spear, and her face got tighter and tighter, and her eyes got glassy. Take a guess, make it up, something's going to hit, I thought. "But that's better than being the *puta* she's gonna be, crack whore in training, somebody's bitch by the time she's twelve—"

Lulu J. looked like her face was about to split open down the middle it was so tight and tense, and then she lifted her arm up and brought it down, and she slammed the fork right into my hand. Later, I didn't remember it hurting, just both of us staring down at my hand, the fork sticking out of it like it was a pot roast. My hand seemed to be moving on its own, twitching, fingers curling up, and didn't feel like it was mine at all. I thought to myself that it wasn't too deep; no bones had cracked, I could still feel the table under my palm.

I heard people talking around us, English and Spanish. I looked over at Lomey by the north door, and he hadn't seen anything, as usual, and so I yanked the fork out of my hand and the blood started, and then I started to really feel it. I patted the top of my hand with my napkin, and it started to throb, and tears were falling out of my eyes again, but I didn't pay attention. I curled my hurt hand against my chest and started eating spaghetti with the other, with Lulu J.'s fork, and I didn't even wipe it off.

She was still staring at me, eyes bulging out of her head.

I said, "Go fuck yourself, *chula.*"

Her eyes scanned my face up and down, and she looked like she was going to start laughing.

"I'm gonna kill you," she said quietly.

"Good," I said, my mouth full. I chewed it as long as I could, and it tasted like worms, but I was hungry for it all of a sudden, and I turned back to her and said, "Then I won't have to look at your ugly fuckin' face anymore."

Her head snapped back like I'd hit her, and she pointed at me, in my face, and whispered, "You not walking out of Infirm this time."

I stared straight ahead and didn't say anything else and kept eating. The food was disgusting but I ate it all anyway, even picked the tray up and tipped it to my mouth and drank the watery sauce up like it was soup.

On Sunday my mother got dressed up in a gold pantsuit with a belt and lace-up yellow heels. She rolled the sleeves up so they looked puffy, and she had on her thick plastic bracelets and jangly necklaces that looked like gold coins.

"Touch it," she said, and she offered me her arm.

I touched her sleeve. It felt like a paper towel.

"That's real silk," she said.

"Wow," I said. "Where'd you get it?"

"Ken gave it to me," she said, walking to the bathroom.

I sat at the edge of the couch and flipped through another anger management pamphlet Gruder gave me. It talked about the three steps to success, and it sounded like a diet plan. Step 1— Take a time-out. Step 2—Think it through. Step 3—Make a choice. I supposed the choice was whether or not to kick the shit out of someone or cut yourself up or hit a wall or break a lot of plates. There was a picture of a sunset on the back.

My mother came back in and made kissy faces, blending her lipstick.

"So what're you doing today?" she said.

My neck tensed up.

"I don't know. I was thinking of going into the city."

She dropped her hands to her sides.

"Not to see Chick Rodriguez," she said.

"God, Ma, I don't know, maybe. I don't know."

She rolled her eyes up to the ceiling like she and Jesus were sharing a moment about how hopeless I was.

"If that's how you want to spend your day," she said.

"Instead of going with you, right?"

"Right," she said. "Instead of going with me."

I stared at the pamphlet again, at the cartoon beach scene. Calm water.

"So no problem," she said, and she held her arms out like she was taking a curtain call. "So you're not coming."

I bit the inside of my cheek.

"Ma, this conversation feels *real* familiar," I said.

"Oh sorry," she said, laughing. "I don't mean to repeat myself. It's just that I'm so old, I'm going senile, right?"

She took her compact out of her purse and popped it open, ran her tongue over her lips and squinted her eyes. I laughed, and she looked over at me and smiled, but only a very little.

"Well, sweet pea, I think I'll wait for Ken outside anyway," she said.

I sat up.

"Ken's coming over? Now?"

Her mouth turned up into a tiny smile, almost mean. She used to get that smile when she talked on the phone to her boyfriends, usually before she'd slept with them.

"He's picking me up," she said.

"To see Gary?" I said, almost out of breath.

She nodded and kept looking at her compact. She knew I was staring at her, and she knew she had me, too, talking so nonchalantly like he was picking her up to take her bowling.

"Does he go with you every time?" I said.

She barely turned to look at me and said, "Yep. Most times."

I started rubbing my temples.

"Has he met Gary?" I asked.

"Yeah, a couple of times."

I felt ready to just about lose my lunch, and my head kept pounding. It had been hurting steady for a few days, never very sharp, but nonstop. All the time it was a thin needle through the temples. It reminded me of when I was a kid and used to have allergy attacks.

"You got a problem with that?" she said.

I clapped my hands together.

"Nope. No problem," I said. "Does Gary like him?"

"He likes him all right," she said. "And Ken thinks he's a good kid."

"He's not a kid," I said, and my voice sounded shaky.

"Kid, man, guy, who cares?"

She snapped her compact shut and shoved it back in her purse, and she headed for the door.

"What do you and Ken and Gary talk about?" I said.

"This and that," she said. "Wish I could tell you more, honey bun, but I don't want to bore you with a goddamn familiar conversation."

CROOKED

She left and slammed the door.

I stood up and felt like my skin was going to peel off me. I started walking around the living room, laughing.

"Ha, ha," I said.

Then I punched the air.

"Ken, Gary . . . Gary, Ken," I said loudly.

"Nice to meet you, son," I said in a monotone voice, the best Ken I could do.

"Nice to meet you, man," I said as Gary, slouching.

I got into it, too, made my hands shake, sniffing big, opening my eyes wide as they would go. Gary was a lot easier to play than Ken.

"So," I said, sliding my hands into my pockets. All cowboy. "You like fuckin' my mom?"

I crouched on the floor in a ball for no reason. My foot was still sore from the glass so I leaned on it and made it feel worse on purpose. It felt like a tiny bone was broken in there.

I stood up quickly and walked to the counter, looked down into the fruit bowl where my mother left her car keys when she didn't need them. I picked them up, and they felt heavy in my hand. There was a shiny gold-and-blue key chain that said RENO. It was supposed to look like the sign you see when you drive in over the city line. The key chain used to belong to Nana; she loved Reno. She liked to play the slots and steal ashtrays and silverware from the restaurants. During the days she'd take tours even though she'd seen everything a hundred times. I went with her once, had a pink balloon tied around my wrist.

I dangled the keys from my finger and then wrapped my hand around them, and then I left. Out in the parking lot, I fiddled with them, shook them around in my hand like change. I looked around when I got to my mother's car, thought I was being watched even though no one was around, and Ken had obviously already picked my mother up.

I got in and adjusted the seat, fixed the mirror and checked myself out.

"What is up?" I said.

I didn't know why I said it. I never talked to myself at Staley. Then I rolled down the window and pulled out, heard the broken glass crunching under the tires. I smoked and hung my arm out the window.

By the time I got to the bridge, I'd seen two traffic cops along the way and a big black Olds I thought was an unmark, and they made me nervous for some reason. I kept looking around, feeling twitchy and paranoid until I thought it out for a second, thinking I wasn't doing anything wrong. I wasn't goddamn Jesse James.

It was stop-and-go on the bridge before the tollbooths. People around me were on phones or nodding their heads to the music they had playing. I stared at the stickers on all the tinted windows. UC Berkeley, Niners, Giants, A's, Mean People Suck, the Jesus fish, the Darwin fish with legs, a shark with a red line through it. Tourists went back and forth on the walkway, and their hair was blowing crazy. There was an emergency phone in the middle, for jumpers. I wondered if anyone ever used it. I looked up at the thick red cables that wound up to the top and looked like they held the whole thing together.

It looked like a big toy to me, like it was built out of Legos or red-painted Lincoln Logs.

I paid the toll and headed for Chick's. Ended up parking across the street from his place when I got there and didn't really realize how excited I was until I stepped out of the car and noticed my heart tapping fast. I ran over to his place and rang the doorbell about five times in a row. No one answered. I held the metal gate and jiggled it back and forth for a minute, leaned back and looked up at the window. It was open; the blinds blew back and forth. I rang once more and figured no one was home for real so I stepped back and decided to get some coffee at Winchell's down the street.

I felt pretty good all of sudden, swinging the keys around my finger, felt like the world was my oyster and all that jazz, what Nana used to call feeling full of piss and vinegar, what my mother called being large and in charge. It was all the same thing anyway, just feeling nice and awake and like a badass, and it got better when I got to Winchell's and the donuts smelled so good and fresh. I bought an old-fashioned chocolate and coffee and sat down at a table by the window. We all went to donut places in high school, especially when we were in the city, because they were open twenty-four hours and never crowded, and you used to be able to smoke. Winchell's, Rolling Pin, Hunt's. The best was Hunt's on Chestnut, bright pink inside, and me and Helen would drink coffee and smoke until four in the morning, just us and a bunch of truckers coming off Lombard.

Then they tore it down and split it up into two little gourmet shops, and Hunt's moved down to the corner, where it was just a pathetic little stand where there wasn't even room to sit, and then it went away all together. Broke my heart, made it easy not to hang out around there, and then it didn't matter anyway because I went to Staley soon after.

There were a lot of people in Winchell's now, I thought probably because it was Sunday morning. A lot of young people in their twenties, reading the paper. Something about all of them looked rich and stupid to me, bright-colored sneakers and V-neck sweaters, fluffy Patagonia pullovers, sipping hazelnut coffee and reading the pink section.

The coffee was good, though, new, from the top of the keg, and the donut was pure sugar and made a grease spot on the napkin. It was pretty easy to see how they fried them in oil like French fries. I started punching my thumbnail through the paper cup at the rim, played with the flimsy handle.

I started tapping the RENO chain against the table, and it made a clicking sound. A girl at the next table with frizzy horsehair and big teeth glared at me, and I kept tapping. Then her boyfriend turned around, wearing a big wooly turtleneck that looked like giant hamster. I blew him a kiss.

I got up right away and took my coffee and left, walked the couple of blocks back to Chick's. The Chinese market across the street was opening, so I walked around a little bit there and checked out the goods. There were some long leafy vegetables that looked like green Barbie hair, and little maroon flakes, and flat see-through disks that smelled like vanilla. The only thing I recognized was peanuts.

Inside there were fish, and the smell reminded me of Tacoma. My mother dated a fisherman once. I couldn't remember his name, but he was the only one who wasn't half bad. He was chubby and short, and really very jolly. He'd bring me and Gary hard candies and cubes of gum. I thought about how he wouldn't have made such a terrible father, even though I guessed he was probably a lot older than my mother when she was with him. He always smelled like fish, like the woods and the lake.

I got a chill walking around the seafood section, looking down at the pink and gray bodies packed in crushed ice. The old Chinese men had gloves on like me and Angie wore, stuffing the fish in, the mouths and eyes wide open.

"Shrimp?" one of them said to me, and he pointed to the prawns next to him. They looked like glass.

"No thanks," I said.

I went back outside to have a cigarette and stared across the street at Chick's building. The more I thought about it, the more I thought that maybe he was there, asleep in bed, crashing. I went across and rang the bell again. I tapped my foot on the stone step and pressed my face to the side of the gate, and then I saw a shadow behind Chick's door and I gripped the gate and smiled, almost felt like hopping up and down.

The door opened, and the blinds rattled behind it, and a short guy came out; he looked like a kid, had on sweatpants and a T-shirt.

"Yeah?" he called from the top.

"Hi. I'm Mel," I said. "I'm a friend of Chick's. He around?"

"Nah, he's not home yet."

"You mind if I wait for him?"

He sighed.

"Yeah, it's cool," he said.

He buzzed me in, and I took the stairs two at a time, and when I got up there I saw how much of a midget he really was. He about came up to my neck and looked about fifteen years old.

"Hey, I'm Colin," he said.

"Hey, what's up?"

Colin shrugged and said, "Come on in."

We went into the living room where the futon was unfolded, the plastic table pushed aside. The whole place smelled like an ashtray.

"Sorry I woke you up," I said.

Colin bent down and grabbed one side of the futon.

"It's cool," he said, folding the mattress over. "Time to get up anyway."

He had a couple of big scars, one going from the corner of his mouth to his ear, the other running up from between his eyes, across his forehead, and it didn't look right. He didn't look like the kind of guy who'd have those kinds of scars; he didn't look old enough.

He pulled the wooden frame up and groaned, kept trying to lock it into place.

"You need help?" I said.

"No," he said, defensive, grunting.

I backed up, and he finally managed it, panting a little bit, breathing heavy, and then he stood looking at it like he beat it in a street fight.

"You can sit down if you want," he said to me.

"Thanks."

I sat down, and he went into the kitchen. I stared at my nails, at the lines of dirt underneath, and then Colin came back and set a pipe and a dime of weed on the plastic table.

"You smoke?" he said.

"Sure."

He opened the bag and started packing, breathing through his nose loudly like he had allergies. He was concentrating hard, too. He stared at the pipe and turned it over in his hands, wiped the end with a tissue. Then he handed it to me with a tiny blue lighter.

I lit up and pulled, and I closed my eyes and thought of a hundred times with Sikes in the basement of his mom's house, how we'd fuck on the sofabed and smoke a bowl after. I used to keep my stash in my sock drawer, wrapped in plastic or tin foil.

I remembered being stoned as hell on MUNI in the city, on the 43 line with Helen, going through the Presidio. The road was curvy, and me and Helen sat on the big back seat and slid back and forth on every turn. We thought it was the funniest thing.

I blew out a long stream of smoke, and it clouded my eyes, and they watered. I coughed and passed the pipe to Colin. He took a hit, and I checked out the tattoo on his forearm. It was a circle with two lines through it, kind of looked like a bull's-eye. "What's that mean?" I said, pointing at it.

Colin exhaled and tugged at the skin on his arm so he could see it better, like he forgot it was there.

"It's a Celtic symbol. I used to be into White Power," he said casually, like he used to be into glam rock.

"So when was that?" I said.

"You know, when I was a kid."

I laughed through my nose without thinking about it, and Colin looked up, a little offended.

"Sorry," I said. "It's just like—" I started to say, and I looked in my lap so I wouldn't laugh again.

"Yeah, whatever," he said. "I know, I look like I'm fourteen."

He licked his lips and seemed genuinely pissed, but I didn't care much and took another hit.

"I'm twenty-one," he said all of a sudden.

"Hey, man, it's cool. I didn't mean to step on your toes," I said.

He nodded again and tightened up his mouth and snatched his pipe back quickly. I yawned and remembered what it was like to be stoned. I never used to like going out, to parties, or out with Gary and his kids when I was stoned. It was better like this, one or two people sitting around with daylight outside. Watching TV, talking trash.

Colin dumped the ash out and tapped the pipe against the edge of the tray. He shrugged.

"You know, it's so easy for girls," he muttered, and I didn't know what he was talking about. "Girls can be all short like that."

I nodded slowly and narrowed my eyes to make it look like it was a very deep thing he just said. He didn't notice, though, just reached under the table and pulled up a bag of cheese puffs.

"Don't worry, these have only been around a couple of days," he said.

I gave him the thumbs-up and had a handful. They tasted like Styrofoam.

"So wait, how do you know Chick again?" he said.

"I went to high school with him."

"Cool."

I took my cigarettes out and handed one to Colin.

"Hey, thanks, I'm totally out," he said. "So, high school?"

"Yeah, high school."

"So do you know that guy who killed someone?" he said, blowing smoke.

I looked up at him slowly.

"Yeah. I do."

"Shit, man, that is *fucked* up. You know, me and my boys, we used to fuck some shit up, beat the shit out of fags and shit, but nobody ever fuckin' died, man. That's cold as hell," he said, shaking his head. "That guy's in Q, right?"

"Right," I said, but Colin didn't seem to hear me; he kept on going, his mouth moving fast like he was in a silent movie.

"He and his brother did it, right?" he said.

"His sister, I think," I said, and I leaned back, laced my hands behind my head.

Colin slapped his knee like an old man and sat up.

"Right, shit, his sister, fuckin' nuts, dude," he said.

Just then we heard keys clanking around at the door, and it opened and shook on its hinges, and there was Chick. He was wearing the amber sunglasses, and he sniffed loudly and wiped his nose. Then he saw me and smiled big and took his glasses off.

"Mel, what is up?" he said quietly.

He fell on the futon next to me and grabbed me tight from the side. His cheek was cold and wet like a dog's.

"What're you doing here, girl?" he said.

He looked tired, and his eyes looked very small.

"I wanted to take a drive," I said.

"Good thinking," he said, rubbing his eyes. "Good to see you," he said, and he smiled gentle. Then he turned to Colin and said, "What's going on with you?"

Colin shrugged. "Nothing. Smoking a bowl."

"You all right?" I whispered to Chick.

He nodded and gave me a crooked little smile that fucked me up inside. He shoved his hands in his pockets and hunched over, his shoulders shaking.

"Someone called for you last night, man," Colin said, packing the pipe again.

"Who?" said Chick.

"Victor, Vic—you know?"

"Yeah, I know," Chick said, almost sounding sad.

He lifted his hands to his face and breathed into them.

"He wanted to know if you were at More's already," Colin said, staring into the pipe with one eye closed, like he was looking through a telescope. "He said you should get a pager like normal people."

Chick winced and said, "Right, that's just what I need."

"You do, man, you have to," Colin said, shaking his head. "You have to be a fucking adult, man."

I rolled my eyes, and Chick laughed. I smiled back at him, and he took my hand.

"Sorry I can't go get a drink or anything, I'm beat," he said to me.

"That's cool, man, I'm chill," said Colin.

We both looked at him and laughed. Chick squeezed my hand hard.

"I'm not fuckin' talking to you, bitch," Chick said.

"Huh?" said Colin. "Oh, right, I get it," he said, squinting.

I leaned back against the futon, and me and Chick stared at each other some more. I put my other hand on top of his and rubbed it slowly, and he smiled; his face was clean and smooth. He had much nicer skin than me, which I didn't really approve of. Me and Helen used to say that you shouldn't date a guy who's better-looking than you or who weighs less than you. I was thinking that Chick and I might tie on the weight thing.

"You want to go lay down?" I said to him.

I didn't mean it in a sexual way, and he seemed to know it. He didn't try to look romantic or excited.

"Yeah," he said, and we stood up.

"You guys don't want any?" Colin said, lifting up the pipe.

"No thanks," I said.

He nodded at me and held the lighter over the pipe sideways, and then he wrapped his baby lips around it. I wanted to knock it out of his hand. But we went to Chick's room instead.

There was still crap all over the floor, and still the rank moldy smell, but it wasn't bothering me as much. The blanket and sheets were in a ball next to the bed, and Chick went right over to the bed, lied down, and curled up with his shoes still on. I slid mine off and grabbed the army blanket from the floor and draped it over him.

"Take your shoes off, boy," I whispered.

He shook his head.

"Nah, I'm too cold," he said, and he pulled the blanket tight around him.

CROOKED

I lied down next to him, and the stitching on the mattress felt scaly and cold on my neck and my arms. Chick turned to me right away and curled up against my side, laced both his hands through one of mine and leaned his head on my shoulder. He rubbed his feet together against the mattress quickly, like he was trying to start a fire. His teeth were chattering like crazy, and it made me shiver.

"What'd you do last night?" I said.

"You know," he said between his teeth. "Raced up."

"Who'd you go out with?"

He shook his shoulders.

"Just some guys. You don't know them," he said, sniffling.

"I'm sure they're really nice," I said.

Chick laughed.

"Oh, yeah, nice young men," he said.

"Who's More?" I said.

He sniffled again and laughed.

"Nobody, Mel. He's just this kid."

He closed his eyes, and his lids fluttered like he was already asleep and dreaming. I got too warm underneath the blanket so I pushed it off and bunched it up around Chick more. His feet were still scratching on the mattress, but they were starting to slow down, and he still held my hand tight. The knuckles on his right hand were bruised, and I touched them lightly with my fingers. I watched his face while he slept, and his lips twitched, and they were pink like the piped-in roses on a wedding cake.

The last time I saw Sikes was during the summer after we graduated. We were in the bar we always went to, usually with Helen, but she was working that night. Me and Sikes didn't have too much to talk about. He was making a stirring-straw chain, bending the edges back and forth, making them mealy and tying the ends together so they looked like red candy licorice.

Sikes looked like a surfer. He was thin and tan and had shaggy blond hair in his eyes all the time, eyes always big and red and stoned, focused deep on the straws, his thick dopey hands weaving them in and out. His mouth was open, his lips red and chapped from kissing me sloppy all day. We'd been fucking around that afternoon, but I wasn't paying attention. It was one of those times when I was looking around, thinking about the sandwich shop where I worked in the mornings, listening to the busted space heater rattle in the hallway.

I was drinking a watery screwdriver, and then I leaned my head down on the bar and closed my eyes, listening to Marvin the bartender talk about how he didn't take his pills, he forgot his pills, he lost his pills.

"I'm sick of taking them anyway," he said. "They can stay lost far as I'm concerned."

"What you lose, man?" Sikes said.

I lifted my head back up and said, "You're a fucking idiot."

Sikes laughed.

"Well okay, Mel, whatever you say," he said like I was talking nonsense.

I never wanted to punch someone so bad, and I didn't know why exactly. I knew I was tired of him never hearing anything the first time, and the way he talked about nothing except pot and bands and how he wanted to move to Portland and live in a van. I scratched my nails against the bar like I was a cat on a couch and turned to Marvin.

Marvin collected all of this Marvin the Martian paraphernalia, so he had T-shirts and a jacket and a hat, and little ceramic figurines from Great America, and a mug he drank coffee out of behind the bar. He had AIDS from being a junkie in the seventies and eighties, had dirt brown trails up and down his arms and said he didn't do the shit anymore, but I never quite believed him. Either he was still shooting horse or he was just extremely relaxed most of the time.

"What you lose, dude?" Sikes said again.

"Not much, just meds," he said.

"His dolls," I said.

Marvin smiled big; he was always eager to talk to me, laugh at my jokes. I was pretty sure he wanted to fuck me.

"Yeah right, my dolls," he said.

Someone flagged him down at the end of the bar, and he left, and Sikes said out of nowhere, "Gary doesn't shoot up, does he?"

"No," I said.

"Oh, sor-ry, Mel," he said.

"He doesn't do *everything.*"

"I was just asking," he said. He lifted up the straw chain and stared through it and said, "That shit's just totally not good for you."

"He doesn't do it," I said loudly. Marvin and some old guys at the end of the bar looked over.

"Right," said Sikes, smiling.

"He doesn't," I said, and I slammed my glass down on the bar, and the ice hopped out, onto my hand and slid away. "Pucks and meth, that's all," I said, trying to stay quiet but I couldn't; I felt my throat straining, getting sore.

"Would you relax?" Sikes said, and he grabbed my arm. "Why're you freaking out?"

He shook his head at me, in pity almost, like I was a crazy person on the street. "I'm not freaking out," I said. "You know Gary doesn't do that shit."

Sikes held his hands up and said, "Forgive me."

He laughed and shook his head again, and I tapped my glass quiet against the bar and tried to breathe slowly.

"Marvin," I called, waving my empty at him.

He came over with a funny look, almost sad, like he was about to give me bad news.

"I can't give you no more comps tonight, Mel," he said softly. "Come back tomorrow."

I shut my eyes, half-sad, half-embarrassed.

"But I'm drunk *right now,*" I said slowly.

Marvin and Sikes laughed, but I wasn't saying it to be funny. I felt right about to cry.

"That's okay, princess," said Sikes, like he was my Dad, patting my arm.

They laughed again. Chuckle chuckle chuckleheads, I thought. All of this was so funny to them, so adult-ly funny, but I didn't think it was any kind of joke, spending every night staring at the mirror behind the bottles, listening to Sikes act like an idiot, standing in front of Marvin who was in the middle of dying, dead in the water, and all we did was smoke pot and drink and try to screw, never had any money to go anywhere or do anything.

Sikes pulled another straw out and bit it like a toothpick, and he started to tie it to the end of his chain. I pushed my stool away from the bar hard and heard it scrape against the floor like a foghorn, and then I walked out quick.

It was cold outside, foggy and wet, and I started walking, eye-ing all the hippies with guitars and pieces of cardboard looking for money, beer, acid.

CROOKED

Sikes trotted behind me, my jacket over his shoulder, and grabbed my arm, turned me around.

"What the fuck, girl?" he said, digging his fingers in. "You just leave without saying shit? That how it goes now?"

"We don't have any money," I said, yanking my arm away.

"So what?"

"Go back, Sikes," I said. "I don't feel like fucking."

"You're so nuts," he said, running his hands through his hair. "You're crazy; you're not a normal person."

I looked at the ground, and it started to swim, and I covered my eyes with my palms. When I opened them, Sikes was still there, and his face was open and needy, eyes wide, mouth open.

"What's wrong with you?" he said.

"Leave me alone," I said slowly and clearly, like I was talking to someone who didn't speak English.

"God," he said, worn-out. "Fine, you know, fine," he said. "I can't even talk to you anymore."

I laughed in his face.

"Not really a problem since you don't have a goddamn thing to say," I said.

I felt like I was foaming at the mouth, like my eyes were coming out of my head. Sikes looked like a kid who had lost his bike.

"Fuck you, Mel," he said quietly.

Then he held the jacket out for me to take, and I reached out and slapped it out of his hand, and it fell to the ground like a wet leaf. He stared at me, looking shocked.

"Fuck you!" he yelled, his voice cracking, and then he turned and ran back to the bar, pushed the door open so hard it slammed against the wall inside.

I stared at the army jacket at my feet and buried my face in my hands for a second and started to lose my balance. Then I grabbed the sleeve of the jacket and started walking, dragging it along the ground behind me. The hippies and burnouts started to look strange and deformed to me, like a bunch of zombies, a bunch of ghouls.

I didn't know where I was going; I didn't have a car. I thought about going to Manny's to find Gary or calling Helen at work. I shut my eyes hard, tried to think of her number at work but couldn't even remember the name of the restaurant. I started scratching at the skin on my wrist. It was soft and moist from the air, and it made me want to rip it up, scratch all the skin off, shred it like chicken. It started to peel off a little bit and get irritated.

I almost tripped over a homeless guy's feet. He was mumbling something, crazy, thin, dirty, smelled like piss and smoke. His jeans were ripped wide at one knee where he was bleeding, or had bled, and the blood looked like rust around the edges, and his leg was bent, curved to the side.

"Fuck you, fuckin' half-breed," he said to me.

I stopped and looked up at the sky, which was all covered with fog; I could only see as far as the streetlight. I knew my hands were shaking, and I was dry and drunk as hell and barely standing straight, and I turned around slowly, and the guy kept mumbling. I saw into his mouth—dark red hole with stumpy teeth.

"You're a fuckin' whore," he said up to me, and then he started laughing.

I dropped my jacket again, and took three long steps so I was standing over him. He tried to sit up, but he was too fucked-up or his leg was in too bad shape, because he struggled a little bit and slid back down. I saw my breath puff out in front of me and looked down at my Docs with the steel toes and just started kicking.

At first he shouted, but then he stopped because I must've

knocked the breath out of him. I kicked him in the stomach, and it gave and felt like mush, and then he started to cough and spit. I kicked him in the chest and he was only grunting now, and he slowly lifted his hands to his face and started to wheeze.

Every time I kicked him, I kept saying to myself, That's it, there you go, all done now, but I didn't stop. I watched him curl up, smaller and smaller like when you burn plastic and it shrivels right up, and then I kicked him once hard in his bad knee. He barely screamed because I didn't think he could get it out; it was a tiny little screech, like air squeezing out of a balloon.

I must've dropped off after listening to Chick breathe for awhile, because I woke up a couple of hours later twisted up in the sheet, sweating through my bra and underwear. I sat up and listened, had the feeling something woke me up but didn't know what. Chick still slept hard, his face pressed into the foam pillow.

I got up, went to the bathroom and peed, and patted my face and my hair down with water. The living room was quiet and dark; I guessed that Colin had since taken off. I went into the kitchen and it stank like garbage, and the walls were old and yellow and peeling. The refrigerator was a mess inside, a lot of food in plastic and balls of foil, and there was an old-fruit smell, like rotting bananas, but I didn't see anything like that.

There was beer on the door, tall boys of Old E, so I grabbed two with one hand and went back to Chick's room. I popped one open and watched myself sip it in the spotty mirror. The beer was sour and heavy and made me feel fat; it filled my mouth up too quickly, and a little dripped out the sides.

I watched Chick in the corner of the mirror, curled up. He looked like he was in pain, his eyes moving wild under his thin lids. His hands twitched, too, and they grabbed at nothing, like they were trying to hold on. I thought maybe he was looking for his gun.

He started to stir, and he stretched his arms out and sighed loudly. He shook his head back and forth, like he was telling someone "no" in dreamland, still clenching up his hands, grabbing at the blanket.

"Chick, wake up," I said.

He opened his eyes suddenly and took a deep breath. He looked confused for a second, stared at me like I was a stranger, but then he started grinning.

"What's up, Mel?"

"Sorry, it just looked like you were having a nightmare."

"What do you mean? Did you wake me up?" he said.

He looked confused again, and I thought it was damn near the cutest thing I'd ever seen. I smiled at him, and he was still confused but smiled back.

"Yeah," I said.

He sat up a little and ran his hands through his hair, and I handed him the other beer. I saw the bruises on his knuckles again; they were light, almost looked like he stamped his fist in an inkpad and it didn't wash off.

"Hey, Chick," I said.

"Yeah, Mel?"

"Why do you have a gun in your closet?"

He shook his head and yawned.

"Good to have, I guess," he said.

"Yeah, but why did you get it?"

"I don't know. This guy I know didn't need it anymore and wanted to sell it, and I had some cash so I bought it," he said.

CROOKED

He wasn't looking at me at all now, leaning against the wall, staring into his beer.

"Everyone has a gun, right?" he said.

"I don't," I said. "My mother doesn't."

Chick sighed, getting impatient.

"It's just for security," he said, and he started flicking the tab on the can.

"Are you a bodyguard?" I said, laughing.

Chick didn't laugh. He looked up at me.

"I meet a lot of people, Mel," he said. "You never know who's going to give you shit."

He looked offended and weird, and it made me want to shut up. I didn't want to chew him out, act like his mother.

"Don't play with guns, Chick," I said quietly.

I sat next to him on the bed and put my hand over his.

"I never use the thing, Melly," he said.

It was strange because that's what Gary called me when we were little, but Chick didn't even know us back then. I liked the way he said it; it made me feel young.

"Don't worry," he whispered, and he reached up and touched my face, ran his fingers from my ear down my cheek, and it gave me a chill.

I stared at his lips, and he was looking at mine, too, and then we kissed a little bit on the mouth, and he tasted sugary. I didn't know what to do with my hands, so I left them in my lap, wrapped them around the beer. He kept touching my face, kept his eyes open, and then we just rubbed our faces together lightly, like I'd seen lions do on PBS. His nose and cheek brushed past my lips, and I kissed them, still with my hands in my lap.

He took the beer from me and put it on the floor, and his, too.

Then he ran his thumb over my lips, and I took his hand and kissed it and put it against my face and smelled his fingers, felt his nails on my lips, teeth, tongue, and he kept his other hand on the base of my neck, tracing down.

Then I got tired of being gentle and started to dig my hands into his sides and grab his shirt. I pushed my tongue into his mouth, and he took it all right. Not many guys wouldn't. I felt snaky, getting worked up. I wanted him on top of me, me on top of him; I wanted to swallow his whole head. I started moving without knowing it, sliding down in the bed, pulling him down with me, twisted my legs around his. I pushed him away for a second and pulled my shirt off. He looked surprised.

"What?" I said.

He smiled. "Nothing."

He pulled me up close to him and kissed the cigarette scar on my shoulder, held my wrist out and kissed my arm up and down, along *juera*. Then he undid my pants and started touching me all over, and it made me right about lose my mind, the way he was kissing me soft and moving next to me, pressing his hips down on mine. It was like a foreign country to me, having a person that close and that warm.

CHAPTER 10

We walked around until we found a bar where Chick didn't owe money. We held hands and smoked, and my stomach and thighs were still sweaty, my privates sore, but not too much. The bartender in the place we found wore a tie and said, "What can I get you folks?" when we came in. My mother said you can tell what kind of a place you're in from how the bartender takes an order. He had thick round glasses and smiled nicely, like we were on our way to the prom.

Chick and I hadn't looked at each other since we left the house, and I glanced over at him now, and he yawned and tugged at his cocktail napkin.

"You okay?" I said.

He kept yawning and nodded, made a little squeak.

"Yeah, I'm good," he said. "What about you?"

"I'm fine," I said, and I looked across at the whiskey bottles.

We didn't say anything then, and I sipped my beer and didn't know why we were being so weird, acting like a couple of virgins. I watched the bartender make a margarita, put the glass facedown on a circle of sea salt.

"You want to do shots?" I said to Chick.

He laughed and said, "Yeah, okay."

I ordered two Cuervos, and the bartender brought us a salt-shaker and two lime wedges on a napkin. The shots tasted like hot lemonade going down, and my eyes started to water. Chick shook his head quick as we sucked on our limes, and he took a tiny black film canister out of his jacket.

"Hold out your hand and close your eyes," he said.

I did.

"Open."

There were two white pucks smearing chalk on my sweaty palm, and I laughed.

"Wow. Just what I always wanted."

Chick smiled and shook two out on his hand and flipped them into his mouth.

"Good and good for you," he said.

"Right."

I held one between my fingers and then dropped it on my tongue. It tasted like aspirin. I drank it down with beer and handed the other one back to Chick.

"One's okay," I told him.

He rolled his eyes and said, "Lightweight."

I started watching a woman sitting a couple of seats down. She had long dyed-red hair, roots coming in black, and she had on pale jeans and some kind of cowgirl top with studs. She waved a twenty at the bartender, trying to be flirty, I thought. She had heavy mascara and dark base, which would've made her look a lot tanner than she really was except I could make out the clean line where it stopped on her neck.

The bartender smiled politely at her.

"Lite, please," she said.

He gave her the beer, and she took a dainty little sip. She was really squeezed into her jeans, too, like my mother, except my mother pulled it off better because hers didn't ride up her ass so much.

She was talking about how she wanted to move to the city but it was too expensive, how she lived in Richmond now and had to take a bus or BART and then walk six blocks to get home. I turned back to Chick and saw he was listening, too, sticking his face in his beer, trying not to laugh.

"Yeah, sure—'the Bay Area's great, lots of room, the weather's great, real cute places to eat,' I told my sister; she's still in Phoenix, and I told her there's nowhere to live around here, and the weather's crappy all the time," she said.

The bartender smiled frozen like he was a mannequin and nodded slowly. I thought he probably never saw this woman before and was being a gentleman, pretending to know what in hell she was talking about. I looked over at Chick, and it looked like he was in pain.

I didn't know what was so funny with him, but seeing his face like that, all tensed up like it was about to burst, like one of those alien stress dolls you squeeze and their eyes and nose and ears pop out like pushpins. I started to laugh and turned away from him.

The Richmond lady kept blabbing, sounded like she was on a speakerphone in my ear. I leaned down close over my glass and fogged it up.

"I just wrote her a letter," she said. She stuck her hand into her purse and pulled out a pink envelope, leaned across to the bartender. "Do you have a stamp back there?" she whispered.

Chick snorted, and I kicked him in the shin. The lady looked at us, and I smiled and felt my eyes watering.

"No, ma'am," the bartender said.

Chick looked as curled up on the stool as he could get, perched on top like a bird on a little twig swing, his feet hiked up on the bottom rung.

I pulled out my cigarettes and then remembered I couldn't smoke them in here, so I just held them up in front of my face. I saw my fingers shake, and they felt thin and weak—little skeleton bones that would grind down to dust if I rubbed them together.

The Richmond lady looked sad all of a sudden; she stared at her envelope, all addressed and ready to go, a clean rectangle return label with a candy red heart in the upper left corner. I tried to read the address but couldn't. My eyes went blurry; the long strokes of her handwriting looked like a mess of pickup sticks.

She saw me staring and turned, and I thought about looking away but didn't want to be so obvious about it, so I looked back at her and pasted on a toothy smile. Her face seemed to shake. I thought she knew me from somewhere, dull eyes coasting up and down my face, shaking in her head like pinballs. Did I know her, I thought, frizzy red hair and cabbage-patch-doll face. Then she broke into a smile and tapped her envelope against the edge of the bar and nodded at me. I leaned over so I was right next to her and could smell her shampoo. It looked like she had something to tell me.

"I like to write letters," she said softly.

Then she leaned back over, and I did, too, because I didn't want to scare her, or lean further in and fall off my chair. I nodded and tipped my glass to her, and she looked pleased.

"I like to write letters 'cause I like to get letters," she said, chipper.

"Great," came out of my mouth.

Chick was almost on the floor, barely sitting, one leg propped up on the stool, his face buried in his arms on the bar. He looked up at me, and his cheeks looked like shiny plastic.

Chick ordered more tequila, and we drank them down fast and sucked hard on the lime wedges. I felt strands of pulp threading through my teeth, burning my gums.

Chick put his palm on the back of my neck, and I leaned my head into it and closed my eyes, felt cold air coming through my nose in two steady streams like water. Chick pulled me up to him so our foreheads touched, both soggy, like two wet stamps pressed together.

"You're my favorite person, Mel," he said.

I laughed because I wasn't expecting it. He pulled away and looked hurt for a second.

"What?" he said.

I shook my head and knew I couldn't explain it. I felt like I couldn't even spell my name.

"Nothing," I said.

We flagged the bartender down and ordered more beer. When he put it in front of me, I stared at the foam on the top disappearing and saw oil circles swirling around. I drank about half of mine right away because I felt thirsty, and then I almost coughed it up because it tasted weird and warm. I covered my mouth.

"Did he heat this up?" I asked Chick.

Chick laughed again with his mouth open but no sound coming

out, gripping tight to the edge of the bar and leaning as far back as he could go on the seat. He looked funny, like a cartoon bunny or a rat, his teeth jutting out like that, and I started laughing, too. I didn't realize how long we were sitting there, giggling like maniacs until my face started to hurt, and I brought my fingers up to my mouth and felt my lips cracking, small tender strips of skin peeling off like scotch tape.

I was late for work three days in a row, and Joe finally noticed and took a piece out of me. He told me to meet him in his office, so first I went to see Wanda. She was his secretary, and she had some kind of nasal problem, always clearing her throat.

She was sitting at her desk holding a small black plastic hand fan, buzzing air in her face. Her hair fluttered, and she blinked her eyes hard and quick, like she was on the beach.

"Oh, he's waiting for you," she said with one eye open.

"Thanks."

I tapped on the door, and Joe said, "What?"

"It's me. It's Booth," I said.

"Door's open."

I went in, and he stood behind his desk with his hands on his hips, and the room smelled foul and dusty. I sat down and crossed my legs and I was fairly relaxed. It felt good to sit; I hadn't been sleeping well at all since my night out with Chick. That first night I'd gotten back to my mother's place around four, drunk and crashing and shaky, and passed out soon after, got up at seven and went to work. Since then it felt like all I'd been doing was drinking beer or coffee, and my stomach wasn't taking it too well.

I yawned wide, and I felt my ears plug up, and Joe went blurry in my eyes.

"Sorry to bore you," he said.

"No, don't worry about it," I said quickly, and then I realized that wasn't the best answer.

"You've been late every day this week," he said. "I've seen your timesheet."

He said it like he'd caught me in the act, like I was trying to pull one over on him. I stared at him. He was wearing a turquoise polo shirt, and it was tucked into pleated pants that looked like they were women's, the way they rode so high and tight.

"Yeah, I'm sorry about that," I said, half-assed.

"You get here at eight-thirty," he said. His bushy eyebrows and mustache crinkled up; he looked like an angry golfer.

"Hey, Joe, I'm sorry," I said, rolling my head around a little.

My neck cracked loudly, and it seemed to piss him off. I pinched my knee hard so I could keep my eyes open and not yawn again. Joe sat down and shook his head.

"Don't fucking apologize to me. This isn't finishing school. Tell me it won't happen again."

He said it slowly—it was the way he talked to Angie and Tino and Rick, all of us really, like we were all handicapped. I heard his chair squeak as he leaned back, looking proud of himself, and my eyes went over his desk quickly—plastic tray of papers, pens, clips, stapler, long pair of scissors with a bright blue handle, dirty and gummy at the base. Joe's mouth was open a little, and I saw his little rodent teeth behind his lips, and I thought if I just had a couple of seconds on him I could cram those scissors right into his mouth and open them up, dig the blades into the ridges of the roof and the tongue, jam them in there like a doorstop.

"Sure thing, Joe," I said.

He kept staring, his eyes all spacey, chewing on his mustache. It sounded like he was biting a hairbrush.

"If you can't handle the work, you shouldn't have taken the job," he said.

"I can handle the work fine," I said. "I haven't been feeling well is all."

He put his hands back on his hips and stared at me, and I started laughing. I tried to turn it into a yawn but then it just got out of control, and then I started coughing because my throat was so dry.

"You done?" he said.

"Yeah, I'm done, Joe," I said. "I really don't know what else you want to hear. I'm sorry; it won't happen again. You want to take the money out of my check, fine. Beautiful," I said, standing up to leave.

Joe looked like he sat on a tack. He stood up and leaned forward across his desk, and it was quiet. I heard the flatbeds in the dock, heard Wanda quacking on the phone about unit sizes.

"Here's a newsflash, Booth," he said. "I can send you back where you come from just like I can send the rest of them out there back to fucking border patrol."

I watched his mouth move, say the words in slow motion, and then he sat back and looked like a fat happy cat, mustache twitching at the ends like whiskers.

"All right now?" he said.

I looked down and felt my eyes water over. I didn't want to cry or howl so I held my breath. Then I let it out in a long thin line and nodded.

"Good," he said. "Get out of here, you and Angie got to get to San Anselmo."

CROOKED

I nodded again and walked out like a zombie, thought, Got to get to San Anselmo to deliver big plastic toilets so someone's fat uncle Freddy can take a dump. Wanda was saying into the phone, "However many you want."

I went to the staff room and stood by the door. Angie came up to me and looked worried, wrinkles on his forehead between his eyes.

"Okay?" he said.

"Yeah."

He didn't seem to buy it, though. He looked at me sideways, then down at my hands. His eyes went soft, and he kept staring at me, squinting and rubbing his chin, like I was a road map.

"What?" I said to him.

He put his hand on my shoulder gently and said soft and low, "Hey, Mami, Joe don't know nothing."

"I'm fine," I said, louder.

Angie looked cagey and nervous, kept looking down to my stomach, or my shirt, and I thought, what is this, what is he looking at—staring at me like I had ketchup stains all over my clothes.

"Sit down, Booth," he said. "I'll get you water."

I looked over at Rick at the table, and he had the same look, too, both of them with outstretched arms and pained expressions, looking at me like I was an orphan.

"I'm fine," I said again, starting to get pissed off. "I just want some coffee."

Angie stood still, though, right in front of me, and so did I. I felt cold. He looked down at my stomach again, and now I looked down, too, and saw what he was staring at. Not my stomach but my hands, shaking bad.

"Oh, man," I said quietly, and I clenched them hard and held them down at my sides.

Rick got up to pour me coffee, and Angie still stared at me with the Virgin Mary face.

"Sit down, Booth," he said. "We don't have to leave yet."

Rick handed me the coffee, standing a good foot away from me, and I reached my fist out and opened it just enough to take the cup. I looked down at the top, coffee rippling in little waves, making my reflection shake and my eyes look huge and black. It streamed down the sides onto my fingers because I couldn't hold it still, so I lifted it to my mouth and drank it down, took it like a shot of whiskey. It scalded my tongue, cooked all the soft skin in my mouth rare.

On the way to San Anselmo, I dropped a lit cigarette three times before I finally put it out. My hands had calmed down a little bit; now they were just twitching in my lap.

"Okay?" Angie said when we were a couple of blocks away from the drop.

I nodded and didn't look at him. Then we pulled up in front; it was the bed-and-breakfast we'd been to before, and Angie got out to find the lady. I rolled up the window and watched him walk up to the porch and knock. The lady opened the door, and she was wearing an oversized shirt with leggings and a belt. She looked weary talking to Angie, shaking her head, no.

It was quiet and hot in the truck, and all I could hear was my breathing. My temples started to hurt again, so I dipped my head down between my legs and heard some kind of jingling, ringing, tiny little bells. It was making me feel ill. The door opened, and I sat up quickly.

"Hey, you okay?" Angie said.

"Yes," I said. "I'm fine." I looked back out to the porch and nodded at the lady. "She got a problem?"

CROOKED

Angie shrugged.

"I guess Joe charged her for all three units last time," he said.

"What does she expect?" I said. "People pissed in all three of them."

"That's what I say," Angie said, throwing his hands up gently so she wouldn't see.

I got out and walked to the back of the truck, and the lady watched us skeptically from the porch, holding her bony hand over her eyes to block out the sun. I ignored her and pulled down the plywood while Angie got on the bed and untied one. We put on our gloves and shimmied a unit down, brought it the same way as last time, through the wooden gate toward the corner of the garden.

The lady followed behind us and called, "Oh, *uh,* excuse me."

Angie and I turned our heads as much as we could without hurting ourselves.

"Could you just, *um,* watch the flower beds, please?"

I looked down and saw I was stepping on the edge of a flower patch, grinding the blue and purple petals into the dirt. I moved over and tried to stay behind Angie and the unit.

"No problem," Angie called back to her.

She seemed satisfied, but still stared at us, every move we made, her hand on her chest. We set the unit down, and I took a deep breath and inhaled some kind of pollen, dust; whatever it was made the back of my throat itch. I held the heels of my hands to my eyes, and that seemed to make it worse, made my lids burn. I kept coughing, hacking like a kitty cat, and then I sneezed loud and messy, cupped my hands over my nose and caught a bunch of mucus.

Angie pulled a wrinkled napkin out of his pocket and said, "Here."

I wiped my nose and my hands, but the napkin was just this tiny square, felt like a piece of toilet paper.

"Go get some water, something," Angie said.

He was concerned again, staring at my hands. I shoved them into my pockets.

"Okay, yeah," I said.

I walked across the lawn to where the lady was standing on the deck. She looked flustered.

"Can I use your bathroom?" I said, my hands tucked tight in my jeans.

She didn't say anything, just looked over at Angie and then back at me.

"Can't you use that one?" she said, pointing to the unit, her arm stretching out over my head.

I mashed my lips together.

"I'd like to wash my hands," I said, my voice cracking. "If you don't mind."

She let out a sigh and looked down, almost sad.

"Through the drawing room, second door on your right," she said.

There wasn't any spit at all in my mouth, and I gulped down nothing, felt like dry ice and I said, "Thanks."

I jumped up the stairs of the deck and went for the sliding glass door when she said, "Oh, um, excuse me."

I turned my head just barely.

"Could you, if you could," she said, pausing, "try to walk around the rugs?"

I stared at her.

"We just had them done," she said.

I didn't know who "we" were, and I didn't know what having

them "done" meant, but I assumed it was a very special thing and I should kiss her ass about it.

"Sure," I said.

I went inside, and the floor creaked under me. There were old wooden clocks hanging on all the walls and they were ticking loudly. All the furniture in the room looked very old, antiques, everything oak, dark red and brown. Lots of leathery brown books—the whole room reminded me of the library in the Clue game. The carpet I wasn't supposed to walk on was blue and green and very soft looking, looked like it was made of fur.

Before the bathroom, there was an open entryway, and there was a window seat with plush blue pillows, and a large birdcage, which was a couple of feet tall and made of long wooden sticks, bound together with twine. It was suspended by a thick bamboo pole that curved at the top, and I didn't think it was real, didn't think it could grow in that kind of formation in the wild.

There were birds inside. I counted six. Four of them were yellow, one was green with a blue head, and one was white. They cheeped at me and wrapped their knotty feet around the bars. They hummed and clicked and whistled. I got up close and pressed my face against the bars, smelled the floor of the cage, sprinkled with seeds and pellets and bird shit.

The white one stared at me and opened its beak and squeaked. It lifted up its wing and chewed at it, poked at it.

The other ones seemed nervous and jittery, all flapping around. The green one settled on one side and squawked and then flew to the other. Two of the yellow ones were all over each other, pecking at the other's head, biting their sides. I thought they were probably getting it on. The white one sat still, though, kept eyeing me, shifted from side to side.

I leaned back and looked out the glass doors, saw the lady still talking at Angie. He was smiling, nodding politely, while she jabbed, opening her mouth wide, moving her arms back and forth at her sides.

I turned back to the birds and unhinged the small square door. They went a little nuts, chirping louder and all switching positions with each other, making bubbly sounds like they were underwater, flutter flutter flutter. I opened the gate only a little bit, and they shuffled around more, gurgling. The green one came up and sniffed at the opening.

"Fuck you," I said to it.

I stuck my fingers into the tiny space, and they scattered. I slid my whole hand in, and it was like I was doing something dirty, in junior high going down someone's pants. I worked my wrist in, my arm up to my elbow, and waved my hand gently back and forth, and all of them screamed and flew to different corners. I felt their tiny feet, cold little claws, feathers brush against the hair on my arm for a second.

When I was a little kid, I used to run my fingers along the seams of my mother's pillows and search for the hard ends of the feathers. I would pinch them and pull them out, and they were small and curved and white, and I'd brush them against my cheeks, nose, eyelids.

I stretched my arm out and reached for the white one. I opened my hand and tried to grab it, but it held tight to the upper right corner, while the others flew around and kept screeching. I thought I almost had the white one, and it knew it and stared at me, its chest going in and out fast. I stretched my arm as far as it could go, pressed my cheek against the side of the cage and swiped for it.

It slipped under my hand; I could feel it smooth on my fingers,

181

and it shot to the other side. It stared at me again and clung to a stick on the left, moving slowly, one step at a time like a tightrope walker.

One of the yellow birds started crying like a chew toy, raised its wings up in a V and shook them. It looked fatter than the others; I thought it probably ate everyone's food. I stretched out my hand and reached for it, fingers moving in like a spider, and I clamped down on it and felt the tiny rib cage in my palm, and then I squeezed it gently. The other birds chirped and flapped, but didn't seem very bothered when I removed the yellow bird; they went back to normal fairly quickly. The two lovers started poking each other again, and the green one gripped the front of the cage and squeaked, but not loudly. The white one stared at me for a second and then started to clean itself.

I held the yellow bird in my fist. Its head popped out the top like a snow globe. It squirmed, and I could feel its heart, small as a stud earring, beating soft and fast against my skin.

I looked out the sliding door once more, saw the lady talking to Angie, Angie still smiling. Yes, ma'am. No, ma'am.

The bird looked at me and twitched and tried to move its wings. Its eyes scanned me, and it twitched its beak which looked like a little pinky toenail. It tried to puff up its chest, but I kept my grip tight and kept pressing. Its legs kicked, tried to scratch at my skin but couldn't reach. The beak opened and closed, and I just wanted to see what it could do, how much it could do, and I kept squeezing my hand tighter and tighter. I could feel the little knot in its chest speed up, bounce against the sides, and I kept squeezing slowly until I felt my nails meet my palm, the bird getting slick and wet, my hand sweating. Its beak opened again, and then it froze. It stopped, and it was still warm, just not breathing.

I opened my hand and held it there. It rested on its back, feet pointed up, beak open. I brushed it against my face; it smelled like birdseed. I lifted my shirt and tucked it between my jeans and my hip, left the shirt hanging out so it looked bunchy.

I went back outside with my shoulders hunched over and curving in, and Angie was nodding, saying, "No problem. Joe'll take care of everything."

"Well I guess that's fine, but that's what you said the last time," the lady said, and she crossed her arms.

I walked up to them and said to the lady, "Thanks very much, ma'am," and I smiled extra sweet.

She touched her neck lightly and tugged at her earring. She smiled back and looked sick to her stomach.

I hit Angie on the shoulder.

"We gotta go," I said.

Angie nodded, and we walked out, and the lady followed close behind. I got into the truck, slammed the door shut and sat down, and felt the bird warm and wet against my skin.

"All better?" Angie said, pulling out his keys.

"All better."

The lady stood at her wooden fence and watched us leave.

I pressed the lighter in as Angie pulled out and took us down the street. I set my hands on the dash and tapped my thumbs together, and then I watched them lie there, perfect and still.

CHAPTER 11

The new girl had a blue kerchief over her head and soft brown arms that were strong but not like a man's, not like Lulu J.'s. I was standing against the wall alone when she came up to me.

"What's your name?" she said.

I opened up my arm so she could read it. She laughed. Her upper lip was crooked, and there was a white hairline scar up to her nose.

"Yeah, I heard about that," she said. "You cried like a baby girl, huh?"

I stared straight ahead and picked something out of my teeth. My head started to hurt again, but the new girl didn't crowd me, and that helped. Everyone crowded you everywhere—at dinner, in the TV room, the gym; they all moved closer all the time, standing in all the lines. I could smell their sweat, hear every word they said about cock and parole.

The new girl leaned against the wall next to me and faced forward, too. She was smoking. I'd only had a couple of cigarettes since I got there, both bummed from Inez in the kitchen.

The new girl held the open pack out to me.

"You smoke?" she said.

I looked her over quick, tried to tell what she wanted, figured she wanted a *gringa* girlfriend.

"I don't like pussy," she said, laughing. "I don't like girls like that."

She held the box out again. Newports. I took one.

"Here," she said, handing me her cigarette for the light, and I felt her fingers brush against mine.

The mint took me by surprise, even though I knew it was coming. It was the best thing I ever tasted.

The new girl watched me and touched her lips lightly. Then she tossed her smoke down and stepped on it.

"See you," she said.

I liked drinking beer on my mother's two square feet of concrete porch, sitting on a stool and lining up bottles on the ground, looking into the ivy bushes, seeing the headlights downtown passing along like little blinking Christmas lights.

I'd tried twice to call Chick but got no answer, so I took the five dollars I had on me and bought two 40's of Old E, and I was almost through the second. Ken had come over to pick up some of his stuff, and my mother was working an extra shift at the restaurant. Me and him hadn't really said two words, and I was getting the feeling he wasn't too crazy about me, that he thought I treated my mother poorly. I felt like saying, You don't know the half of it, slick. You just don't know the half of it.

CROOKED

I finished off the last of my 40 and swished it around in my mouth, and then I went back inside and dragged the stool behind me. It hit the door on the way in and the whole thing vibrated and made a racket. Ken came out of the bedroom with a duffel bag.

"Oh," he said, pointing to the door. "Was that you?"

I nodded and thought about how there wasn't any beer left in the fridge.

"Hey, you want a cigarette?" I said.

"No, thanks," he said.

I lit one for myself and leaned against the counter; smoke trailed in my eye and burned. Ken patted his hair down and sat in the Hawaii-Five-O chair and flipped through a tiny leather book with "Addresses" in gold on the front. He held the book close to his face and turned the pages slowly.

"Do you need to use the phone?" I asked him.

"No, thanks."

"You don't have to ask, you know," I said, rocking on the balls of my feet.

I laughed.

"I guess Sally already told you that," I said.

"Almost as much."

I sighed and didn't know what else to say; I was just trying to be friendly and make some conversation, but he wasn't making it easy. He looked very thoughtful just then, like a kindergarten teacher, or maybe a friendly janitor.

"Hey, Ken, you want to get a beer with me?" I said.

He looked up from his little book, his mouth open, mustache hanging down over his lips.

"Now?"

"Yeah, now," I said, laughing. "No, next week. Yeah, now."

He looked down at the book and moved his mouth around like he was chewing something.

"You sure you need another?" he said.

I closed my eyes.

"Yes, I am," I said. "Would you like to join me?"

Now he rubbed his chin.

"All right," he said. "Let's get a beer."

"Perfect!"

I got my jacket and pulled the four dollars I had in the pocket of my work jeans, and me and Ken went out to his car. The back seat was full of metal parts, equipment, something that looked like a big fish tank.

"What's that?" I said, tapping on the glass.

"It's an incubator," he said. "For a baby."

I didn't know what to say to that.

"Right," I said.

We got in, and Ken zipped his jacket up and breathed into his hands.

"So you sell that stuff to hospitals?" I said.

"Yeah, and private practices."

"Like doctors, private doctors?"

"Pediatricians, yes," he said.

I nodded, and Ken started the car, and let it hum and the windshield defrost. He didn't seem interested in talking at all, and it made me pissed, him making me do all the work. It wasn't like he was the first person on my list I'd like to have a beer with; there just wasn't anyone else around. I stared at the incubator in the side mirror.

"You know Sally had a C-section, right?" I said.

Ken nodded. "She told me."

CROOKED

"You see her scar?" I asked.

He nodded again, and we pulled out of the parking lot. I reached for my cigarettes and then stopped. I didn't know if it was okay to smoke in his car. I couldn't remember if I'd seen him smoke.

"She had to have one because we were all clogged up," I told him. "Me and Gary. Trying to come out at the same time."

I watched the trees outside and bit the inside of my lips, thought to myself, Stop telling him this shit.

We got to the 3 A.M. Club and parked in the little lot out back, and then we went in. Ken pressed his hair down again and looked a little nervous.

"Is this okay?" I said, pointing to the sign above the door, where it said 3 A.M. Club in fat letters.

"Yeah, sure," he said.

We sat at the bar and ordered pints of Anchor Steam because they didn't have any Bud or Coors. Ken paid for them when they came, and foam stuck to his mustache when he took a sip and looked like tiny shaving-cream dots. He wiped his mouth with a napkin and scrunched it into a ball, held it in his hand. We didn't speak. Some easy listening was playing—"Brown-Eyed Girl."

"This place used to have better music," I said.

"That right?" said Ken.

"Yeah. Now all it is is this crap," I said, pointing up to the corners, where I thought the speakers might be. "'Margaritaville,' crap like that."

Ken smiled politely.

"You know, there used to be a little variety about it," I said. "The Israelites song by Desmond Dekker."

Ken rolled the napkin ball around on the bar with his palm.

"You know that song?" I asked him.

"Yeah, I think so."

And that was it for conversation from Ken for a while. We sat quiet, and I wondered what exactly my mother liked about him so much.

After a couple of minutes, he said, "I like country myself."

"Oh yeah?" I said. "Like what? Like Hank Williams?"

Ken shrugged.

"Oh, yeah, he started it all. Johnny Cash, Merle Haggard, stuff I used to listen to with my dad and my granddad," he said.

I felt very emotional just then, about Ken and his family sitting around on Sunday morning after church, listening to old country, Mama singing Patsy Cline.

"Where'd you grow up, again?" I asked.

He flattened the napkin out and smoothed it down with his fingertips.

"Down south," he said. "Receda, Anaheim, mostly."

I couldn't think of what to say about that. I stared into my beer; Ken looked straight ahead like he was alone.

"It's weird how everyone has a pool down there," I said.

"Yeah?" he said.

"Yeah," I said, sighing. "Hey, I'll be right back."

He said okay, and I went to the bathroom and stared at my face for a while. I thought I looked pale, actually thought I looked green in the light of the bathroom, the same color as the green goo in the soap dispenser. Then I got to thinking, Where the hell am I, and why the hell am I out drinking with Ken, and that made me think about Chick again.

"American Pie" was playing when I came out. I called Chick on the pay phone next to the bathroom and leaned against the door and listened to the muffled rings on the other end. I stood there and heard it ring about ten or fifteen times, and then I hung it up hard and heard the bell make a whiny sound, and then I walked back to the bar.

"Call someone?" Ken said when I sat down.

"Yeah," I said. "He's not home, though."

"That your friend Chick?"

I was about to say, Yeah, that's him, motherfucker's never home, but then I thought I'd never told Ken the first thing about me, what I did, who I hung out with, and I figured my mother must've filled him in, and I didn't like it. It was like he was spying.

"Nope," I said. "Not Chick."

He didn't look like he believed me, but I didn't much care, and we finished our beers soon after, and Ken pulled his jacket off the back of the barstool.

"You taking off?" I said to him.

"I was thinking I might," he said. "Let me give you a ride."

He stood next to me and put his jacket on, clasped his hands in front of him and yawned.

"I'm not ready to go yet, but, you know, thanks," I said.

I pulled my wallet out and peeked in, figured I could get something cheap and go from there. Ken still stood next to me.

"I think you should let me take you home," he said quietly.

I laughed and patted him on the shoulder.

"That's sweet of you, but I'm gonna have one more," I said.

He smiled, and I could see the tips of his teeth. They were very white.

"I think you better come with me," he said. "Tomorrow being a work day and all."

I nodded and made it look like I was actually thinking it over.

"I don't think you should worry about me," I said to him.

I hadn't ever realized how big he was, how tall and fit. He didn't move, stood there solid like a telephone pole, and I waved down the bartender.

"Your mother worries about you," he said suddenly. He leaned his head down to mine and said, "She grinds her teeth in her sleep every night because she worries about you." Then he stood up straight again. "She had to get a plastic mouth guard especially made for her," he said. "By a dentist."

I laughed and said, "I'll be sure to reimburse her."

I closed my eyes and shook my head, thought maybe when I opened them, Ken wouldn't be there anymore. I started gripping my knees.

"Another?" the bartender said, and I looked up.

I didn't get "Yeah" out fast enough, because Ken leaned over the bar and said, smiling sweet as all hell, "We're all done, thanks."

I heard the words and stared at the back of Ken's head, and my hands felt like rocks in my lap. The bartender took both our glasses away with one hand, and I watched a Heineken bottle on the bar, and for a second I saw myself bringing it down on Ken's bald head, saw it breaking and splitting into the red bumpy skin on his neck, saw the red pinprick dots drizzling down.

"Let's go," he said, nodding toward the door.

I blinked hard and heard "American Pie" coming out of the speakers. "Bye-bye, Miss American Pie, drove my Chevy to the levee but the levee . . ."

I stood up and faced him, and I had to rock on my feet for a second and get my balance. I patted down the collar of his shirt, smoothed it down outside his jacket like my mother would do. Remembered Gary saying I prefer to beat people right to death with kindness.

CROOKED

"So here it is," I said, cocking my head to the side, almost in a sexy way. "You can leave and do whatever you want with the rest of your night, and I'm going to stay here and have another beer, and then I'm going to go from there," I said, and I looked right in his eyes.

We stayed there for a second, and then he backed off. I smiled and felt fierce, and I sat back down.

He shrugged and said quietly, "You don't need any more to drink, Mel."

"Don't worry about it, Ken."

I shut my eyes and felt a dull pain in my mouth, on my tongue. I was biting it and didn't realize it, a little bit tucked in the back corner like tobacco.

Ken sighed.

"Good night," he said.

"Night, Ken," I said cheerfully.

I tapped my fingers on the bar and leaned over again, tried to get the bartender's attention. I saw her at the other end, talking to some guys in baseball hats and turtlenecks, and I watched Ken walk away out of the corner of my eye, and then I saw him at the end of the bar. I scooted my ass to the edge of the stool and leaned over far and saw Ken talking to the bartender, not moving much until he pointed at me, and she turned and looked at me and nodded.

Then he headed for the door, but before he got there, he turned to me and gave a little salute, two fingers tapped against his forehead. I stood up slowly and watched him leave, and then I went to talk to the bartender, my foot catching around the leg of the barstool, and I dragged it with me for a step and shook it off like it was toilet paper.

"Hey," I said loudly.

She glanced at me and seemed bored, and then she walked over to where I was, dragging her feet. Her eyes were heavy, and her hair was pulled through a little ring on the top of her head and looked like a plant.

"What that guy say to you?" I said, slurring.

"That you've had enough," she said.

I laughed and crossed my arms, hiked them up on the bar to show how casual and in control I was.

"Look," I said, like it was our little secret, "I just met him and I didn't want to go home with him, and he's pissed."

She looked at me with a weird soft look, like I was a nice disabled person, all pity and sorry, and I felt my breathing speed up and my head floating with sludge, and she said in·one breath, "He said you're just out of prison and on parole, and if I serve you anything but coffee and water he'll call the city on me."

I backed away from the bar.

"Sorry," she said, shrugging.

I nodded and shoved my hands in my pockets, walked out quick and went around to the parking lot, speeding up until I was running, and Ken was still there, leaning against his car, waiting for me. I stopped short and stood there panting, gritting my teeth, and I pointed at him.

"Need a lift?" he said.

"No," I said, and I stumbled up to where he was standing. I pulled my jacket off, one arm at a time and set it on the hood. "I don't need a fucking lift, Ken."

Ken looked over at my jacket and back to me and scratched his forehead. He stared at me blankly and leaned back on his car.

"Jesus!" I yelled, laughing. "Jesus Christ, Ken, would it kill you to have a fucking *expression?*"

CROOKED

I lost my balance and staggered a couple of steps back.

"Come on," I shouted, clapping. "Let's go, big Ken, me and you, let's duke this shit out."

"I don't fight with girls, Mel," he said calmly.

I laughed again, swaying back and forth a little, stared him right in his watery dish-towel eyes.

"I don't fight like a girl, Ken," I said.

"I'll bet."

"You get in a lot of fights, Ken?" I asked him, wiping my mouth.

"I've been in a few, yeah."

I kept laughing and started pacing a little bit, staring at his round lightbulb head and his hair combed into a ring on top.

"Oh yeah?" I said. "Yeah, you come out all right?"

He shrugged. "I did okay."

"Did. O-kay," I said, and my head rolled back and felt like it was moving without my doing. I stared at the stars.

"So come on," I said, getting dizzy, putting my head back down. "Let's do it."

I got up close to him and poked two fingers on his shoulder. He shut his eyes and looked tired and hassled.

"I'm not fighting you," he said.

I stepped closer and stood right in front of him, looked at the lines in his face.

"You first," I whispered. "Here," I said, and I scraped my finger on my chin.

The skin felt soft.

Ken looked away from me and up at the sky, like I wasn't there. I pushed him again, with both hands this time, and I lost my balance and went back a few steps and shouted.

"Let's go, Ken!" I yelled. "Let's go, man, come on, pretend you're knocking me right out of the picture," I said, feeling like I was on wheels, rolling around the pavement. "Now you can be all alone with Sally."

I started coughing like an old man. Ken unzipped his jacket and laid it down next to mine.

"There you go, Big Ken, Big Daddy Ken," I said, bouncing up and down on the balls of my feet. "Ken is the fucking MAN, King Ken, King Kong Ken!"

He put his hands up, palms open, and said, "I'll make you a deal—you can take a clean shot at me, and then I can take you home."

I shook my head.

"What," I said, "what is that bullshit?" I dropped my hands to my sides. "You let me hit you—what kind of faggot shit is that?" I said, my legs unsteady, splaying out like stakes on a pup tent.

He closed his eyes.

"Get in the car, Mel," he said, monotone, sounded like an answering machine.

I grinned at him.

"Mel, if you don't let me take you home right now, I'm calling your P.O.," he said.

"Good luck, big guy," I said.

"Fine," he said, crossing his arms. "I'll call a cop."

"Oh, you fucking go for it, Ken, you call a cop. You call a cop and tell them a little girl's fucking with you in a parking lot—you're a pretty tough guy, call the cops on a little girl like me," I said, and spit leaked out the corners of my mouth.

Ken rubbed his eyes and said, "Mel," and he said it like he wasn't talking to me all, like he just thought of me out of nowhere.

CROOKED

"Yeah, what? The fuck you want now?" I said, walking up to him.

He looked up fast and pushed me with the heel of his hand in my chest, quick but not hard. I fell back a little, and then I swung at him.

One time Jeannie held up a towel a couple of feet from the wall and told me to aim for the wall. It was a little trick, to aim for something behind what you're hitting, a little trick to play on your mind, get yourself to hit a thing harder.

I hit Ken pretty hard, I thought, not aiming for anything behind him in particular, but I got the side of his nose and upper lip. They cracked against my fist and hurt my knuckles. He snapped back and leaned over the hood, and he stayed there for a second and came back up slowly, hands at his sides. Blood filled in small lines on his lip, and he ran his tongue over it, touched it, held up his fingers in the light so he could see.

I rubbed my knuckles and held my hand out and watched it shake. My nose was running.

"You ready now?" Ken said quietly.

My heart was knocking like nuts against my ribs, and that was all I could hear when I closed my eyes, that and my breathing. I wiggled my fingers out and stepped back.

"Yeah," I said.

Then I got in the car and rolled my jacket into a ball, put it against the window and used it for a pillow. And I passed out so hard on the way home that Ken had to turn on the radio to wake me up.

Our mother had met Cal Trimmer almost as soon as we got to the Bay Area and started dating him right away. He did contracting in the East Bay and had very clear glassy eyes, and he was losing his hair, but he shaved it short anyway. He was really fit, too. Not tall, but lean and strong; I could always make out the definition of his arms and chest under his T-shirts.

Gary and I didn't see him too much. We didn't see our mother too much, either, but every once in a while I'd run into Cal in our little kitchenette, him reading a newspaper at the flimsy table we ate off, smoking, drinking black coffee. He never said anything to me, didn't seem to notice me except when I'd take phone messages for him, and he'd say rude and quick, "Sally there?"

At one point I got the impression that Cal and my mother weren't doing so well as a couple. He wasn't calling so much, and she was home more often. Then there was one night when she was working, and I was smoking a bowl in the living room, curled up on the couch. It was a Friday or a Saturday, and Sikes and Helen weren't around, and Gary was out buying cigarettes. I lit up on the pipe Sikes bought me for my birthday; it was a brown ceramic dinosaur with googly eyes, and it got hot in my hands when I held the lighter to it.

The TV was off, but I was sitting in front of it anyway, and I thought about making some phone calls but it was already midnight, and it was almost no use going out now. So I just kept taking hits, closing my eyes and moving my tongue around inside my mouth; it felt sandy.

I was starting to pass out, head getting heavy, and I shook awake like you do when you're almost asleep and you swear you're suddenly falling down stairs or tripping on a curb. I dropped the pipe and all the spent ash on my lap and the couch, and I shook my head, knew my mother would have a fit about it.

I rubbed the ash on the cushion, swirling it around in circles, watching the gray and black spread thin, and then I heard noises coming from the pool area. The super called it the courtyard, but it was just the dirty swimming pool and Rubbermaid garbage cans lined up in a row.

I heard the cans being knocked around, dull sound of them hitting the concrete, cans and bottles. I thought for a second it was Gary, wouldn't put it past him; he'd knocked the things over before. Or raccoons. One time I'd faced off with one when I was waiting outside for Sikes, and the little bastard hissed at me and opened its bony mouth to show off its fangs, and I panicked and threw my cigarettes at it.

Now, though, it sounded like too many, like all ten cans knocked down at once. I sat straight and wasn't sure I'd heard anything, and then I stood up and felt like I was about to faint for a second. I went to the front door and stepped outside, onto the walkway, and I peered over the wooden railing.

I saw three brown garbage cans and one bright blue recycling can, on their sides, milk cartons and coffee cans everywhere, rotten fruit smell starting to drift up, and I saw a figure there, someone stumbling around.

I ran down the stairs breathing heavy and saw it was Cal Trimmer, drunk, wading through the garbage. He looked up at me and pointed, started laughing.

I wasn't scared of him, but I didn't know what to do. I stared at his thick finger and leaned away, like he was going to poke me with it.

"Where's your mama?" he said.

He stopped staggering for a second and stood straight up, rolled his head around on his neck.

"She's not here," I said.

He was big, not so much taller than me but his arms hung off him heavy, blond hair covering his skin.

Then I saw one of the neighbors in a window—a biker, real hairy and wore jeans and leather, and I thought my mother had slept with him when we first moved in. I saw his light go on, and the blinds hike up a bit, but then they closed again.

"You lyin', girl?" Cal said.

"No," I said. "She's working."

He looked about to pass out, eyes fluttering, mouth opening halfway. He groaned.

"Just go home, Cal," I said.

I didn't know what else to do so I started picking up the garbage. I grabbed a couple of two-liter plastic soda bottles, not looking at Cal any more, but then I saw his hands moving. I looked up, saw him unbutton his pants, pull his dick out.

I'd seen a few dicks before, and I'd felt differently about each one, but they never made me feel sick just to look at them like Cal's did now—maybe because it was a little hard, swinging in front of him like a paperweight.

He wasn't coming near me, didn't seem like he really knew I was there. Any other time I would've laughed. Maybe if he tried to make a move on me or started pissing I would've screamed. But he didn't. His head just rolled back again and his mouth hung open, and I could see his tongue moving over his teeth and his lips.

He started tugging on his piece, pulling at the tip with his thumb and forefinger wrapped around, and I thought I would throw up. I thought about all the dicks I'd seen, in person or in porns, but his looked different, the way it stretched around, rubbery.

I didn't know for how long I stood there, him pulling at himself like that. The bottles squeaked in my arms and that was the only sound for a while, that and his heavy breath, and then I heard quick footsteps behind me.

CROOKED

"What the fuck is this?" said Gary.

His eyes batted up and down Cal, and I could see the bones in Gary's face, everything blank, and then it all registered; everything started moving, twitching, and he dropped the brown paper bag he was holding, and then he flew at Cal.

Gary screamed, not any words—it sounded like an animal, like a whale or a dinosaur, dying from the inside out.

Gary lunged at Cal with both arms raised above his head like they were goal posts, planning to beat them down on him, I guessed. Cal still looked dreamy and stoned off his dick but when Gary got about a foot away from him, Cal snapped out of it and grabbed his wrists.

He was so much stronger than Gary, Gary only fifteen and bone thin, only used to fighting kids in parking lots. Cal shoved Gary off and threw him far and hard into the bags of garbage that had fallen out of the cans, and Gary snapped back and hit his head against the concrete.

"Your mama's a goddamn whore," Cal said, pointing at him.

His dick was still hanging out, still swinging.

I dropped the plastic bottles, and they bounced and tripped at my feet, and I stared at Cal's dick, rotten little stick, and I got pictures in my head of my mother underneath him, arms and legs spread wide, him all grunts and sweat, both of them like a couple of dirty dogs skitching around in the mud.

Then I made a noise, too, but it was quiet, more like I was crying, because I wasn't stoned enough not to be scared and because Cal was making me look at his dick and because my mother really was a goddamn whore. And then I went for him.

My idea was to land one on his mouth but I'd never been in a fight before, except with Gary, so I swung blindly and Cal dodged it and grabbed my tiny balled-up fist and hit me across the mouth with the back of his hand.

You really notice the difference if you've never been hit by a man before and then you are. When me and Gary fought, it was all pulling and scratching and kicking, never punching. And my mother never hit me as hard as Cal did right then.

His hand felt like a tray of ice cubes. He hit me so hard I flipped around as I fell and put my hands out in front of me, my arms jamming up in my shoulders when I hit the ground. I shook my mouth out like a horse and saw Gary sitting up.

I turned and saw Cal, hands still on his dick even though it'd gone limp by now, shrunk small, and he kneaded it back into his jeans and wiped his mouth. For all our noise, no one had come out of their apartments, and there wasn't a big mess of anything, just plastic bottles rolling around, hollow, green water in the pool rocking.

Cal looked like a cowboy standing there, buttoning his jeans, swaggering all cocky. He cleared his throat, coughed up like he was about to spit but didn't, and then he left.

He didn't say any final offensive thing, didn't kick us when we were down, nothing like that. I stood up and felt sore all over, but Gary stayed on the ground, linked his arms around his knees and cried. His face was red and screwed up into a bunch of lines, and he kept crying and drooling and moaning low. I stood in front of him for a while and then just went back upstairs, because it didn't seem like he was coming up any time soon.

CHAPTER

12

I woke up with my mother standing over me. I was on the couch, fully clothed—shoes, bra, everything, feeling like I'd died. She was wearing a white blazer with shoulder pads.

"I'm leaving in two minutes," she announced, and then she went into the kitchen.

I sat up, head full of crabs, and I was sweating bad, too, my underarms, my stomach, my crotch. I closed my eyes and felt dizzy, and then I took a deep breath and stood up and walked to the kitchen, uneasy, holding my arms out for balance. I headed to the sink.

My mother didn't look at me, just rolled her eyes up to let me know I was in the way. I pulled a mug down and turned on the water, drank it and leaned over the sink, rested my hands on the edge. I wanted to put my head down on the cool metal.

"Are you coming or not?" my mother said.

My mouth was dry and sore, and the corners felt like they'd

been taped down. I didn't think I could speak, so I nodded. Things were double unless I stared at them. I focused on the dishwashing liquid; the bottle was fuzzy, so I picked it up and squinted at the label—"DAWN." The letters were big and blue, little sparkly stars floating around.

"Give me a second," I said.

"I'll be in the car," she said, and she walked out the front door and slammed it behind her.

I went to the bathroom and ran the toothbrush over my teeth, leaned my head over the sink and drank out of the faucet, washed my hands and patted water on my face.

I stared at myself in the mirror, eyes barely open, puffy, blood vessels bursting, little pink pillows on either side. I opened the medicine cabinet and took three Bayer and two of my mother's orange Vitamin C tablets. They were chalky but I got them down without throwing up.

My mother had started the car, and I got in and closed my eyes. She pulled out of the lot, sharp turns all the way, and I gripped the side and tasted the tinny flavor of the Vitamin C and thought I was going to toss it all over the window.

"Hey, Ma, can I bum a cigarette?" I said.

She grabbed her purse roughly and dropped it in my lap, staring straight ahead through her huge sunglasses. A minty smell came out when I opened the purse, and there were all of these little plastic cases—for lipstick, pills, tampons. I found the cigarettes and her pink lighter and got started.

My mother started coughing dramatically.

"Could you open the window at least?" she said.

I rolled the window down and blew smoke out, but the wind whipped it back in our faces.

CROOKED

"Could you aim away from me, *please?*" she said.

I couldn't believe she was serious, her smoking three packs a day her whole life, everything in the house reeking of smoke and lemon Lysol to cover it up. Her breath was like a barbecue pit. I started laughing at her.

"Christ, Ma, what is your fucking problem?" I said.

"My fucking problem, darlin' pie, is that you stink like a god-damn bar and all's you do is drink yourself stupid, *and* you hit Ken in the face."

"He told me to hit him in the face," I said.

Her voice cracked and she said, "He said you were all jacked up and went picking fights with him."

"I was just fooling around, Ma," I said.

She laughed, pushed air through her nose. "Yeah, well that's great," she said under her breath. "Ken's fat lip isn't fooling around, right?"

"Ken can handle himself just fine, looks to me," I said. "He doesn't need you to bitch me out."

She didn't answer, just took her glasses off, and she stopped short and rough at a light.

I blew smoke out the window and cracked my neck to the side, said, "Fine, Ma. I'll tell him I'm sorry."

I felt her hand on my chin, all bones and filed-down nails, and she jerked my face to hers, and my neck cracked loud and warm and felt like hot water in my ear. She was all the way gone, her whole face closing up, rubber lips waving like a dog.

"He don't need me to take care of him, and he don't need your goddamn apology, girl," she said, out of breath. "You're god-damn out of line, and you live in my fucking place, so clean your-self up."

She threw my face out of her hand like it was the plastic hood from her smokes, and then the light turned and she looked away from me. I didn't move, kept my head right where it was.

"You can go shack up with Chick Rodriguez for all I care," she said, and that was it.

We pulled up to my work, and I opened the car door and turned back to her one more time, and her face was all stone. I got out and saw Tommy John standing by the side door, smoking. My mother stared at me for another second, her mouth turned down, and I shut the door, and she put her sunglasses back on and leaned over. I bent down, thinking she was going to say something, but she rolled up the window instead, and then she drove away.

"Who's that?" Tommy John said.

"No one."

I walked past him and into the dock and heard someone loading in the rear, lifting three or four on a dolly, and it was extra loud to me and sounded like a blender. I squinted my eyes to the lights and I could see my hand clearly now, the big gray and blue bruise looked like a paint splotch on my knuckles.

I went into the staff room, and it smelled dusty to me, yellow lights humming and flickering, making buggy noises. I put my hand over my eyes and nodded to Angie and Tino at the table.

"Morning," said Angie.

"Hey," I said.

They kept talking in Spanish, and I poured coffee and stirred in some powder creamer, broke up the floating clumps with a straw. I got a bag of chocolate-chip cookies from the vending machine and sat at the table and put my head right down on it. Angie and Tino laughed.

"You have a rough night?" Angie said.

CROOKED

"Yep."

The table was cool on my cheek, sticky from soda, tiny crumbs everywhere. I heard my head beating, under my temples, behind my ears, and I started to space out; my mouth tipped open. Closed my eyes and colors started pooling, turned into my mother holding my face.

Angie shook me, his hand on my elbow, and I snapped awake.

"Huh?" I said.

Joe was standing at the door, propping it open.

"I need you two," he said, pointing at Angie and me.

We didn't move immediately. Joe rubbed his mustache.

"Now," he said.

Angie smiled, and Tino looked in his lap, trying not to laugh. Joe held the door open, and we stood up and went outside. Tommy John was still standing by the side door.

"Let me ask you two this," he said, and he pulled my sleeve, pulled us over next to the pay phone.

I tried to focus on his face, my stomach full of malt liquor and tiny lumps of powder creamer turning circles. I could smell Joe's breath and it smelled dead to me, like he wore dentures, like he'd been eating rotten lunch meat and coffee and Tic Tacs.

"Either of you got anything to tell me?" he said, eyes going between me and Angie.

I thought of the bird and rubbed my knuckles, thought of the smooth feathers getting damp. Look him in the eye, I thought. Something telling me to look him in the eye.

"I don't think so," I said, my voice sounding bouncy and young and weird.

Angie's eyebrows went heavy; he frowned and shook his head.

"Marjorie Welch?" Joe said.

Angie shook his head and shrugged.

I held my breath.

"San Anselmo?" Joe said.

"What?" said Angie.

"The flowers?" Joe said slowly.

I almost started laughing and let my breath out so fast I snorted.

"Good you're getting a bang out of it, Booth," said Joe. "She wants us to pay for the flower bed she says you two crushed."

"I don't think we did," Angie said.

"She thinks you did. There's not too much damage, and I got her down to a hundred, so that's fifty off each of your checks next period," Joe said.

Angie shook his head quickly and rubbed his mouth, started breathing so loud I could hear it.

"Hey, Angie, what do you want," Joe said, holding the clipboard out. "I've got to give her something."

"We didn't do that," Angie said. "She told us to watch out and we did. We watched out."

"Hey, man, I know," Joe said, trying to smooth it over, like he was just one of the guys. "You got to take a little hit on this one."

"It's not right, Joe," Angie said loudly. "It's bullshit."

"That's enough," Joe said, getting impatient. "I don't have time to make you feel better. You got a problem, take it up with the union."

He sounded so smug, knew goddamn well me and Angie weren't in any union.

Angie was getting red and started swinging his arms back and forth a little. Joe looked up at him.

"What the fuck's your problem?" he said.

"This is shit," Angie said, pointing at him.

CROOKED

Joe narrowed his eyes.

"Let's just watch it now," he said quietly.

"We didn't step on the fucking flowers," Angie said.

He kept pointing, and his finger suddenly looked long, extended, like it'd been pulled out and stayed there, like Silly Putty.

"Get your goddamn finger out of my face," said Joe.

The two of them stared at each other, Angie so much bigger and wider than Joe; any other place he'd kick the shit out of him, I thought.

Then Angie backed off and turned around, started walking toward the staff room, but funny, like all his weight was in his chest, pushing him forward. When he got to the door, he stopped, didn't open it, just leaned his head on it, and I could still hear him breathing. Me and Joe stood still.

Then, real quick, Angie snapped his head up, brought his arm back like a slingshot and punched the door hard and made it shake. He turned around and looked on fire to me, glaring at Joe, all red behind his eyes.

"You go on and put a dent in that door," said Joe, making it sound like a dare. "You go on."

Angie looked like a bull, looked like steam was about to rise right off him. He was sweating, fists tight at his sides, hunched over like he was ready to charge. Joe had his arms crossed, self-righteous as a preacher, buck beaver teeth coming up to gnaw at his lip. He ignored Angie and turned to me.

"You got any problems, Booth?"

I shook my head.

"All right," Joe said, and then he left and went back to his office.

Angie lifted his fists in the air, looked about to scream and then put his hands through his hair, grabbed wads of it and tugged. I walked over to him, my heart still going nuts.

"Hey, look," I said quietly. "You should fucking walk out, man. Fuck that shit, right?"

He looked at me, hands still in his hair, shaking a little.

"You're a nice white girl," he said. "Nobody cares you been in jail."

There was a rock in my stomach now while I looked at him, lips spread apart, eyes dark and round. Angie was the best person I'd met in a long time.

He shook his hands out and said something to himself in Spanish, and then he went into the staff room and slammed the door behind him.

"He's right," Tommy John said, a few feet away.

"Nobody's fucking talking to you," I said.

I saw Angie through the window, leaning forward against the vending machine, forehead pressed to the glass. I made fists.

I went to the pay phone and dialed Chick's number, cradled the phone on my shoulder and stared at my reflection, long and green in the metal square around the keypad. Then someone picked up.

"Hello?" he said, tired, scratchy.

I jumped and held the receiver tight with both hands.

"Chick? Where you been?" I whispered.

"Chick ain't here," he said.

I closed my eyes; my lips felt hot on the mouthpiece.

"Yeah, hey, Colin, right?" I said. "This is Mel."

"Hey, Mel, look, it's totally early now, you know."

"Yeah, I know, sorry. Hey, do you know where Chick is, though?"

The phone started to shake in my hands, and Colin yawned on the other end.

"Uh, no, he hasn't been around for a few days," he said.

I wrapped the metal cord tight around my palm.

"You sure?" I said, not hardly hearing myself.

Colin laughed.

"Yeah, I'm sure. Look, you kind of woke me up here—I was, like, asleep and shit."

"Oh, yeah," I said, out of breath. "Sorry." I pulled the cord tighter around my hand, started to feel the rings scrape my knuckles. "Hey, Colin?"

He sighed.

"Yeah?"

"You know where he might be?" I asked, kicking the wall lightly. "You know people he hangs out with?"

"I get it," he said, laughing. "You mean, like, girls?"

I wrapped the cord in another loop.

"No, I don't mean girls," I said, louder. "I'm not talking about girls."

"Yeah, okay," he said, trying to tease me. "Whatever."

"I don't mean goddamn *girls.*"

I jerked the cord a little, and it wiggled loose in the base of the phone. Tommy John watched me from the staff-room door.

"People he might be hanging out with," I said. "You know?"

"Uhh," Colin said, and he yawned again. "I don't really know any of those guys—"

"What guys?"

"Shit, I don't know," he said, getting pissed. "I don't know, you know, I'll, like, leave him a note you called. Bye-bye," he said chirpy and fake, and then he hung up on me.

"Colin?" I said, sounding squeaky.

He was gone; I heard some clicking. I stared down at the

receiver in my hands, shaking, but I held it tight, saw my fingertips go white but didn't feel it. My eyes watered. I felt hot.

I took tiny little breaths like you see goldfish take, thin gills going back and forth a mile a minute.

I put my right foot against the wall under the phone and hoisted myself in the air a little, got the metal cord tight around my hand and yanked the shit out of it. It choked my hand good, split the swollen skin and made it bleed, and I pulled it once more and jerked it out of the box, and then I fell back on my ass and shouted.

Thin blue wires stuck out of the box like pine needles. I sat on the ground like a baby with the receiver in my hands, Tommy John and Angie and Tino all staring.

Duke was still staying with his uncle in San Rafael, where he lived on and off during high school. I took the bus there after work and brought a quart of V-8 juice in a paper bag. There were brown wind chimes dangling from the roof of the porch, and there was a TV sitting next to the door, with no tube. I kneeled down to look closer, and stuck my head in a little, and it smelled like a busted bike chain. Then I saw ants all over the rim and pulled out quick.

I stood up and shivered and brushed my arms down. I felt them everywhere for a second, in my armpits, behind my knees, up my nose. I turned and rang the bell, hoped Duke's uncle wasn't there so I wouldn't have to make small talk. I heard steps, and Duke opened the door.

"Mel!" he said, and then he gave me a bear hug. "What's going on?"

"Nothing," I said, and I went in after him.

The light was dim and made the whole place look yellow. The carpet was beige and had brown spots on it, and the couch was old leather and looked slippery. Everything smelled like smoke and incense.

"You get here okay?" he said, going to the kitchen.

"Yeah, you know, I was here a few times," I said. "Fourth of July, right?"

I sat down at the thin kitchen table, white Formica with tiny gold specks. The chairs were puffy, gashes in all of them down the middle of the seat, yellow stuffing coming out.

"You want anything?" Duke asked.

"Do you have beer?" I said, and I took the tomato juice out of the bag and set it on the table.

"Right. Red-eyes," he said. "Cool."

He made us pints of red-eyes and stirred them with a long wooden spoon. We drank them out of Tupperware marked with little milliliter lines because they were the only tall glasses he had.

"What happened to your hand?" he asked.

I'd wrapped some toilet paper around it, and it wasn't bleeding anymore, just bruised and swollen, and the tissue made my fingers look stubby.

"I had an accident at work," I said, and I looked up at the ceiling and traced my eyes around the light fixture. It was shaped like a flower. "Slammed it in the truck door."

I didn't think about lying to Duke; it just came out. I knew I couldn't look at him and tell him what really happened. He started talking about what he'd been up to, and I didn't listen. I thought about Chick.

"Hey, you know where Chick is?" I said, interrupting him.

"Uh, I don't think so," he said. "He's not at his place?"

"Not lately."

Duke rubbed his eyes.

"He called me the other day, like, Monday," he said, yawning.

I burped tomato juice.

"Yeah?" I said, trying to sound casual. "Monday?"

He shrugged. "I don't know. I think so."

I tapped my Tupperware on the table and watched the juice slosh around.

"Hey, you want to go into the city?" I said.

"What, like, now?" Duke said, craning his head around to look at a clock on the counter.

"Yeah, like now."

"But I got a cold beverage," he said, holding his drink up, smiling like an old man.

"We'll take them with us," I said. "They're in Tupperware." I flicked my fingernail on the side. "Fresh as a daisy."

He didn't look too convinced. I started sweating.

"Let's go later," he said. "We can make a night of it, make fun of the kids."

He said it all sweetly, earnestly, excited to hang out with me and drink. He smiled, his face wide and stupid like a big moose, not having any idea how crazy I was inside, ready to lose my mind, knock the Tupperware over and watch it spill everywhere. I didn't want to hurt him but part of me did, walk behind him and slam his head down to the table, take his car keys and go.

I got up and walked around and clamped my hands down on his shoulders.

"Come on, Diamond Duke," I said, laughing. "Let's go find Chick, get this shit started."

I laughed for him, kept saying to myself, try and sound like young people sound, like kids did in high school. Talk light, talk high. No big deal, no big deal, I thought. Nothing's a big deal.

"Not now, Mel," he said. "We got to wait for Steve to get back anyway. He's got the ride."

I put my hand to my forehead, and it was hot. I made a fist and knocked on the side of my head like it was wood. Turned around and banged it lightly against the refrigerator.

"Hey," Duke said. "Hey, Mel, quit it," he said gently.

He took my elbow very lightly and pulled me away. I stared at him, and it made him nervous; he sat back down. I didn't sit down; I stood in the middle of his kitchen and didn't move.

"You all right?" Duke said.

"Hey, who does Chick hang out with anyway?" I said.

Duke shrugged.

"I only know a couple of them, you know. It sounds like they're assholes, though," he said.

"Does Chick do running?" I asked. "Is that what's happening?"

Duke's mouth got small.

"Yeah, I think. Sometimes."

He looked worried.

"It's okay," I said. "I'm not his mother."

Duke nodded and looked sad. I wasn't upset about Chick running; I'd figured as much. It was his only marketable skill. Would've been Gary's, too.

CHAPTER

13

The new girl was waiting for me in the hall outside the pit with another Mexican and a husky black chick.

"This is Aracelia and Paulina," the new girl said.

The other girls didn't say anything. Aracelia was short and pretty, small bones in her face, a mole under her eye, almost glamorous. Paulina was big, big arms and breasts stuffed under the blue nylon shirt.

"I'm Jeannie," the new girl said, and she pulled the kerchief off her head. Her hair was wet from the shower.

My eyes went back and forth between them.

"You take five minutes, we take some shit out of you," said Jeannie. "You come out without crying or dying, we'll help you a little bit," she said, and her South City accent made all the words run together.

It was hot in the hallway, and I could smell the trash from the pit. I stared at the three of them and touched my arm; every day little clumps of blood peeled off.

I stepped away from the wall slowly and nodded, held my arms at sides with the palms out. Jeannie stepped forward with a tiny smile. It was sexy. Somebody's gonna hit you, and you can't get away, Gary said, just close your eyes and play dead.

I closed my eyes and Jeannie's bony fist hit my teeth. The cleft of my lip slammed against the top row, felt like my two front teeth were imprinting themselves in wet cement. My head tipped back and I lost my balance, tasted blood in my mouth and went down.

I lifted my hands to my lips, and they circled around. Aracelia kicked me in the stomach with her tiny feet, and I lost my breath, and then Paulina's hard boot in the small of my back. I held my arms over my face, but Paulina leaned down and yanked one off me, held my wrist away, while Jeannie leaned down and cracked me across the nose fast.

I wasn't making any real sounds, just little grunts, but it was still the most noise I'd made in days and it felt strange. My head was full of blood now; I couldn't breathe through my nose.

They kept kicking me up and down, and I stayed, my body curled up like a fortune-telling fish in your palm, feet and arms and head curving in. I looked up and tried to see, too much light in my eyes, and I saw Jeannie, looking down at me, almost gentle, almost sweet. She kicked me hard in the ribs, and I thought I felt a bone snap, like a cheap glass Christmas ornament.

I couldn't hear anymore, not even the squeak of their shoes on the linoleum floor, and I couldn't smell the trash anymore from the pit, couldn't taste the blood, feel my nose or my lip, and I thought if I'm dead right here that isn't so bad. There were white powder-puff clouds in front of my eyes, and I felt real warm, like I was in a sleeping bag, like I'd been drugged, too tired to wake up.

"Hey, girl; hey, girl," someone said, and I thought it was Gary.

I thought I was passed out in my bed in the apartment, and we were still in high school, and I was late, Gary standing over me with two lit cigarettes in his mouth, saying, "Hey, girl, we're late, move your ass." He'd yank my foot under the blanket.

I jerked and gasped a little and lifted my head up slowly and looked at the floor and saw blood spreading, felt it dripping off my face like sweat. I choked on it, felt it go down my throat and up my nose. I couldn't close my mouth all the way, my lips busted up. I squinted up at the light.

"Hey, girl, you sleeping?" Jeannie said.

I shook my head and touched my lips, and they felt huge, blown up like water wings. Aracelia and Paulina stood against the wall, all three of them breathing hard, Paulina's big chest going up and down.

"Here it is," Jeannie said to me. "You can't be a real Reina, but you can be, like, a little Reina, Green," she said, reaching her hand down to me.

I didn't know if she was calling me Green because my eyes were green or because I was a *gringa*. Green-ga. I stretched my hand out and took hers, and she pulled me up fast. I had to hunch over to the side because my rib was jammed out of place, and as soon as I got up I almost went back down, my knee all cracked up.

"What's your name?" Jeannie said.

I looked past her at Aracelia who smiled shyly, almost like she didn't just kick the shit out of me, and Lina had a smirk on, too, arms crossed, looking like she'd just gotten laid.

I shrugged, and said quietly, my throat tickling because it was the first thing I'd said aloud since I talked trash to Lulu J., "Green's fine."

CROOKED

*   *   *

By the time me and Duke got in the car, we were feeling it. We'd split the six-pack and got into just a little bit of his uncle's Wild Turkey, and Duke somehow convinced him to let us take his ride.

I slid into shotgun and tried to pull the seat up and banged my knee hard against the dash.

"FUCK," I said.

"What're you doing?" Duke asked.

He burped and yanked his seat belt over him, and he kept trying to whistle between his teeth but it just came out a long line of S's. He pulled us out of the driveway and skinned the back tire against the curb when he turned, and I held the side like I was bracing for a crash.

Duke pushed a tape into the deck, and it was some kind of dance music—thump thump thump. I closed my eyes.

"Turn that shit off," I said.

"No, wait, listen, this is a friend of mine," he said.

It kept pounding, eerie organs in the background. I plugged my ears with my fingers, and it only helped a little.

Duke hunched over the wheel and bobbed his head to the music. I stared at him like he was a ghost.

We got to downtown San Rafael, and I rested my head on the window.

"Is there still that liquor store on D?" I asked.

"Huh?" Duke said loudly.

I leaned in and turned the music down.

"Liquor store? On D?" I said.

Duke thought hard.

"Oh, yeah," he said. "Why?" he asked, kitty-cat grin on. "Looking to buy some hooch?"

I busted up laughing. I loved old-fashioned-sounding things like that, like "hooch."

Duke made a sharp turn and pulled over at the next corner in front of Simon Wines & Liquors. I opened my door before the car stopped and let my foot drag on the pavement.

"More power to you," said Duke, and then he got a five out of his wallet and stuck it in my hand.

There was sawdust all over the floor of the store, all wooden crates and boxes stacked up, kind of an Old West feel. I ran my hand along the wine bottles, and they were warm.

In the back there was the wall of liquor up to the ceiling, and I put my hands on the Maker's Mark and Bushmills, and the price tags read $20.99, $18.99—all above our budget. It was going to be either Jack or Jim. Always between Jack and Jim. No need to fight over me, boys, I thought. You can all have a piece.

I took a fifth of Jack and walked up to pay, set the bottle down and took a couple of silver-dollar mints out of the bin on the counter. I held one between my fingers and stared at it and shut one eye, stared at the counter man's face behind it.

"Can I see some ID?" he said.

I exploded, laughing.

"You sure can," I said, coughing. "Of course you can."

I handed him my license, and he looked at it and then up at me, doubtful. Then he gave it back, looking bored now, and he scanned the bottle in. I watched for the digital numbers on the register like they were lottery balls coming up.

"It's on sale for $9.99," he said quietly.

"Great," I said, practically shouting.

I gave him the cash and looked up to the corner of the room, next to the round mirror at the camera pointing down at me, metal fixtures attaching it to the ceiling like bug legs. It made me nervous.

He put the Jack in a tall paper bag quickly and handed it to me without looking, like we were doing something illegal.

I didn't say anything, just took the bottle by the neck and walked out, pointed a finger gun at Duke and got back in the car.

"We good?" he said.

"Yep."

I opened the bottle and took a tiny sip and handed it to Duke.

"Friday night," he said.

We headed for the bridge, and Duke turned his music back on.

"Could you turn that rave shit off?" I said.

"Mel," said Duke. "Give it a chance."

I shut my eyes as we went up Waldo Grade, saw the last of the jammed commuter cars coming into Marin from the city.

I stuck the bottle between my legs and twisted the bag around the top, looked in the side mirror for cops. I winced when I felt the whiskey hit my stomach and fill my nose. I remembered Gary said to me once, when we were young, "Shit, girl, if you can take a shot of Robitussin you can take a shot of this." I angled the bottle up and took three good pulls.

"Damn, Mel," Duke said.

I coughed as we got to the rainbow tunnel. My mother always told us to hold our breath when we went through the rainbow tunnel; she'd heard it was good luck. Of course it was child's play to Gary. He could almost make the whole trip across the bridge without breathing.

I didn't hold mine now because my heart was beating fast from drinking so much so fast. There was some kind of choir on the tape, chanting.

"Those aren't real people," Duke shouted, pointing to the deck. "This guy, Dave, completely manufactured that sound."

We came out of the tunnel, and I nodded, swallowed some more whiskey and stared at the hills, fog rolling over.

"Hear that?" Duke yelled to me. "That's almost religious, you know?"

It didn't sound religious to me; it sounded like little dead children.

We got to the bridge, and Duke swerved, and I hung on and stared at a cyclist. I unrolled the window and let the wind hit me, fog spray. I opened my mouth and felt water on my tongue, my teeth. The music still pounded, and now it was louder and it sounded like there were laser bullets flying and a weird laugh track. I leaned forward quickly and pressed EJECT, and the tape popped into my hand.

"Hey, what're you doing?" Duke said.

Then I threw it out the window like it was a Frisbee. I watched it spin in the side mirror and tumble into the bike lane. I was a little upset it didn't make it over the railing, into the Bay.

"What the fuck, Mel?" Duke said. "That was my only copy."

I laughed at him.

"Yeah," he muttered, "real funny. You can't just throw people's shit out the window."

"I'll buy you a new one."

"I told you," he said, annoyed. "It's my friend's. You can't buy it in a store."

"Fine. I'll call your friend then."

Duke shook his head.

"I can't bug him for shit like that," he said. Then he said quietly, "That was old stuff, too."

CROOKED

"Fine," I said loudly. "What do you want? A goddamn hand job? Jesus."

Duke looked a little surprised. He blushed, and I blew air through my lips so they flapped like shutters. We didn't say anything for a while and got in line for the tollbooth. The sky was dark now; the fog was in. Me and Duke were dizzy drunk, and it was only eight-fifteen.

By the time we got to Chick's, we were halfway through the fifth and had already discussed how we couldn't feel our toes. Duke kept moving his seat back until he was almost lying down, arm stretched out to the wheel. I was laughing at him, and I laughed all the way down Clement but when Duke found a space a block away from Chick's, my stomach turned knotty.

I stepped out of the car and held the bottle in my arms like it was a baby. Duke seemed to take a long time getting himself together; he couldn't lock the seat upright, couldn't get untangled from his belt. I stood on the curb and chattered my teeth, hugged the bottle to my chest.

We walked to Chick's place and didn't really say anything to each other. Duke rang the bell, and we heard the buzz upstairs. The light was on in the front window, and I saw a shadow, someone moving around. I felt my hands start to shake; the bottle was wiggling around in my arms, and I started moving my lips, talking myself down. You're okay, I said in my head. You're okay.

Duke was staring at me, so I quit it. The right lens of his glasses was foggy, and I laughed.

"What?" he said.

"Why is just one lens foggy?"

He shrugged.

"I don't know. It does that sometimes."

Then the door opened at the top of the stairs, and I hopped the step and pressed my face against the gate.

"Chick?" I said.

"Nah, he's not here," said Colin, leaning out.

I banged my head against the gate.

"What's up, man?" Duke shouted.

"Not much—what's up with you, Diamond Duke?"

He buzzed us in, and I felt exhausted, suddenly, like I didn't have enough energy to even climb the stairs, hardly enough to sit in the cold flat and wait for Chick. Duke bounded up and shook hands with Colin.

"Howdy, Mel," he said to me.

He smiled, and I nodded hello and looked down.

I followed them into the living room and sat on the futon, and it sagged. Duke and Colin talked about nothing, what's going on, what's happening, what're you doing, man. You know, working, living.

Colin was wearing surf shorts and a T-shirt that was too long for him. His face looked bumpy and red like he had a rash. I stared and squinted and couldn't tell if it was just the light in the room.

"Y'all drinkin'?" Colin said.

"Hells yeah," said Duke.

They kept talking, and I unscrewed the cap on the whiskey and took a sip, and some dripped down my palm. I stood up.

"Where's Chick?" I said, interrupting.

"It's cool, Mel," Duke said gently, reaching his hand out like he was about to pet me.

I ducked out of the way, and Colin laughed.

"Do you know where Chick is?" I said, slower.

CROOKED

Colin cocked his head and rolled his eyes up to the ceiling, and it made me think he was lying.

"*Uh,*" he said, pretending to think. He hunched his shoulders up and dropped them. "Nope," he said, trying to be cute. "Out with friends, you know—*guy* friends, Mel."

Then he got up in my face and put his hand on my shoulder, played like he was consoling me. "You're a sensitive girl," he whispered.

I jerked my shoulder back, and his hand fell off.

"Touchy," he said, and then he turned back to Duke.

I stared at a pimple on his neck.

"You can hang out if you want. I don't know when he'll be back," said Colin.

"Cool. Thanks, man," Duke said.

Colin grabbed a comic book from the TV tray and adjusted his crotch like he was wearing a cup.

"I gotta go lay one down," he said to Duke.

"Cool," said Duke.

Colin didn't say anything to me, didn't look my way, just went into the bathroom and closed the door. I heard the little metal hook latch. Duke stretched his arms above his head and yawned.

"You want to wait?" he asked.

"Sure. For a while," I said. "Hey, come here."

Duke walked up to me and bent down. I couldn't tell if it was me or him that smelled so god-awful, like whiskey and mousetraps.

"Hey, do you think he's lying?" I said. "Do you think he knows where Chick's at?"

"Shit, probably," Duke said, and he paused. Then he whispered, "Colin's kind of a dick."

I nodded, my eyes fixed on the bathroom door. I tugged on Duke's sleeve.

"Go see if there's beer in the kitchen," I said.

"All right," he said, and he took the bottle from me. "Gimme."

I smiled, and he went into the kitchen, and I kept my eyes on the bathroom door. I stood up and walked up close to it and stared some more, my head sunk to the side. I could see the light sneaking out under the frame. Thought about the thin metal lock.

I backed up and turned sideways, and then I ran for it, slammed into the door leading with my shoulder, and it flew open. Colin sat on the toilet with his shorts around his ankles, mouth open, and I stumbled to the sink.

"What the fuck are you doing!" he yelled, trying to hold the comic book over his privates.

My shoulder tingled, and I rubbed it with my hand and stepped up to him, and then I clenched my bad bleedy red hand and hit his nose and knocked him right off the toilet.

"What the fuck, what the fuck," he whined, squirreling around on the tile next to the tub.

My hand stung a little, but it didn't really bother me. I held it in front of my face to get a better look at it, and it didn't even look like it was mine, all swollen and fat, blue veins puffing out.

Colin held his nose with one hand and tried to pull his shorts up with the other, but I squatted on top of him quick and grabbed his arm, bent it around.

"Ow, ow!" he yelled.

I held his wrist like it was a baseball bat, twisted the skin and pinned it against his back, and then I tightened my thighs around him, sitting on his bare ass. He felt like a bundle of sticks.

"My nose," he mumbled, still squirming.

CROOKED

"Relax, it's not broken," I said.

I could see the side of his face, his thin long nose starting to swell up red and bulky.

"You crazy bitch, you're a fuckin' crazy bitch," he said, slurred, mouth pressed against the floor.

I pushed his wrist down, and he shouted.

"Okay, little man," I said, and I leaned down to his ear.

Duke appeared in the doorway.

"Mel, what are you doing?" he said, out of breath.

"Dude, get her off me; she's fuckin' crazy," Colin said.

I grabbed the hair at the back of his neck and pulled his head up.

"Where's Chick?" I said to him.

He tried to pull his head away, shake it out of my hand, wiggling like a fish.

"Get her off me, man," he said again.

I glanced up at Duke and smiled at him, and he busted up laughing. He clapped his hands and fell against the door frame.

"Where's Chick at?" I said to Colin.

I dug my fingers into his wet scalp, and it felt all grainy.

"I don't know, I don't know," he cried, and his voice was nasal and tight.

"Who's he out with?"

"Victor, I think."

"Who's Victor?"

"Shit, man, I don't know. They get wasted together."

Duke was almost crying in the doorway, swinging the whiskey bottle around like he was directing traffic. I let go of Colin's head, and it smacked down flat on the tile.

I climbed off him and stood up and held the sink for balance.

Colin scrambled around, curling up like a ribbon, trying to yank his shorts up, grunting. He finally got to his feet and hunched over.

"Dude, don't fuck with Mel," Duke said, still laughing.

"My fuckin' nose," Colin said.

I pushed past Duke and went to Chick's room and turned on the light. Took a deep breath and smelled pot and sweat and sneakers, everything locked in, windows sealed tight. I stumbled to the dresser and started picking up scraps of paper, knocking them off, trying to fix my skunk-drunk eyes on Chick's squiggly handwriting, names and numbers, looking for Victor. Gene. Ed. Jordan. Buster. And then Mel Booth, on the back of a Manny's matchbook. Mel Booth, it said, letters gone over a few times in ballpoint pen.

My eyes felt heavy suddenly, and I dropped the matchbook on the dresser and went to the closet. I stared at the clothes hanging on the wooden bar and batted at them like they were bugs. Everything smelled like foot powder. I kneeled down, pushed the socks and T-shirts around until I found the blue shoe box, and I opened it.

The gun was still in there. I picked it up carefully with my middle finger and my thumb like it was a live crab. I snapped the release, and the clip fell into my hand.

I slid the clip back in and tried to tuck it into the back of my pants, but the waist wasn't tight enough, and the piece started to slide down to my ass, so I grabbed it and took off my jacket and wrapped the gun in it real gently. I stood in front of the mirror and slouched to the side with the jacket balled up under my arm and tried to look casual. I winked at myself.

I walked back out to the hall, and the piece felt heavy in the jacket, and I thought about the cop shows where the cops go into the drug lord's den with their guns drawn, holding them next to their faces, pointed up to the ceiling. Goddamn fool way to handle a gun, Nana would say. Blow your stupid brain right outta your head.

Colin sat on the futon in the living room holding a can of Coke to his nose, leaning his head back. He saw me out of the corner of his eye and squirmed around again, tried to jump to his feet but fell off the futon instead, right on his ass.

"Shit, fuckin' shit," he said.

Then I heard the toilet flush, and Duke came out, buttoning his jeans.

"You piss on the seat?" I said to him.

"Shit yeah."

I smiled at him and felt halfway okay at that second. Didn't feel hungry or thirsty or sick for once.

"Let's get out of here," I said quietly.

"Yeah, go on now, get outta here," Colin said feebly.

I whipped around and said, "What the fuck did you say?"

Colin said, "No, I just mean, like, I don't know when Chick's coming back, you know." He coughed and shriveled up on the futon.

I turned back to Duke. "No use waiting."

He shrugged, and then we heard keys in the door. The three of us turned and stared and didn't move.

Chick was laughing, and the first thing I saw was his arms, slim and brown. He walked in and saw I was there and looked happy for a second, tiny eyes going back and forth over me, and then he got panicked. There was a Mexican kid behind him, bandanna over his head, big jeans and hightop shoes, thin brown mustache.

"Hey, Mel," Chick said softly. He looked at Duke and said, "What's up, man?"

They said hi, then Duke started talking to the Mexican kid, and

Chick came up close to me. I could smell his breath, like coffee and smoke, and his eyes were wet and soft like a puppy, pupils shaking. He kept licking his lips.

He put his hand on my arm and rubbed it a little.

"How you been, girl?" he said.

"Fine."

The Mexican kid was talking to Duke and walking back and forth like he was doing the two-step, arms lifted in front of him, obviously a little tweaked. Chick jerked his head around.

"This is my boy, Victor," he said to me. "This is Mel."

"What's going on, Mel?" Victor said.

"Not much," I said, still looking at Chick. "What about you?"

"Nothing, johnny," he said, cutting the air with his hand. He was breathing hard.

Chick smiled shyly at me, trying to get me to smile back, I thought. I didn't. Then he looked over my shoulder at Colin.

"What the hell happened to you?" he said.

"He fell down in the bathroom," I said.

"What?" said Chick.

"Nothing, dude," Colin said.

Chick was confused but looked back to me, and his forehead straightened out. He wiped his face with his hand, sleeve pulled over it, and we both stared at it, sweat soaking it through.

"I have to go," I said.

"You just got here," Chick said.

"No, I really have to go."

I heard Duke and Victor talking behind me, hushed.

"Hey, let's talk," said Chick, and he nodded to his room.

I shifted on my feet, right to left. Chick's bottom lip shook, like he was about to cry. He scratched his head, forearms.

I nodded slowly, and Chick turned around and said something to Victor in Spanish. I heard *cerveza.*

Me and Chick walked to his room, and Duke smiled at me as we went, gently, like he was my father. In Chick's room, he sat on his bed and patted the space next to him, smiling. I put my balled-up jacket on the floor near the door and sat beside him and didn't look over. His leg started up, knee vibrating up and down.

"Hey, Mel, I'm sorry I didn't call you all week," he said.

I turned my eyes down and stared at his ratty sneakers with holes in the heels. I sighed and shook my head.

"I've been a little busy, that's all," he said gently, which made it all the worse, the way he was purring to me, trying to sell me some line of trash.

"I don't give a shit, Chick."

He took my hand and tried to lace his wet fingers through it, but it was my bad hand, and it stung so I pulled it away.

"What happened to you?" he said.

"I hit my mother's boyfriend."

Chick laughed. "No shit?"

He kept laughing, manic and speedy, started scratching at his arms again.

"Goddamn, that's badass, girl," he said.

I turned to him and tried to look him in the eyes, but I was too drunk. They kept crashing together in his forehead so I looked down again.

"Count on you to fuck some shit up," he said, rambling. "Old man hit the fuckin' floor, right—"

"Shut up," I said. "Just shut up."

He stopped.

I rubbed my eyes, my temples. I stared at the door, and it

looked like it was rippling. I dipped my head down and let my shoulders go lax, put my face in my hands. My fingers were sticky and smelled like dirt. I let my head sink to the side and felt like I could fall asleep right there.

Then I felt Chick's lips on my neck. I opened my eyes, and he was blurry; his hand curled around the other side of my face, and he started kissing me. His lips were wet and tight, and he held my head firm. It reminded me of being with Sikes just then, only because I felt like I wasn't there at all, like it was a daydream and I was actually still straddling Colin in the bathroom. I used to do that all the time with Sikes—space right out while we were fucking, not thinking about other guys, really, just about being on the beach, or in the woods up by the lake where Nana used to live.

Chick laid me back, put one hand behind my neck and was kissing me faster now. My eyelids fluttered, and I didn't know what to do with my arms or hands so I folded them up in front of me. His hand went under my shirt, up to my tits, touching one, then the other. I let him, and I threw my arm around his neck sloppy.

He got on top of me and planted himself between my legs. I kept my eyes open, and his eyes were closed, and he held my face tight. I could feel his heart tapping fast through his chest.

He took his jacket off, still kissing me and threw it behind him. I stared at the ceiling again. He lifted my shirt up, and I raised my arms and let him slip it off me. He pushed his whole body hard on me, pressed his hips against mine and touched my face, my cheeks.

Then he lifted his head up, eyes back and forth, frantic. He looked worried now, his mouth open, tiny saliva line between his lips. He buried his face in my neck.

"What's wrong?" I said.

He sighed.

"Nothing," he said, and he lifted his head up. He touched my lips lightly. "Not you, not you—I'm just all fucked up, you know?"

He looked scared, beady eyes.

"What do you mean?" I said.

"Me and Vic did a lot of shit over at More's place, that's all," he said. "Sometimes I can't get it up when I'm all fucked up."

I let my head fall back on the bed and slid out from under him, pushed him off gently. He tumbled over and propped himself up on his side. I straightened the underwire of my bra.

"I'm sorry, Mel," he said.

I sat up and started to feel a little sick in the stomach, thought about all the tomato juice from the red-eyes.

"Forget it," I said. "I have to go, though."

"No, come on," Chick said. "Don't let it ruin everything."

"It's not that," I said. "Maybe we have the wrong attitude."

He sat up and looked confused.

"Not about your dick," I said. "Just this right here. Me and you."

He looked down and picked at his fingernails.

"We're not engaged, you know?" I said quietly.

He nodded. We sat there.

I leaned over and grabbed my shirt and put it on.

"Hey, Mel, I'm, *uh,* I'm sorry," he said.

"Forget it," I said.

I stood up and scooped up my jacket and held it in a bundle in my arms.

"Chick?"

"Yeah?"

"Victor—is he okay?"

Chick shrugged and didn't get it.

"Is he giving you shit?"

Chick laughed. "Who told you that?" he said. "Duke?"

"Didn't say who, just that—"

"No," he said, leaning back on his elbows. "No, Mel, Vic doesn't give me shit. Diamond Duke's afraid of these kids me and Vic go out with." He shook his head and laughed fast again. "Duke just don't know how to talk to people, know what I'm saying?"

I didn't answer him. I just looked at his eyes. They were huge, but he didn't seem to be looking at me, just in my direction, like he was a blind person.

"Promise me something, Chicken," I said.

"What's that?"

"Don't do any more tonight, okay?"

He stared at me for a second and nodded, gave me a thumbs-up, and I smiled and knew he was lying.

CHAPTER

14

The next morning I was hung over as hell when I went to see Gruder. He was late, so I tried to stay awake best I could, propped my head up on my hand and kept the hurt one limp in my lap. I closed my eyes, and they twitched at the edges, and I kept feeling like I was tripping on something, over a curb, something. My mouth dropped open; my neck started loosening up, and I could've gone to sleep right there, but then Gruder came in and made a racket.

"Sorry, Melody," he said, carrying a newspaper and a thin paper cup of coffee. He took his legal pad from the desk, sat down, and said quietly to himself, "Melody."

He sounded sad and dreamy, like I wasn't there in his office but somewhere else and in bad trouble, like I'd been in an accident.

"Heard you damaged some property at work," he said.

"Did Joe call you?"

"Yes, he did. He said you destroyed a pay phone."

I looked at my fingers.

"Is that what happened?" he asked.

I took a deep breath. "Yeah."

He stared at me, waiting for more.

"That's just about the size of it," I said.

"Why did you feel the need to do something like that?" he said.

I shook my head and tapped my fingers against his desk.

"I was a little frustrated," I said.

Gruder nodded. "Why's that?"

"I was trying to call a friend of mine."

Gruder stared.

"He wasn't home," I said.

Gruder coughed. "Okay," he said. "Anything else?"

I stared at the ATTITUDE sign on the bulletin board.

"Well yeah," I said. "Joe cut me and Angie, the guy I make drops with, Joe cut our paychecks fifty bucks each because a customer said we stepped on her flowers."

Gruder kept staring.

"We didn't step on her flowers," I said. "She had a chip on her shoulder because she thinks Joe cheated her."

"Joe thinks you have a chip on your shoulder," Joe said.

I laughed and let my head drop down.

"Yeah, I guess you could say that," I said.

"What else?" said Gruder.

"Nothing. There's nothing else."

He nodded slowly, and I knew he didn't believe me. I thought of the wet bird in my hand.

"What did Joe say to you?" he asked.

"Didn't you talk to him?"

"Yes, but I'd like to hear what you thought about it."

My stomach growled, and I pressed it with my palm. I sighed.

"That he had to call PacBell to come replace it, and if there was any cost it would come out of my paycheck," I said, without any tone at all, laundry-list style.

Gruder stared. I could feel my hands start to shake so I grabbed my knees.

"What?" I said. "Why are you looking at me like that?"

Now he reached for a pen, and I laughed.

"Great," I said. "You better make a note of that."

He wrote something down, clicked his pen, and tucked it into his breast pocket.

"He told me he'd have to let you go if you acted out again," Gruder said.

"Oh yeah?" I said. "He say it that nicely, too?"

"No, he did not," he said. "I told him you might be willing to attend an anger-management workshop."

I laughed again and leaned forward.

"You're kidding, right?"

Gruder smiled uneasily, and it made me want to punch him.

"No, I'm not," he said. "I think it will show Joe you're serious about improving your attitude."

I let my head hang down again and dropped it into my hands. My stomach was burning. It felt like I had swallowed Elmer's Glue.

"I know this isn't easy," Gruder said.

"You know *shit,*" I said, and then I stood up. "This isn't any kind of a life out here—it's like some fake thing."

I felt my voice wavering, and I coughed. I got dizzy, too, held my hand against my forehead, wiped the sweat off.

I guessed Gruder had heard this kind of thing before. He

leaned back in his chair and held his hand out gently, like he wanted me to give him five.

"Please," he said. "Sit down."

I was tired, and my back hurt. My spine felt like a plank of wood, and I closed my eyes and felt sick, smelled meat in my nostrils.

"I really have to go," I said quietly. "Can I go?"

He nodded slowly.

"Sure. If you like."

"I would like. Yes."

"All right then," he said, took his pen from his pocket and wrote something else down.

My hands felt heavy, like there were magnets in the tips.

"Happy Thanksgiving, Melody," he said.

"Right," I said. "You, too."

I peeled off down the hall, pressed my thumb hard on the elevator button, two, three, four times. In the elevator I stood in the corner and leaned my head against the cool perforated wall. People stared but I didn't move.

The sky was all bright gray when I stepped out of the building. I blinked hard and covered my eyes, saw the big brown-and-orange A&W sign across the freeway, and it made me think of root-beer floats. They were my favorite thing when I was a kid. I could down three right in a row if you put them in front of me.

I walked up to the crosswalk and tapped my fingers against my palm, kept saying the words "anger management" over in my head. Thought about how Joe probably had a goddamn good laugh picturing me sitting in a circle, holding hands with Ritalin kids and wife beaters.

At the counter in A&W, I ordered a bacon cheeseburger and a root-beer float, and the girl said it was $5.79. I flipped through the three dollars in my wallet, picked out the loose change in my pocket and figured I had to pick one or the other.

"Just the burger, then," I said.

It looked a lot smaller on my tray than it did in the neon picture menu. In the picture, the patty was round and shiny, and the bacon was so long and crisp it curled up the sides of the bun like petals. My burger looked like it had been stepped on.

But I ate it anyway. In about four bites. I thought of my mother saying, "You showed that who's boss." That's what Nana used to say when you ate something really quickly. I stood up and knew I felt weird but couldn't put my finger on why. I placed the tray on top of the garbage can and walked outside, felt full of energy, like I could run back to my mother's apartment, and then I realized what it was: I didn't feel sick.

Thanksgiving morning was cold. My mother was padding around the apartment in a fuzzy yellow towel and white sport socks. The TV was on with no sound, showing the parade in New York, and there seemed to be forty or fifty high-school marching bands, all wearing tall hats with big feathers, majorettes with tiny leotards and smiling like Miss America. It reminded me of Helen Healy. She was in band in high school; she played the flute. She always ended up dating drummers because drummers marched right behind the flutes.

"Would you look at that?" my mother said.

She didn't say it to me directly, just out to the air. I looked to the TV and saw a huge cartoon baby floating above the crowd. Its eyes were crossed, tongue sticking out.

"What is it?" I said.

My mother squinted.

"Some kind of cartoon character," she said.

"It's ugly as hell," I said.

It was. I realized it was a big balloon, but the head seemed deformed and bloated. It looked dead to me.

My mother lit a cigarette and poured herself coffee. She coughed, and it sounded like there was junk in her throat.

"You sick, Ma?"

"Nah," she said. "I just smoke."

I laughed and said, "Right."

I picked up my cigarettes from the coffee table and lit one, and my heart started beating fast; it always did when I smoked without eating anything first. I felt my chest closing in a little.

"You're working tonight, right?" I asked.

"Yeah. The restaurant has that, what's that called?" she said, staring into space. "The fixed-price menu. You know, twenty dollars, you get salmon or bass. Sides are traditional—potatoes, cranberries," she recited. "Cornmeal stuffing. Everything except the bird."

"Ken going?" I said.

"Nah, he went down south," she said, and she folded a paper napkin in front of her, smaller and smaller squares. "He's got family there."

She turned away then, opened the hatch on the coffee machine and pinched the filter with two fingers, dropped it in the trash under the sink.

"You can come in if you want," she said. "I can probably get you comped."

I stared at the back of her head, straw hair tied in a knot, fake French twist she saw in a magazine.

"I don't know," I said.

"Oh yeah?" she said, facing me again. She pulled another long cigarette out of the box. "You got plans?"

CROOKED

"No, not for dinner. I was thinking," I started to say, and then I stopped and took a little breath. "I was thinking I might go see Gary."

She smiled, and I could tell she didn't even realize it; all the skin on her face just lifted like someone was operating it from a remote control.

"Yeah? You going out there?" she said.

"I think so."

"Well, okay," she said. She looked satisfied, like she just sold me something, and it made me embarrassed. I stared at my nails. "Hey, why don't you take the car?"

"Huh?" I said, almost laughing. I couldn't remember a time she ever offered her car to me or Gary, not once ever. "How're you going to get to work?"

She shook her head at me.

"I can call one of the girls, get a ride," she said.

"Only if you're sure."

"Positive."

She seemed more awake now, and she turned on the water in the sink and started spraying it around. I stood up and felt the air rush out of me, the top of my head tingling.

"He knows I'm working today," she said. "This is gonna be some big surprise for him—he's not expecting anybody."

"Yeah?"

"Yeah," she said, turning around to face me. "But you don't have to worry. Today's what they call an open day. You don't have to make any appointments. It'll probably be crowded."

I shrugged.

She came out from behind the counter and stretched her hand out to me, near my face, and I winced and didn't even think about it. She laughed.

"I'm not gonna hit you," she said quietly.

Then she stopped laughing right away and pulled her hand back. She looked down and seemed pretty to me just then, no makeup on her face, almost a little delicate. Then she patted me on the shoulder, awkward.

She started back toward the bathroom to get dressed, stepping very lightly. I could hardly hear her.

"Mel?" she said.

"Yeah?"

She paused for a minute.

"Bring him cigarettes," she said. "He likes Marlboros and American Spirits."

I spilled nearly a full cup of coffee on my lap in the parking lot of San Quentin. It scalded the tops of my thighs.

"Shit," I said, and I tried to fan my legs with the flimsy napkins I had.

I patted my jeans down, tried to soak some of it up, but it had turned cold by then anyway, and it looked like I'd wet my pants.

I rolled down the window and sat in the car for a few minutes, smoking. The lot looked full of cars, but there didn't seem to be any people around. The sky was full of fog and had gotten bright, and I leaned my head back and scratched at the roof, at a tough black patch where my mother must've put out a cigarette.

When I was six and screaming one time about something I don't remember, my mother told me to shut up, and I kept on, and she grabbed my arm and pressed her cigarette into my shoulder, and it burned through the shirt and fried the skin. I still had the scar in a pickle shape, right next to my underarm.

I got out of the car quickly and tied my jacket around my

waist, tried to cover the wet spot. I walked to the visitor's entrance and showed the card the dayman had given me to the attendant, and he let me in. He pointed me down a hallway, yellow linoleum, and it smelled like disinfectant, lemon or pine. It made me think of Staley.

There were a few people in the waiting room. I noticed a woman with a bunch of kids. She looked tired or drugged, her head kept rolling back, and the baby on her lap chewed a plastic ring. The oldest boy stood next to her, wearing chinos that were worn-down at the knees, brown grass stains along the sides. His hand was on his mother's shoulder, like he was posing for a picture.

I went to the window and printed my name and signed it, wrote down Gary's name, the number on my visitor's card, the time—2:50. Then I sat down next to an old man and across from a teenage girl wearing a Giants windbreaker, hair pulled tight on her head. She picked at her ear and looked at her finger and wiped it on her jeans. It left a little blood smear.

The old man next to me was reading a newspaper. He was staring at an article about another fire in the East Bay. He gripped the paper tightly, and then he noticed me looking and smiled.

"A lot of damage, huh?" I said, nodding at the paper.

"What?" he said.

"The fire. In the East Bay," I said.

"Oh yes," he said. "Yes."

He folded the section he was reading and put it on the chair next to him, and then he picked up another and held it upside down. His hands were clamped down on the edges, and his eyes scanned all over the upside-down words, and he smiled at me again, and I got that he wasn't reading any of it at all.

And I thought that he was probably coming to see his son, and the teenage girl was coming to see her boyfriend. And the boy with his hand on the drugged woman's shoulder was coming to see his dad.

The boy had picked up the baby now and was shaking it around in his arms. He rocked it back and forth hard, and the baby screeched.

"Joffrey," came through the speakers, and I hopped in my seat.

The boy reached over and shook his mother's shoulder; she sat up straight and looked around, almost afraid, like she'd been caught. She stood up and brushed down the wrinkles in her skirt, and then went through the green door. The boy followed her.

I closed my eyes, and my stomach was growling, but I was weirdly full. I felt nauseous and covered my mouth, felt air bubbling up. I thought I smelled hamburger meat.

"Booth," the voice through the speakers said.

I jumped again, and stood up and went to the green door, and the old black guard looked at my visitor's card again, and another G walked me in.

We walked behind the other visitors, past the drugged woman and her children. She was crying, and the boy was holding the baby and pinching its cheek hard. The baby twisted around. I glanced at the man who sat across from them through the glass. He had corn-rows, and he leaned forward and wasn't saying anything and looked pissed off. The G pointed me toward a booth labeled "5."

I nodded and sat down in the orange plastic chair. I could hear the woman to my right, in booth 6. She was talking dirty. She said, "I wanna suck your cock so bad, baby, I wanna put it in my mouth . . ." I could see the man she was talking to rubbing his crotch with his elbow. His mouth was open.

I felt sick to my stomach again and lifted my shirt to my nose, and it smelled like smoke. I stood up quickly and thought I'd walk out and puke in the waiting room, vomit all over the old man and his newspaper. I'd lie to my mother and tell her I had a gorgeous conversation with Gary, and I wouldn't have to hear any noise about it from her until she came to see him next. But then a door opened on the other side, and Gary came through it, and a guard walked him over.

We stood facing each other, both of us standing, staring. His hair was longer than it ever had been, almost to his shoulders, and his right eye was screwed up, pinched at one side, like it was sewed shut, and it made the other one look huge. He sat down in the chair across from me and smiled, and I saw his bent teeth. He rested his hands on the counter in front of him, and his arms looked thin but lean and tight, sticking out of his orange jumpsuit, which looked too big for him. He nodded at me and at the chair, pointed to the phone.

I sat and grabbed the phone receiver, and I heard static like there was a sock over his end, and then Gary picked his up. We didn't say anything, but I could hear him breathing, and it sounded like it did inside a Halloween mask, hollow in your ears.

"What happened to your eye?" I said, my voice echoing somewhere in the phone.

"Someone tried to remove it with a spoon," he said.

His voice was different, lower. It always used to crack, especially when he was racing, scratchy because he'd talk and smoke so much, get excited.

"What happened to your pants?" he said.

"I spilled coffee on myself. In the parking lot."

He nodded.

"That's awfully silly," he said.

"Yes, I know."

The phone smelled strange on my end, like gum and Lysol, shoes in a bowling alley. Gary licked his lips and stared at me. I didn't know what to say.

"So," he said. "How are you?"

I laughed and didn't mean to.

"You know—good."

I couldn't look at him anymore, couldn't look at the lines in his face, kept remembering the last time I saw him, at the sentencing. Three for me, life for him. I'd kept turning my head around to see him, trying to see his face. He was looking straight ahead.

I stared at the white counter, and it was all scratched up, like someone had scraped it with a key.

"I brought you some cigarettes," I said.

Gary smiled.

"Keep them," he said. "They won't get to me anyway."

He rubbed the bridge of his nose and coughed.

"Why did you come if you have nothing to say?" he said calmly.

My hands were sweating. I put the phone in the crook of my shoulder, and wiped my palms on my jeans.

"I don't know," I said. "Ma wanted me to."

He laughed through his nose.

"Since when do you do things Sally wants?"

"Since she lets me sleep on her couch."

"Right," he said. "So Mel," he said, sing-songy. "What've you been doing?"

"Nothing."

"Nothing?" he asked. "Not one thing?"

I wasn't used to him speaking slowly. It sounded like he was drunk to me, or sick.

"You know, working," I said.

"What do you do for work?"

"I deliver Porta Pottis."

"Ah," he said. "That must be fantastic."

"It's fine."

He nodded and scratched at his pinched eye. The skin pulled back like rubber. I looked away.

"What else you been doing?" he said.

"Nothing. Hanging out."

"Where?"

"I don't know," I said. "Nowhere. With Chick and Duke."

Gary leaned forward.

"Oh, yeah?" he said.

"Yeah."

"So, you fuck Chick?" he said.

"Yeah, I did. So what?"

He smiled wide and shook his head at me.

"What?" I said again, getting louder.

"Nothing," he said, still smiling, frozen. "He comes here every few months, Chick," he said. "Duke doesn't." Gary raised his eyebrows. "He doesn't want to see me."

I shrugged.

"Like you and Helen, right?" he said. "She doesn't want to see you either, I bet."

I started chewing my pinky nail.

"She hasn't called me up," I said. "But I didn't call her up either."

"She didn't come to see you when you were up at Staley, though, right?" he said, as if we were ten years old, like he was shoving the rule book in my face. Right?

I didn't answer him.

"What about Sikes?" he asked. "Where's he at?"

I tugged on a sliver of skin with my teeth, and it started to split away from the nail, and it stung.

"Why are you so goddamn nervous?" Gary said.

I took my finger out of my mouth and said, "Prisons make me nervous for some reason, Gare."

"Right, well," he said, sighing, leaning back in his chair. "They make me feel great, so I can't say I know what you mean."

"Hey, you asked me," I said slowly.

"I know," he said. "I know."

I started scratching at the end of the counter, along the chipped bits, and we were quiet. I couldn't even hear him breathing. The woman next to me whispered to her boyfriend, "Fuck my hole, baby." I looked back up at Gary, and he wiggled his fingers in a wave at me; his mouth started to twitch.

"Quit it," I said.

He shook his head and smiled.

"Breathe," I said.

He tapped his fingers on his chest, counting. A vein in his neck pulsed out.

"Fuck off, Gary," I said, and I hung the phone up hard.

He exhaled and closed his eyes. Scratched his head and pointed at my phone. I picked it back up.

"Here's the thing about them, though," he said.

"Who?"

"Duke and Helen—they think they're better than us."

"That's crap," I said.

"It's not crap. It's completely true. Ask Duke—he'll say he's got other problems, but it's actually just because he's a better guy than me."

"That's stupid."

Gary laughed again. He was talking faster now, and it sounded familiar, like he'd practiced what he was going to say to me a hundred times.

"It's true," he said. "Why do you think Helen didn't call you when you got out?"

"I don't know."

"Yeah, you do. Don't be dumb on purpose. She doesn't think you're worth her time. You're not as good as she is."

I shook my head. "That's not right, Gary."

"Oh yeah?" he said, and then he got up close to the glass between us, the tip of his nose almost pressing against it. "Why doesn't Helen call you, Mel?"

"I don't know," I said slowly. "We drifted apart—it happens."

"It happens. Yeah, I guess it does." He leaned back in his chair again. "It was some coincidence though, right?"

"What?" I said.

"That you drifted apart around the same time you got convicted."

I leaned away from the glass quickly, and he stared at me and moved his tongue around the corners of his mouth. It was short and square and looked like an eraser.

"Do you want me to leave?" I said.

"No. Do *you* want you to leave?"

"I think I do."

He smiled, crooked teeth and red gums.

"That's why you didn't come to see me either, right?" he said, leaning forward again.

He hunched his shoulders up far, almost to his ears. It reminded me how he could sleep in any position, sitting straight up on a bus, a train, in the back seat of a car, on a park bench. He was flexible, could fold up his arms and legs like he was a paper fan. He could suck in his stomach so it caved in past his ribs, made him look like a starving person.

"I'm so very below you," he said. "And you're squeaky clean now, right?" Then he laughed. "You turn into a Catholic?"

I stared at the counter, and my breath got short. I tasted tin in the back of my throat.

Gary tapped the glass, and I looked up, and his face was huge, everything about him—eyes, mouth.

"It's like you weren't even there," he said.

I felt the worm again, inching up from my stomach, wriggling around in my mouth, thick as a garden hose.

Gary put his hand on the glass and pressed his palm on it so it looked yellow and soft. I put my hand up against his and didn't think about it. The glass was warm. I felt tired and calm.

I looked at his eyes, green like mine, thought about his sugary-smelling breath, red face, zip-up sweatshirt, riding our bikes around. He left me in the dust every time, skidding sharp around corners, marking up the curbs with the diamond prints of his tires. They were black and fat; if you touched them with your hand, they'd smear like charcoal. I could tell by looking at them where he'd been, follow where he'd gone to.

He stared back at me with his one screwy eye, and then he looked sleepy, too. The woman next to me was saying, "Fuck my pretty little asshole, baby."

"Look at that," Gary said quietly and nodded to our hands. "They're the same size."

I took mine down and put it in my lap.

"They're not the same size," I said. "You have longer fingers."

CROOKED

"No, I don't," he said, and he kept his palm on the glass. "Put yours back up. They're exactly the same."

"No, they're not," I said, louder.

"They are, they completely are," he said. Then he shrugged and pulled his hand away. "You know it's true."

He gave me a smart-ass smile, like when he used to hold me down and give me Indian sunburns, twisting the skin on my arm tight, saying, You're so dumb, you know it's true, dumb girl.

"Hey, Gary," I said. "Fuck you."

He kept smiling and said, "Go home, Mel."

Then he hung up and waved his hand, calling the guard over like he was a waiter. The guard came, and Gary didn't look at me, and he stood up and left, and I sat there, still, with the phone in my hand. The woman next to me whispered, "That's right, baby; that's right."

I had to work the next day; apparently the day after Thanksgiving didn't come as a ready-made paid holiday. Angie was taking the day off unpaid, so Joe matched me up with Tommy John again.

I got there earlier than usual and headed for the staff room, past the pay phone I'd ripped up. PacBell hadn't come to replace it yet, and the wires still stuck out of the hole next to the keypad.

I clocked in and tried the door to the staff room, but it was locked, lights off, empty inside. I looked around and didn't see anyone, and then Joe came out of the office, chewing at his mustache. He did that when he was thinking hard.

"Hey, Joe, can I get in here?" I said, tapping the door.

"Oh—yeah."

He took out his ring of keys and let me in. I turned on the lights, and they flickered and started humming.

"Booth?" he said to me.

"Yeah?"

He stood at the door still, propping it open, had one hand on his hip.

"You remember Marjorie Welch?" he said.

I turned away from him and pulled out the box of coffee filters, flipped my thumb through them like they were playing cards.

"Yeah?" I said.

"You see any birds at her house?" he said, sounding distracted.

My hands tensed up around the handle of the keg.

"Any what?" I said, turning my head just the slightest bit.

"Birds," he said, louder.

I flipped the button on the coffee machine and watched it go orange, and I turned around to face Joe. He looked at me, confused, like he'd forgotten what we were talking about.

"What kind of birds, exactly?" I asked.

Joe shrugged.

"You mean, like, turkeys?" I said. "For Thanksgiving?"

"No, Booth, not turkeys," he said, getting annoyed.

"Can't say I saw any birds," I said, scratching my chin. Really think about it hard, Green, I said to myself. "Why?"

Joe rubbed his eyes. "Marjorie Welch is missing a bird. She left a message."

I nodded, pursed my lips, pretended to think.

"Maybe it flew away," I said.

Joe seemed to be in a trance for a second, staring past me.

"Oh, no, wait, I *do* remember some birds," I said.

Joe perked up.

"Yeah, I took one out of the cage, and it tried to bite me, so I snapped its little neck," I said in one breath.

Joe looked at me.

CROOKED

"Then I threw it in one of the johns," I said.

Joe kept staring at me and then shook his head quickly. He rolled his eyes and made his mustache accordion up.

"Yeah, all right, Booth, that's hilarious; thanks for nothing," he said. "Tommy John's got the assignments," he said, closing the door. "Don't take your time today, either."

"Sure thing, boss," I said after he left.

Tommy John came in soon after, wearing a T-shirt and jeans that were a little bit too tight.

"Good morning, Miss Staley," he said. He came up close to me and leaned over my shoulder. "Coffee done?"

"Nope."

He sat down at the table and stretched his arms above his head, yawned loudly. I stared at his hands, dry skin between his fingers.

"What'd you do for Thanksgiving?" he said.

"Nothing," I said, sitting next to him. "My mother had to work."

He pretended to be shocked, put his hand over his mouth. I ignored him.

"What about you?" I asked.

"Saw some friends."

I nodded.

"Hey, where are we going today?" I said.

"Just picking up," he said. "Two and two."

"Uh-huh," I said, laughing.

"What?"

"Joe made it sound like a lot," I said.

"Yeah, I bet he did," Tommy John said.

He stood up and went over to the coffee stand and pulled out two wax cups.

"What do you take?" he asked.

I didn't know what to say at first. Tommy John had never poured me coffee before.

"Lots of cream, little bit of sugar."

He pinched the sugar packet at the top and shook it out, dumped in two spoons of the creamer. I liked watching his big fingers handling the tiny packet, thin plastic spoon, liked seeing his hand wrap around the small cup. He passed it to me.

"Thanks," I said.

He put three sugars in his cup and leaned against the stand.

"We using Angie's truck?" I said.

"Yeah, it runs better," he said. He stared into his cup for a minute and smiled, said to me, "What do you think Joe did for Thanksgiving?"

"I don't know, got a hooker, maybe."

He smiled at me now, and I did back at him, and then he turned it dirty, his brow got heavy, and he rubbed his teeth a little with his tongue. I looked away and drank my coffee, smiled down into my cup so he wouldn't see.

In the truck, Tommy John turned on some Motown station and sang along to "Papa Was a Rolling Stone."

"Who sings this?" I said.

"Temptations."

"Nah," I said. "Isn't this from the seventies? Isn't it Sly and the Family Stone or something?"

Tommy John laughed.

"No way," he said, like I was crazy. "It's the Temptations."

"It doesn't sound like the Temptations."

"Okay, Staley, you wanna bet?" he said. "You wanna bet it's not the Temptations?"

"Sure. What do you want to bet?" I said.

As soon as I said it, my chest got tight and hot, and I couldn't get my eyes off his hands locked on the wheel, couldn't stop looking at his fingers, at the lines the bones made on the tops of his hands, like tree branches split thick.

"A beer," I said.

He laughed and said, "Whatever you say."

The song was almost over, starting to fade out. I stared out the window and thought of my Daddy for a minute. Papa was a rolling stone. Me and Gary didn't remember him too much, seeing we were only about three when he took off. The only thing that was really clear in my head about him was the tattoo of a snake on his forearm. He would flex it, make it wiggle. I couldn't even picture his face except for a couple of photos my mother had lying around, when he was young and handsome and looked like Elvis, and she was slim and pretty and had a body like a Barbie doll.

Then the song ended, and Tommy John and I both listened, hunched forward, but it led right into another, and we leaned back.

"Shit," I said.

"Just hold tight, Staley," he said, grinning. "Don't you worry."

"I'm not worried," I said. "I don't have anything to be worried about."

I rolled down the window and started smoking, and I suddenly felt pretty giddy.

"Can I have one?" Tommy John said.

I pulled a cigarette out and handed it to him. He lit it; I watched his cheeks, the shape his mouth made when he inhaled— tight little diamond—watched the smoke come out of his lips.

The song finally ended, and we eyed each other, listening hard. The voice on the radio said, That was Marvin Gaye with "Trouble

Man," and before that we had "Papa Was a Rolling Stone" by the Temptations.

"Fuck," I shouted.

"Aha!" Tommy John laughed, pointed at me with two fingers around the smoke. "Pay up, Staley."

"You fucking cheated me, man," I said.

"That was a goddamn sucker bet, Staley, and you fuckin' danced right into it—you owe me a goddamn beer."

"Fine."

I was laughing, too, harder than I even realized because soon my throat hurt, and it felt raw and chapped, and I told Tommy John to pull over at the next store.

"Before the job?" he said, glancing at me.

"Yeah," I said. "How long's the pickup going to take, anyway?"

"Couple hours."

"Well what the hell else are we supposed to do all day?" I said.

He laughed and said, "I sure like the way you think, Staley."

We peeled off the freeway and found a Safeway. Tommy John pulled in and let me out in front, and I stared at the Safeway-brand soda machines and wondered why they couldn't just put beer in vending machines.

The store was cold and filled with old people. I walked to the back, to the liquor section where nobody else was and took my time in the aisle. Seeing the liquor bottles calmed me down. All that dark brown and yellow, green and blue glass looking so clean, stacked right up to the ceiling almost. There was something beautiful about it, so many bottles, so many different kinds, unlimited options.

Beer wasn't as nice-looking or colorful, but it did the trick. Some of the labels on the microbrews were pretty detailed, had

CROOKED

flowers on them, or animals, but I couldn't stand the taste of them. Below the micros were bottled Coronas and Heinekens, which I liked but were a little rich for my blood.

Then I saw the six-packs of cans with aluminum so thin you could puncture the side with your thumbnail and didn't hardly have to push. Meister Brau, Schlitz. I grabbed a six of Old Milwaukee, on sale for $4.99.

When I got back outside, the sun was out bright. I watched Tommy John as I walked to the truck, watched his head move along to the song, eyes closed, his lips moving.

"What you get? A six?" he said as I got in the cab.

I nodded and pulled it out of the bag, and the plastic rings dug into my fingers.

"Let's pull over somewhere," I said. "Not here."

Tommy John smiled.

"Shit, I never knew you were this much fun," he said. "Some girls you can kind of tell with, but Staley," he said, spacey, like he was talking to himself, "Staley's a mystery."

Tommy John drove to the lot behind the Safeway, where there weren't any cars, just a couple of orange Dumpsters at the border, concrete dividers, and then woods. Not real woods, but trees and grass and a patch of bushes. You'd almost think, sitting there in front of the trees, that you were camping somewhere up north until you listened for a second and heard the cars driving on the freeway that curled around the other side.

I handed Tommy John a beer, and he held it up for a toast.

"To Staley being a loser," he said, cheery.

"I'm not fucking toasting to that."

"Suit yourself," he said, and he lifted the can up anyway in a little salute.

I looked in the side mirror and didn't see anyone, not a soul in the back lot. The sun was hitting the hood of the truck, and it bounced into my eyes, and I blinked hard.

"Where is everyone, you think?" I said.

"On vacation somewhere," Tommy John said, slurping up foam from the top of the can.

The beer was cold and tinny and tasted like sparkling water to me. Tommy John kept the radio on, and I tapped my fingers on my knee. I looked at his legs, saw that he had a hole in the side of his jeans, a rip at the seam. I could see a square of his pale skin.

"Hey, can I ask you something?" I said.

"Sure," he said, and a little bit of beer spilled on his lip. He touched it with his tongue.

"What'd you do to get into Folsom?" I asked.

He smiled and looked down in his beer.

"Didn't Angie already tell you?"

"He just said it was for assault," I said. "I don't know any of the details."

He sighed.

"Okay, Staley," he said. "Not like it's any big secret." He took a long sip and set the beer down, then put both hands on the dashboard and stared straight ahead, like he was trying to move the car with ESP.

"There were these kids I grew up with—" he started.

"What were their names?" I said.

"Why do you want to know that?"

I shrugged. "I like to get a mental picture of things."

He smiled a half-smile, only in one corner of his mouth. It just about drove me crazy.

"Mick and Pat," he said. "And Mickey had this girlfriend, and she wasn't too smart, not that bright, and a little bit ugly, to tell you God's truth," he said, and he glanced at me. "Nice anyway, nice enough, but she wasn't so smart. I thought she was a little, you know, touched," he said, tapping his head. "Maybe born that way, but Mickey liked her because she was . . ." He coughed, and his voice got lower. "She was a little easy—she was hungry for it, always hanging all over Mickey and crying if he didn't call her and crap like that."

He stopped. I thought he saw something in the trees ahead, but there was nothing.

"Lots of girls were like that, where I'm from, but it was worse with this chick because she was kind of dumb. And the other thing is that Mickey was always an asshole mostly, but I don't know, when you grow up with guys, you can't always tell they're assholes. 'Cause they're your boys, you know?" he said, turning to me. "You know what I mean, Staley?"

"Oh," I said, not realizing I was supposed to answer him. "Yeah."

"And there's this one time, at Pat's little sister's birthday party, she was turning eighteen, I think, and we were all in the backyard, all of us drinking since noon, smoking weed, shooting hoops, fucking around, and Mickey decides to break it off with this girl right there.

"And the sad thing was that this girl was already on the outs with all the other girls because they all thought she wasn't too bright," he said, and then he laughed. "Like they're fuckin' brain surgeons, you know what I'm saying."

He stopped again.

"Hey, where was I?" he said suddenly.

"Mickey decides to break it off."

"Right. Mickey decides to break it off. It wasn't even dark yet, but everyone's fuckin' wasted, man, I mean, nobody knows what fuckin' day of the week it is, and there was this, shit, what're those things called—those, like, animals filled with candy?"

"Piñatas."

"Yeah, there was a piñata, and people were taking swings at it, but no one could knock it down because everyone was so fuckin' drunk, so they just ripped the shit down and tore it open." He laughed again. "It was full of those nasty butterscotch candies, too. Tasted like goddamn *piss.*"

I started laughing, too.

"And Mickey gets in a fight with this girl, and tells her to get the fuck out and calls her a dumb bitch, and some people laugh, and some people just ignore the whole thing, just keep crawling around on the ground looking for candy, like fuckin' babies, and I don't know, man, I just lose it. I just fuckin' lose it."

He paused.

"What happened?" I said.

"I don't remember it all that well, but from what I gather, I pick up the baseball bat they were hitting the piñata with, and I go up to Mickey—he's turned away from me, and I crack him over the head with it."

He stopped for a second.

"And then he goes down, and I hit him again on the back, and Patty tries to stop me, tries to, you know, pull me away, so I swing at him, too, and get him in the stomach, break a couple of ribs, I guess. And then everyone's on me. Every guy who's there, every guy I grew up with—kicking the shit out of me, staring at me like I'm a circus freak."

We were quiet.

Then I said, "So Mickey didn't die?"

"Nah, but I fucked him up good, I guess, and now he can't see so good out of one eye, but he's fine," Tommy John said. "From what I hear."

He picked up his beer and started drinking it again. I looked ahead, the leaves on the trees blowing around.

"What was the girl's name?" I asked.

"What girl?"

"The girl, Mickey's girlfriend."

"Oh, the girl," he muttered. He closed his eyes. "Shit, I don't know. What the fuck was it—Katie, Kelly, Kally? Is Kally a name? Do people name their little girls Kally?"

"I really don't know," I said.

"I don't know her name," he said. "I forget."

He looked peaceful then and closed his eyes. I looked at his arms and reached out, touched the Jesus tattoo on his shoulder. He opened his eyes and turned to me, and his eyes were real big. He looked at my hand on his skin, didn't flinch, didn't move.

"What're you doing, Staley?" he asked, calmly.

"Is it a problem for you?"

He shook his head slowly. "No."

I glanced out at the trees and looked in the side mirror again, and then I stood up as much as I could in my seat, and put my hand on his shoulder, tight. He looked surprised but didn't stop me, didn't say anything, smiled and leaned back so I could swing my leg around and straddle him. I planted my knees on either side of him, put my arms around his neck. He put his hands on my thighs; they were warm.

"Hey," I said to him.

He nodded.

"This is all you get," I said.

"Don't worry, Staley," he said. "This is all I want."

The bottom of the wheel dug into my back, but I leaned down anyway, held his face to kiss him rough while I undid his belt. He pulled me tight to him, so tight I could barely breathe, hands on my hips, under my shirt.

I chewed on his upper lip the whole time.

CHAPTER

15

I woke up standing in the middle of the parking lot wearing only a black T-shirt and underwear. The T-shirt was from a bar my mother used to work at called Sunny Springs; the words were in cracked white letters across my breasts.

I was staring up at the sky when I came to, heart beating fast as a rabbit, feet were freezing. I stared at my hands and then looked around and saw all the cars, saw my mother's, the only light coming from the little cones above the ground-floor-apartment doors.

I rubbed my hands on my arms, shoulders; I'd obviously been out there for a few minutes. I went to my mother's apartment, watching the ground, dodging tiny piles of green glass.

The front door was open, just a crack, and it was dark inside. I pushed it and went in, shut the door behind me and locked it. There was a breeze in the living room; I couldn't tell from where. It felt like a wind tunnel. Then I saw the sliding door was open, so I walked over on my toes, quickly, and sealed it shut, turned the lock.

The tops of my thighs were sore, and it made me wonder how long I'd been standing out there. I was shaking, not cold really, still breathing hard. I looked at my blankets on the floor and didn't know what to do, didn't feel tired enough to sleep.

I decided to wash my hands. They felt sweaty and greasy to me, so I went to the bathroom and turned on the hot water in the sink, blasted it on my hands until I couldn't feel them. I bent over and lifted one of my feet and inspected the bottom. It was black.

I turned on the shower and took my clothes off and got in. I sat on the floor, felt the warm porcelain on my legs, my ass. Took a washcloth and rubbed it on the bottoms of my feet in tiny circles. The dirt peeled off and spun down the drain. I touched the little scar on the ball of my foot from the glass I stepped in.

I thought about how long I'd been sleepwalking in the parking lot and the bushy area out back, tracking dirt in, most of the time locking the doors but sometimes not, dragging my feet and stepping in glass, standing or walking or running so much my legs hurt the next day. And I had no memory of any of it. It was like something I was reading about in the paper.

I thought I had a fever when I came home from work the next day. I wasn't wearing heavy clothes, and it wasn't hot out, but I felt right about to faint the whole day. I took off all my clothes except my bra and underwear and lied down on the couch and drank a glass of water and smoked. I didn't feel like watching TV, didn't feel like moving.

I closed my eyes and tried to rest, and I almost fell asleep a couple times, but then my head would start to sink to the side or my arm would slide off the couch, and I'd jerk back awake and be shaking like crazy.

I was smoking the Marlboros I'd bought for Gary, and they tasted thick, and I stared at the picture of us as kids I'd brought in from my mother's room. I thought about our hands pressed against the glass.

Then the phone rang, and it was Duke.

"Hey, Mel," he said. "Where you been?"

"It's been like a week, Duke," I said, dizzy from standing. "You my mother?"

"Did you get my message?"

I remembered it vaguely, Duke's fuzzy voice on the machine, saying to call—he had to ask me something.

"Oh, yeah," I said, and I sat down in the Hawaii chair.

I pulled the phone cord over, and it wouldn't budge so I leaned over the arm, the phone on the floor, and the cord went taut.

"I don't know where Chick is," he said. I could hear him blowing out smoke.

I laughed.

"You know what, Duke, what else is new?" I said.

"No, I know, I know," he said. "Colin says he hasn't been home in four days. No calls, nothing."

"Well, I sure as shit haven't heard from him," I said.

My head felt like it was filling up with fluid.

"No, I know, I figured as much," he said. "I just thought, me and you could try to track him down, make sure he ain't dead."

I tried to sit up straight in the chair but the phone cord strained; I bent my neck down like I was a giraffe, trying to give it some slack.

"Duke, are you really worried?" He was quiet. "It's just that I'm sick, and shit," I said.

"Yeah, you don't sound too good," he said. Then he sighed. "It's cool, Mel, I'm getting all paranoid. I think it's the *drugs.*"

I laughed, and he did, too. I stared down at my stomach and pressed it. It had gotten a little rounder in the time I'd been back. My arms had stayed pretty toned up from lifting the units at work, but I hadn't done anything for my stomach. I had a little paunch now, and it looked healthy to me, like a little loaf of bread.

"Where are you? You over there?" I asked.

"Yeah, me and Colin are smoking a bowl," he said, and I rolled my eyes. "Can you get your mom's car?"

"I don't know—she's not home yet," I said.

Then I got quiet for a second and looked out the sliding doors, sky getting dark. I stared at the picture of me and Gary. It was on the coffee table. Me and him squinting into the sun. I tried to remember what it was like, the backyard in Tacoma, the picnic table, the kitchen. All the kitchens smelled the same in our neighborhood, like the produce drawer in the refrigerator. I almost got myself emotional but didn't, mostly because I couldn't remember ever feeling like the age I was in the picture. I couldn't even imagine what it felt like to be a kid like that.

Then I thought how I couldn't ever imagine my mother as a kid living with Nana either. Couldn't see her as a young thing meeting Daddy, how she must've been so crazy about him, crazy in a way I hadn't even seen yet. Before she ever laid a hand on me and Gary.

Or before Chick and Gary were speed freaks, before me and Helen weren't virgins, before Jeannie ever beat the shit out of anyone, before everybody was drunk all the goddamn time. I knew that all happened, that there was something before. I remembered little bits of it but it felt like it was all on another planet where you can grow up pretty and stay clean and nice and not necessarily get fucked with.

Tears leaked out the sides of my eyes, but I didn't feel like I was crying. They just felt like cold drops.

Then I said, "No, forget it, I'll take the bus."

"You sure?"

"Yeah, I'm sure," I said. "Fuck it."

"Well, all right," he said, laughing. "All right."

"Give me an hour, hour and a half, something," I said.

"Yeah, see you then."

"Bye."

We hung up, and I went to the wardrobe and opened the top drawer. Took out Gary's Nacho Mama's T-shirt and pulled it over my head, and I could see the outline of my bra through it but didn't care; pants, socks, shoes, jacket.

I rested the back of my hand on my forehead, and it still felt warm to me but I couldn't tell if I had a fever. I didn't feel great, but I knew I wasn't dying. I kneeled down in front of the wardrobe and lifted up three pairs of underwear and took out Chick's gun and poked the nose of it into my jacket pocket. I tried to let go of the handle and let it rest there but it kept slipping.

I went to my mother's closet in her room and slid the door open, smelled baby powder and perfume. She had a hundred fake silk and satin blouses, shirts with shoulder pads, costume jewelry snapped on or animal stripes. At least ten pairs of Payless shoes, all the spikiest, pointiest heels you ever saw, even the summer sandals.

I looked through the jackets at the far right side, flipped past the fake fur coat Nana left her. There was a white pleather jacket with a thick buckle, a dark denim, finally a blue raincoat—long, deep pockets. I pulled it off the hanger and tried it on and sniffed the vinyl at the shoulder. I opened one of the Velcro pockets and put Chick's gun in gently, rested my hand on it.

I wrote a quick note to my mother on a napkin that said, "Out with Duke. Don't worry.—Mel," and then I picked up my house keys and my wallet, stood at the front door and took one last look around, then shut it hard and locked it, pulled the hood of the raincoat over my head and left.

I had my own place for a few months after high school. I'd saved a little bit of money from temping and working at Patsy's sandwich shop, and my mother even loaned me a couple hundred dollars for the security deposit because she wanted me and Gary out of her hair so bad. Fat chance about Gary, though; he was still sleeping on her couch most nights, or he crashed at Chick's place, or Duke's uncle's, or mine.

One night in October he came to my place without calling, rapped on my door in the same way every time—knock knock knock knock knock—five right in a row, fast and furious, like someone was on his tail.

I was doing dishes and thought I imagined it at first, zoning out, staring at the plastic slats in the window in front of me. Then he knocked again—one two three four five. I dried my hands and went to the door, looked out through the peephole and saw him all distorted in the round glass—big head and a body the size of a fly. He knew I was looking at him so he smiled fakely, and his teeth looked big as storm windows.

I opened the door, and he stepped in, wet from the rain, hair slicked down. He wore jeans that were falling off him and an old corduroy jacket with suede patches on the elbows. All his clothes draped off him because he was so thin. It was like he'd wrapped himself in sheets most of the time.

He ground his shoes hard into the rug, unbuttoned his jacket, and hung it on a doorknob.

"There's a mat outside. That's what it's there for," I said.

"Oh, right. Sorry," he said, and he shook his hair out like he was a dog. "I bought you a present," he said, and he handed me a small brown paper bag, wrinkled and damp, the top twisted closed.

I pulled out an egg roll wrapped in wax paper. I opened it up and took a bite; it tasted like salt and cabbage.

"Thanks," I said.

"Don't mention it."

He sat on the couch and stretched his legs, tapped the floor with his feet.

"You fucked up?" I said.

"No way, José," he said.

He always said no even though he always was, and I always knew it, but it was a little thing we had.

"Guess who died," he said, crossing his arms, hands under his pits.

"Who?" I said, my mouth full.

"Cal Trimmer."

I stopped chewing, and the food felt stuck in my mouth, too big to swallow. Gary took a deep breath and held it.

"You're kidding," I said.

He let his breath out and sighed loudly.

"Yeah," he said somberly. "Yeah, I am kidding."

Then he started laughing at me, first just a little chuckle but then quickly louder and louder until he was howling like a dog while I felt the egg roll solid in my throat like a bunch of mud. I ran to the bathroom and spit it into the toilet, coughed and retched but didn't vomit. Lettuce strands and tiny orange squares, oil rings floated on the surface. I walked back to the living room, and Gary was laughing quietly again, shoulders curled in forward, the way mine used to be. It was our, mine and Gary's, natural position to sit—with both feet planted on the floor, shoulders turned in, head slightly tilted. I'd made a little effort in high school to sit up straight like normal people, pin my shoulders back, but it made my chest ache, so I always sat a little hunched over, not as bad as Gary but not perfect.

I started to smoke, and Gary looked at me hopefully. I threw a cigarette at him, and it landed in his lap with a pat.

"Thanks," he said. "I'm out."

"You're always out."

"Yes, I know," he said. "But see, I'm only smoking when kind friends give me cigarettes. Then I'll just naturally cut back and save money."

"You'd cut back and save money if you quit," I said, scraping my nails on the plastic tablecloth. "And people wouldn't think you're an asshole."

"That's funny," he said, not laughing.

We were quiet and smoking, and I shut my eyes and heard Gary saying *Cal Trimmer* again in my head. I winced.

"That was a really shitty thing you did before," I said.

Gary squinted and looked to the dark patch on the rug where he'd wiped his feet. Then he looked at his shoes.

"That thing you *said*," I told him. "About Cal Trimmer."

"That? Come on, that's no big thing," he said. "You're too sensitive, girly."

I didn't answer him, just got up and went to the refrigerator and pulled out beers.

CROOKED

"Silver Bullet," Gary said.

I stood in front of the window above the sink for a second and watched the rain leak and slide across the slats, split in two at the ends.

Gary walked over and sat at the table, put out his smoke in the ashtray with a couple of quick stamps. He ran his hands over his hair and stared at the water on his palms. His fingers were shaking.

"All right, so Cal Trimmer didn't die," he said, making a fist.

His eyes looked huge just then, liquid dark green, greasy seaweed on a rock. But when he looked up at me, with his long baby lashes, I couldn't turn him down for anything. I could see how he got girls to do some of the shit he got them to do because he had this look like he was a very little kid who needed your help so bad, but at the same time he could look like a great big daddy, so sick and sexy it would just kill you.

He smiled at me and winked, leaned forward in his chair and said, "That bastard's alive and well, and I think me and you should take a chunk out of him."

Colin let me in at his and Chick's place, and the whole room smelled like weed.

"Hey, Mel, what's up?" he said quietly.

His eyes were thin and red, and his nose was still swollen, the bridge almost as wide as the bottom, still looked like a Vienna sausage.

"Hi," I said.

"Mel!" Duke shouted.

He was sitting next to the TV holding a bong, not looking worried about much of anything, and he waved hard in the air like I was a mile away.

There was a girl on the futon slumped over to the side, wearing a long green skirt that looked like a parachute. Her hair was shaved short in the back, and she was scratching her head very slowly.

"Oh, um, this is Shelene," Colin said.

"Hi," I said.

"Hey," she said.

"Sit down, Mel," said Colin. "You want a beer?"

"No."

Colin sat down on the futon next to the girl, and Duke leaned out of his chair and passed him the bong.

"Oh, you want a hit?" Colin said to me.

"No," I said again, and I gave Duke a dirty look.

Duke mouthed, "What?" to me. I shook my head.

"Colin, do you know where Chick's at?" I said.

He laughed.

"No, man. I don't know. I never know where that guy is."

He kept laughing, and I had to look away so I didn't hit him again. Stupid grin, little bean for a head I wanted to knock right off his body.

I turned to Duke and said, "Why am I here?"

Duke coughed and shrugged, and I stood up and headed for Chick's room.

The window was open, the room was cooler, the blinds blowing in a little. I went to the dresser and started looking at the scraps of paper.

Duke came in holding a can of Bud and shut the door behind him.

"Colin said we should call Victor," he said, yawning.

"Do you know Victor's phone number?"

"No."

CROOKED

"Do you know his last name?" I asked slowly.

He shrugged.

"Great, Duke."

He stood next to me and started picking up scraps of paper and matchbooks and cards and held them right in front of his face to read them. I felt about to lose it, like I was going to rip all the shit out of Duke's hands and tear it all to pieces. I leaned forward and stretched my arms out and swept all the little papers off the dresser, and they fell to the floor.

"Why'd you do that?" Duke said.

"Because there's nothing fucking here," I said, and I slapped the wood hard and it made my palm hot. "I've already been through all this shit."

Duke sipped his beer and stared at the dresser.

"I thought you'd at least know how to get in touch with Victor," I said, making little fists at my sides.

He shook his head, matter-of-fact.

"Nah, I thought he might show up. Sometimes he just shows up here when Chick's not here, sleeps in his bed."

I buried my face in my hands.

"I thought you knew *something,*" I said through my fingers. "I thought you knew some goddamn thing. Why the fuck am I here?"

"You know, just as, like, a place to start," he said, sniffling. "There's this kid he does work for sometimes—"

"What's his name?" I said, cutting him off.

"*Um,* More, I think."

"Is that his first name or his last name?"

"*Uh,*" said Duke.

"Goddammit!" I yelled.

I grabbed the Bud out of his hands and hurled it at the wall above Chick's bed in a wild pitch. It hit with a crunch and dropped to the pillow. Beer gushed on the sheets.

"You don't know SHIT, so why the fuck am I here?" I said to him.

Duke ran to the bed and picked up the can, licked beer off his hand.

"What the fuck's wrong with you?" he said.

He said it like I just kicked a puppy. I hit my head with my palm a couple of times and grabbed my hair by the roots. I took a breath and held it and counted to ten. Twenty.

Duke laughed.

"Whatever you say, Gary," he said.

I let the air out and stared at him.

"That's totally something Gary would do," he said, pointing at the wall. "That's totally his shit, Mel. Not yours, ever," he said quietly.

"Yeah, well, you don't know me all that well," I said.

"Right," he said, smirking. "You're out of your mind, you think that's yours."

"You don't know shit, Duke."

"Yeah, okay, I just know you, and I just know Gary."

I headed for the door, past him and said, "You don't know me at all, and you haven't seen Gary in three years at least."

I walked fast to the living room, Duke right behind me.

"Neither have you," he said.

"Actually, I have," I said.

In the living room, the girl was sitting on Colin's lap, and when me and Duke came in, he pushed her off and stood up quickly, and the girl squealed.

"When'd you go?" Duke said.

"Colin," I said. "Do you know Victor's last name?"

"Oh, you know, I totally know," he said, making a fist, hitting his chin lightly. "I totally do, it's on the tip of my tongue."

Duke put his hand on my shoulder and tugged me.

"When you see Gary, Mel?" he said.

I said, "I'm asking Colin a question right now, Duke. Gimme a minute."

Colin's eyes batted between me and Duke, and his cheeks started to flush red. I stepped closer to him.

"Come on, Colin," I said, soft as I could make my voice. "What letter does it start with?"

I heard Duke breathing behind me, felt his hands on my shoulders, and he turned me around quickly.

"When did you see Gary?" he said, in my face.

"Thanksgiving, Duke," I said loudly. "Jesus."

Colin took a step back, away from us.

"I thought you didn't want to see him, that's all," said Duke.

"He's my goddamn brother," I shouted. "I didn't realize I had to clear it with you."

"It's just that Gary Booth can talk a lot of trash when he wants to," Duke said, and then he pointed in my face, his long finger with grease on the end right about to touch my nose, and he said quietly, "I didn't think you were goddamn stupid enough to buy any of it."

I could feel the spit from his tongue on my lips.

"Gary Booth?" said Colin.

"Only about you," I said. "How you think you're so much goddamn better than me and him both, and I think I agree with him to tell you the truth."

Duke laughed.

"Mel, if you think that—" he said, and then he stopped for a second. "I don't know what the fuck to say to you."

"Wait, Gary Booth from Chick's high school, who killed that guy . . ." Colin said.

I turned around to face him, and his little head looked right about to explode.

"With his sister," I said.

"That's you?" Colin said weakly.

"Yeah, it's me. You got everything, now?" I said.

Colin shrugged, tried to play it off and not look stupid.

"Yeah, I mean, I knew. It never, like, registered," he said. Then he coughed.

"Hey," said the little girl on the couch. "Baby, don't let her scare you," she said, standing up.

"Shelene, like, don't," said Colin.

Shelene was trying to stand still, and her arms were waving in an uncontrolled way, flapping. She swayed around on her legs like they were stilts.

"You think you're something 'cause you did some time?" she said to me.

She was wearing a tank top and had acne on her chest. She laughed in my face and burped.

"You think that makes you a badass?" she said. "It don't. It just makes you white trash."

We were all quiet. Colin covered his mouth. I stared into this punk girl's face; she was younger than me, I thought, probably just out of high school, and it flashed in front of me for a second, her life, what music she listens to, what she does on the weekends, hangs out here with Colin probably. She looked so young to me, almost pretty, but her nose was turned too far up and her forehead was huge.

"Hey, Colin," I said. "Tell your girlfriend to relax."

"Shelene, come on," said Colin, pulling her arm.

She waved her arms again, trying to keep her balance but didn't and fell back on the futon.

"I'm sorry," he said. "She's fucked up."

"Do you know Victor's last name?" I said to him.

"I don't think so," he said. "Shit, you know, I'm such a wad, I totally used to know it."

"Do you know anyone who knows him? Him and Chick?"

Shelene stretched out on the futon and started twisting around like a slug.

"Yeah, a couple guys," Colin said.

"Do you know their numbers?" I said.

"Uh, yeah. I got them somewhere."

He stared at me blankly. I stepped up close to him and held his chin tight in my hand. The bones in his face felt skinny and right about to bend and snap like a straw basket.

"Why don't you go call them?" I whispered.

He looked like he was going to shit his pants, pale lips shaking. I took my hand away, and he backed up toward the kitchen.

"Right," he said. "I'm, like, on it."

Then he turned and ran into the kitchen, and I heard him pick up the phone. I sat on the couch next to Shelene, and she was passed out. I pushed her legs aside a little bit, and she flipped on her side and grunted.

Her bag was at my feet, and I opened it and found some cigarettes. Winstons. Normally wouldn't touch the stuff, but I didn't have any on me.

Duke sat on a chair, and I held the box open to him. He laughed.

"God helps those who help themselves," he said.

I nodded, and he picked up matches from the plastic table and twisted one around, lit it by flicking his thumb. Gary taught him how to do that.

I dropped the cigarettes back into her bag and started rooting around. There was a thin paperback book inside, *The Scarlet Letter.* I held it up to Duke.

"How the fuck old is this girl?" I said.

Duke laughed, and I leaned forward and smoked and rested my elbows on my knees. We heard Colin talking in the kitchen in a quiet voice. Me and Duke didn't say anything. Both of us watched the little girl next to me sleep. Her mouth was open, and she was barely breathing. Looked pretty dead to me.

Gary had asked me to get him a scratch pad and a pencil, but he wasn't really writing anything down, just tapping the pencil between two fingers, bouncing the eraser end off the table.

Soon he pulled out the ten-of-hearts card he kept in his wallet and lined up some of the yellow stuff from a small plastic bag, and combed the lines with a dollar bill and then rolled the bill up. He snorted one up and sounded congested. He leaned his head all the way back and sniffed, then came forward and did the other.

He flipped his hair back like it was a wet rag.

"You could say, 'Hey, you dropped something, mister,'" he said, scribbling "mister" on the pad.

He reached for the bag again.

"Hey," I said. "You're all done for now, right?"

Gary laughed.

"Oh, this isn't for me, Melly."

He pushed the card toward me, and it picked up crumbs and grease from my ratty tablecloth.

"I don't want that shit," I said.

He laughed again, and his bottom lip went wild. It looked like there was a bunch of little muscles, little crabs twitching underneath the skin.

"What, you have better plans for tonight? Drinking alone? Again?" he said. He pushed "again," too, knew it brought up how me and Sikes weren't on speaking terms and how I barely left my apartment anymore.

"I have to work tomorrow," I said.

"Yeah, I know what you mean," he said, scratching the pale hairs on his cheek. "Takes a lot of effort to make sandwiches," he said. "No, I mean it. Pre-cision job."

"At least I have a goddamn job."

"Right. Lucky you," he said. "Just enough lettuce shreds," he said, winking at me. "Equal parts mayo and mustard. That's important work, Mel."

He grinned and looked like a skeleton. Then he started laughing again, Adam's apple vibrating in his throat like he swallowed an eight ball.

"Hey, Gary," I said. "Shut the fuck up."

He laughed harder and leaned back, and his thin plaid shirt hiked above his belly button. He placed his hands flat on his stomach, and he was so skinny it made his fingers look broad, thick.

He kept laughing, and I went through the next day in my head. I knew I'd finish the six-pack of Coors Light in my refrigerator if me and Gary didn't finish it together, and then I'd go to sleep too late, maybe one or two, sleep restless, toss and turn, get up at four with a dry mouth and a headache, drink some water, take a Unisom and some Advil, pass out until nine when I'd wake up no matter what. Drink coffee and smoke until work at noon where I'd stand behind the cold glass case and look down at wet strips of turkey, roast beef, cheese. Fold it like ribbons on tough sourdough bread while it slipped around under the thin plastic gloves on my hands. Then I'd leave and stop at the supermarket for more beer and something for dinner, usually peanut butter and bread, or hot dogs, or a cup of yogurt and corn flakes, and I'd come back to my little room and eat in front of the TV, watch whatever was in front of me, hopefully *COPS* or a news magazine and drink beer until I was tired enough to sleep.

Gary's eyes were wet like a seal's. I put my finger on the ten-of-hearts card and pulled it closer, stared at the yellow lines—they looked like cornmeal.

I curled my shoulders in and let my head drop, brought my face down to the card and plugged one nostril, pressed my thumb against the dry skin there, always flaking off, and I took one line in, and it felt like it was burning a hole. I sniffed and thought I was going to sneeze, and I waved my hand in front of my face, trying not to, but it felt like my sinuses were going to bust open.

"Don't sneeze, Mel," Gary said. "You'll lose it."

He grabbed my hand and held it tight, stared at me.

"You don't have to sneeze," he said slowly, like he was trying to hypnotize me. "You don't have to sneeze."

My nose was hot, and there was a tickle at the back of my throat, but staring at Gary so earnest, gripping my hand with his cold fingers, made me not think about it. I took a deep breath.

"There you go," he said. "Come on, now, clean this shit up," he said, glancing at the card.

I coughed, and my eyes started to water, and then I leaned my head down and did the second much quicker. I sat up and closed my eyes, and felt the first line down the back of my throat—tasted like aspirin.

CROOKED

Gary picked up the card gently and set it on his palm. It wobbled back and forth.

"Lick," he said.

I held the edges of it like it was a wet Polaroid and licked it clean, tiny grains on the roof of my mouth.

My teeth hurt, and my lips hurt, and I didn't know why. I touched my chin, my mouth and realized I was smiling; my lips felt plastered on my face, the corners turned up. I could hear my heart.

Gary squeezed his beer can, making a dent in the side and then releasing it. We used to break pop cans open when we were kids, crush them with our feet, stomp on them, and then bend them back and forth until they broke tiny slits at the sides, and the last few drops would trickle out. You had to be careful; it was like shotgunning that way, sharp aluminum sticking out; you could cut the shit out of your lips.

Now Gary pressed the can lightly with his thumb. Click click click. In, out, in, out, right where the mountains were. Tap the Rockies. It sounded like finger snaps on a Spanish dancer. I started laughing.

It seemed to be all I could do, just laugh my ass off, feeling sweat stains spread under my arms. I wiped my face with the back of my hand, still laughing, eyes spilling over with tears while I squinted at Gary, grinning, blurry.

I squinted at Colin's scratchy writing on the corner of a magazine cover.

"Is this it?" Duke said, looking past me, out the window.

"382 Serrita," I said. I saw the numbers painted in white above the door. "382 Serrita," I said again. "Pacifica."

"Pathetica," Duke said. Then he laughed, and we got out.

The lawn of 382 Serrita didn't look very good; a lot of the grass was overgrown and yellow, and there was a weird little statue of a squirrel. It held a ceramic chest full of dirt.

Duke and I stepped onto the porch, and I could see a light on inside through the brown wood shutters.

Duke wiped his hands on his jeans.

"Is this his parents' house, or what?" he said.

"How the fuck should I know?" I said loudly.

"Shh, Mel."

"What did Colin say?" I whispered.

"He didn't say anything."

I pressed the doorbell with my thumb, and we waited. I saw a shadow, and heard someone right behind the door.

"Who're you?"

It sounded like an old woman, raspy voice, thick accent.

Duke and I stared at each other. He pulled the bandanna off his head.

"Hello, ma'am," he said, lowering his voice, trying to sound respectable. "Is Victor at home?"

We heard quiet rustling on the other side.

"No, Victor no home," she said.

I felt my headache come back, crushing temples. I flexed my fists.

"Do you know where he might be?" I said, sounding too loud and bossy.

Duke glared at me and shook his head.

"I, oh, I don't know," she said. Then she called out, "Jackie!"

We heard more footsteps, and another voice, younger voice, hushed Spanish. Something about the way they talked made the hair stand up on my skin. I crossed my arms, rubbed my hands over them.

CROOKED

Then the door opened, and there was a teenage girl wearing a big sweatshirt and faded jeans. Hoop earrings, brown lipstick and eye makeup, and her hair pulled back tight. She scratched her upper lip lightly with her thick painted nail. The old woman stood behind her, about five feet tall, her face all folds and wrinkles; her eyes looked tucked far behind the lids.

"Okay, Abuela, okay," the girl said, waving the old woman away.

The old woman sighed and threw her hand up, said something quickly in Spanish and walked off. The girl turned to us.

"You friends of Victor's?" she said.

I could see a cooking show on TV, with no sound, behind her head. I could see the pan from above, three pieces of chicken fitting together in the middle, breast tucked into leg into thigh.

"Yeah," Duke said. "We, *uh,* called, but nobody picked up."

The girl nodded and looked bored. Duke kept going when he realized she wasn't going to explain.

"We're actually looking for Chick Rodriguez," he said.

The girl's eyes widened. Her cheeks were full and brown.

"Oh, you know Chick?" she said.

"Yeah," said Duke.

"They're not here," she said, leaning against the door. "They're in the city, I think."

I let my chin drop to my chest and breathed heavy.

"Yeah? You know where at?" said Duke.

He sounded polite when he said it, like she was someone's mother in high school. She clucked her tongue on the roof of her mouth and shrugged.

"You know, like, Jason, right?" she said.

"I think so, yeah," said Duke.

"I think they're there, at his place."

"Where's that?" I said to her. "We need the address."

She looked me up and down, the way Jeannie used to right before she said, Don't you get in my face, Green.

"They forgot to take you along, right?" she said.

Duke tugged my elbow.

"Nah, we just need to talk to Chick for a second," he said.

He sounded quiet and smooth, and the girl's face softened.

"Any chance you know the address?" he said, smiling.

She smiled back and clacked her long nails on the doorframe.

"Maybe," she said. Then she crooked her finger to Duke and said, "You can come in for a minute."

Duke started in, and I began to follow him when the girl blocked my way. I was so close to her I could smell the spray in her hair and chocolate on her breath.

"You can wait here," she said, holding her hand up. So I could talk to it, I guessed.

I stepped back on the porch and said, "Sure," my jaw tight. I watched them walk through the living room. Duke looked huge next to her and made all the furniture look miniature—tiny tables and chairs, looked like it was built for elves. The girl said something to the old woman, and she and Duke disappeared down a hallway.

I stared at the back of the old woman's head while she watched the cooking show with no sound.

There were bugs in the air. I heard them—it sounded like they were right at my earlobes, and saw them out of the corners of my eyes. Mosquitoes, gnats—I didn't know, but it felt like there were about ten of them at once buzzing around my head. I swatted the air in front of me, and then I thought I felt one on my face, so I slapped the side of my head, loudly. I stared at my palm looking for bug insides but didn't see any.

CROOKED

Then I glanced up and saw that the old woman had turned around to look at me; she seemed confused, and I smiled and tried to act normal, like I belonged on her porch, slapping myself.

Duke and the girl came back soon, Duke with his hands deep in his pockets. He leaned over to the old woman and waved.

"*Adios,*" he said.

The old woman ignored him and kept staring at the TV, and Duke scratched at his ears like a cat and then walked outside and stood next to me. The girl stayed in the doorway.

"Thanks a lot, again," he said.

She nodded.

"Yeah, thanks," I said.

She gave me a quicker nod, more like a tic, and then she rubbed her chin with her shoulder and shut the door. I watched the light from inside thin out on the cement porch floor until it was gone.

Duke pulled at the corner of my raincoat, and I swatted him away.

"What's your problem?" he said.

"Just quit doing that," I said. "Makes me feel like I'm on a goddamn leash."

"Sorry."

We walked down the porch steps.

"We know where we're going?" I said.

"Back to the city," he said, sounding tired. "We can bail if you want, Mel. I'm kind of beat."

I stopped walking. Duke kept on.

"Hey, motherfucker," I said, and he turned slowly to face me. "You called me, you know?"

"Yeah, I know, I thought it's getting late and everything—"

"No," I said. "Fuck that. I'm not just going home and going to fucking sleep now," I said. My heart was starting up fast again, rattling around in my throat.

Duke slid his glasses down to the edge of his nose and rubbed his eyes.

"All right, okay," he said, his voice all nasal. "Jesus, okay, let's go."

He turned away from me and walked toward the car, and after a second I followed him. It was all quiet except for the mosquitoes, and a couple of crickets.

Me and Gary were in the car across the street from the building where Cal lived. It was a supposed to be a luxury type of building, but it looked more like a project—all cinder blocks, each apartment with a balcony and a row of iron bars to keep people from falling. We were sniffing up lines of Gary's stuff off the ten card sliding around on a tape case, and I thought about how much he'd had because he was so jumpy, more than usual. He kept making fists with his hands and stretching them out again.

"It could be another Cal Trimmer who lives here," I said.

"Nah, it's him," said Gary, sounding sure.

He started scratching and rubbing his lips and his chin, like he was putting on aftershave. It sounded like wood on wood.

"Would you quit it?" I said.

"What?"

"Touching your face like that."

He grabbed the wheel instead, and we sat there without speaking.

I couldn't feel my lips, kept combing my teeth over them. I looked down at my hands and thought they were someone else's. Someone else's shaking white hands, veins starting to pop out, skin getting dry and tight and old. I had to make a fist hard just so I could feel my knuckles stretch out, the nails in the palms.

"Maybe he's not coming home tonight," I said.

"He'll be home soon," Gary said, looking at his watch, "like ten, fifteen minutes."

I didn't ask how he knew. I looked over at him again, wide hands still on the wheel. I started thinking about how we sure used to kick the shit out of each other when we were kids. I had the scar on my forearm to prove it.

"That's him," Gary said, leaning forward.

A man wearing jeans and a tan jacket was getting out of his car in the parking lot across the street. He took something out of his trunk and was moving slowly, but I still couldn't see his face clearly at all.

"How can you tell?" I said, squinting.

"That's his car," said Gary.

Gary looked excited. He was making fists again, unconsciously, I thought. His mouth was slightly open, his huge eyes staring straight ahead, completely autopilot. I thought about how many times exactly Gary had been here before to watch Cal. Maybe he came here alone and sat and stared all night, sniffed that shit up his nose and smoked cigarettes down to the dirty wet filters, thinking about all the things he could do to him.

"Let's go," he said suddenly.

I followed him. I was still buzzing myself, my jaw aching from clenching it, nose running. As we got closer, I still couldn't make Cal's face out very well, but I saw that he was carrying a turntable under his arm. I could see the lid.

"Come on," Gary said.

We crossed the street, walked quickly. I was cold all of a sudden, sweat frozen on my face. The only thing I could hear was Gary's steps, and mine and a couple of crickets. Then Cal looked up, and I could see him.

It had only been three years since he slapped me into the garbage bags at my mother's apartment, but he looked a lot older. He'd shaved off his mustache, and his face was red. He was also less fit, belly hanging over his jeans, waddling a little. I thought how he really let himself go, didn't come out too well after all, and I thought especially clearly just then that my brother, Gary, hadn't come out of anything too well. Some people don't come out too well.

Then we were on him. I grabbed the turntable out of his hands, and he was so surprised he let it go pretty easy. I touched his hands, and they were cold and grainy like they'd been in sawdust. He looked old and confused, didn't scream or yell, looked at me like he didn't know me.

"Hey," Cal said, pointing at me. Like he recognized me.

Gary socked him in the gut, and he fell. He started coughing and closed his eyes hard, one shaky arm stretched across his stomach, the other barely holding his weight off the ground. Gary was too strong for him, now. I didn't much know what to do, just held the stereo, the cord unraveling like a snake, lid falling open.

Gary picked him up by the collar and hustled him into the vestibule, and I set the turntable on the ground and followed them in. Cal was back on the floor, still coughing, spit coming out of his mouth in a long string. Now Gary hit his nose, and Cal fell on his stomach and coughed blood.

"W-what are you—" he started to say.

Gary hunched down and pulled him up by the collar again, hit him once more, and this time he must have busted something in his lip because there was blood everywhere now in red dots on the

CROOKED

linoleum, on the glass door, on the silver-ridged mailboxes set deep in the wall.

"Please," Cal said.

I could hear the loose teeth in his mouth knocking together.

Gary looked fierce, white and sweating, his fists still tight, shaking. Humming like a car. He looked at me and nodded. Cal coughed and gasped and tried to say something else. I shook my head, and Gary bared his teeth and bit his lip.

"Come. On," Gary said quietly.

I shook my head again, and Gary looked like he did when we were kids, like a crazy dog, eyes bulging out of his head, lips and teeth so huge it looked like he could just chew the veins right out of your neck. I thought about twisting his arm back, trying to pin him, and how he'd flip me over on my stomach and knock my head on the ground. You can't beat me, Mel, he'd say. Then it all came over me—Indian sunburns and wadded spitballs shot out of rubber bands at my head, us sinking our teeth into each other, our mother burning the shit out of me and him both, Denny waving the gun around, and dead Evan Trambleau, every cocky redneck at the kitchen table with no shirt and no shoes, and Cal with his dick out.

I kicked him in the stomach, and it felt like flour. He kept coughing and let out a short gurgly scream, and then his arm buckled out from under him, and he fell on his stomach, chin hit the ground with a crack.

I felt water on my face, dripping into my eyes, sweat, something, and I reached my hands up and touched my cheeks lightly, realized I was crying, wasn't making any noise but crying still, pools down my face, all the skin tight and sore.

"Get the record player," Gary said, pointing outside.

I nodded and left the vestibule, and heard the glass door seal shut behind me. I was shaking bad and looked at the blood on my shoes and pants. I bent down to get the turntable and felt all the blood rush to the top of my head, and it made me dizzy. I held the turntable in one arm, and the cord unraveled again and I picked it back up and wound it tight around my hand.

I turned to see Gary on his knees, arm around Cal's neck, Cal's face red and puffy, bleeding. Gary moved behind him, on top of him, on Cal's back like they were wrestlers. Cal's eyes were pasted shut, and he didn't look like a person, his face twisted up like that, eyes sealed tight like a giant worm.

Then Gary swung his other arm around Cal's belly, like he was going to give him the Heimlich, and he dragged his fist fast across his stomach, and Cal's tongue pushed out of his mouth suddenly. It looked like a fat pink fish.

There was too much blood when Gary pulled his fist away. It seemed to come out of Cal's stomach in a sheet, the way smoke used to drip out of my mother's mouth when she did a French inhale. Gary let his grip go, and Cal slipped out of his hands and fell to the floor.

I didn't get it. Didn't know why there was so much blood until I looked up at Gary and he had blood all over him, blood soaking the cuffs of his coat and his hands from the wrist up, soaked through the knees of his jeans. Then I saw the pocketknife in his right hand, dripping blood, but also with something else spread on it, something gummy—muscle, fat, innards, looked like dried glue.

Gary folded the knife up and tucked it into his jacket pocket. His hair was in his face again, and he flipped it away from his forehead and looked down at Cal. Cal's fingers twitched.

Gary stepped over Cal and walked toward me, pushed open the

glass door, and the smell hit me—it was meat, steak. I covered my mouth and lost my balance, and blood slid out under the door, onto the sidewalk, under my boots.

Gary took my elbow, kept me up straight. I tried to speak.

"Gare, Gare," I said.

He got a gentle look on his face and ran his finger down my cheek; it was just about the most tender way he ever touched me. He smiled.

"Me and you got it good, Mel," he said.

I pointed at the body and couldn't talk, just pointed, and Gary wrapped his hand around mine and brought it to his mouth and kissed it.

"Let's go," he said.

He kept holding my hand, and I couldn't remember the last time he'd done that either, and he guided me across the street to the car. I heard nothing and saw nothing, just stared at the turntable under my arm, letting Gary lead me.

Duke and I kept circling, passing by the squat house in the Sunset where Victor's sister said to come. I looked out the window, fog rolling in low. Then I had an idea.

"Let me off in front," I said to Duke.

"No way, Mel," he said. "You're not going in there alone."

"Don't be an asshole. I'm not gonna get raped."

He got shy, me saying "rape." He hunched forward in his seat.

"I know you're not," he said. "It's just better if we both go in together, you know?"

"Why?" I said. "We're not picking a fight, right?"

"Yeah, I know."

"Then let me out," I said again. "Come on, Duke," I said gently.

I touched his arm, his forearm where his shirt was rolled up, below his elbow.

I ran my finger back and forth on his skin, and he looked at me sideways, nervous.

"Look where we are, man," I said. "Not exactly a high-crime area."

I said it soft and sweet like I was his girlfriend, and he turned the corner and slowed down.

"Go down Pacheco," I said, pointing behind us. "There'll be parking down there."

Duke nodded.

"You sure you're okay?" he said.

I reached up and touched his face, cupped his cheek in my hand. He looked down, embarrassed.

"I'm sure, Diamond Duke," I said.

He started to blush and shook his head out of my hand.

"I'll be right behind you," he said.

"Right."

I got out of the car and walked around to the driver's side, leaned down to the window. Duke smiled but still looked uncomfortable, big dumb flat face spread out like a pancake.

"What're you so worried about?" I said.

"I just worry about you, Mel."

I laughed.

"Yeah, those Booth kids," I said. I lowered my voice and wagged my finger at him and said, "Keep your eye on those Booth kids."

Duke laughed, and I stepped back and waved him off.

"Go park," I said.

He smiled and took off.

There was a strip of yellow grass next to the curb, and I could hear the blades crunch under my feet. I looked up at the house, and it was off-white stucco with dark blue trim and seemed to take up a lot of space on the block.

The front door was wooden with thick diamond-shaped glass panels down the center, and the wood was old and peeled and water damaged. The white arch above the doorway was dirty yellow, spider-webs in the corners.

I pressed the doorbell and heard it hollow inside. I heard a dog bark, and it got closer. I heard its paws clacking along the floor until it was right on the other side. It looked like a brown blob through the glass. It pushed its nose against the edge of the door and sniffed loudly.

I rang the bell again, and the dog barked again, and sniffed. I waited. No one came.

I knocked softly, and the dog growled loud, and it didn't sound like any kind of dog I ever heard, really low and fierce. I knocked once more quickly, just barely tapping, and the dog barked like crazy and hurled itself against the door, threw all its weight, and the glass rattled. I stepped back, thought the whole thing was going to break.

The dog was pacing, groaning in its throat, like it was gearing up to crash right through. So I ran at it, led with my shoulder like when I busted in on Colin in the bathroom, and I slammed against the door and shook the whole frame. The dog went nuts now, barked and barked, sounded like it was getting hoarse.

I rubbed my shoulder and started laughing a little bit because I didn't know what came over me.

Then I heard footsteps and saw a figure through the glass, heard some whispering.

"*Who* are you?" someone said.

"I'm a friend of Chick Rodriguez," I said. "He around? Him or Victor Bracero?"

There was more whispering. The dog was growling softly.

"Who are you?" the voice said again.

"I'm a friend of Chick's," I said to the door.

Nothing.

"Look, I just need to talk to Chick for a second, and I heard he was here," I said in one breath.

There was a pause, and then the door opened, and the first thing I saw was the dog. It had hardly any hair and a pointy snout, short stocky legs, and the skin on its tail was red and raw and chewed down. It barked and drooled at me, and the kid yanked it by a chain collar around its neck.

I stood back. The kid was around my age, limp green hair on his head and a black T-shirt, cutoff jean shorts, skinny. Another guy stood behind him, taller, bigger, square shoulders. He looked me over with his arms crossed.

"Who are you, again?" the big one said.

The dog tried to jump at me, and the kid with the green hair said, "Down, Zeke," but the dog got up on its hind legs and pawed the air.

"I'm a friend of Chick Rodriguez," I said, staring at the dog's black lips.

"You said that," the big one said.

"My name's Mel," I said, and the dog barked.

"Chick call you?"

"No," I said, and I had to shout a little over the dog barking. "Hey, any way you could get the goddamn dog out of my face?"

"You don't like dogs?"

"I don't like dogs who want to kill me," I said.

He smiled.

"Get him out of here," he said to the kid with the green hair.

"I'm trying, More," the kid said.

I could see thin muscles in his bony arms twitch while he tried to yank the dog away. The dog's tongue flopped out of his mouth, hung over the side like bologna.

"I'll do it," the big one said.

He grabbed the chain collar and yanked it away from the kid. The dog yelped, and the big one bent over and pointed in its face.

"Sit the fuck down," he said to it, like it was a person.

The dog sat and panted, and the big one turned back to me.

"How'd you know Chick was here?" he said.

I thought about Victor's sister and tiny little grandma. I shrugged.

"Lucky guess."

"Right," he said.

He stared at me.

"I'm More," he said. "That's Jason," he said, pointing to the kid.

"Hi," I said.

Jason smiled fakely and played with his bottom lip. More nodded toward the front door.

"You try to break my door in?" he said.

"Yeah," I said. "Sorry about that."

He nodded slowly.

"That's cool," he said. "Come on up."

He clicked his tongue and both Jason and the dog hopped to their feet and headed down a hallway. I followed them, past the living room where the TV was on but no one was watching it, up a staircase that creaked as we climbed. I stepped with just the tips of my toes, tried not to make noise.

I followed More past a room full of exercise equipment, all shiny metal, and then into a room with the blinds drawn shut and dim light on from a halogen lamp, a mattress on the floor and a ratty pillow, and I felt my heart in my throat for a second.

"Chick," More said. "You have a visitor."

I saw Chick sitting straight up in an easy chair, feet planted on the floor, hands gripping the arms, head back. He didn't respond.

Jason sat on the pillow on the floor and folded his legs up under him. More walked to Chick and snapped his fingers in his face.

"Chick, wake up," he said. Then he sat in a chair, opposite Chick, a few feet away and said, "Victor took off hours ago."

Chick lifted his head slowly and squinted at me, didn't seem to recognize me. Then he smiled. "Hey, Mel," he said. "How'd you get here?"

I squatted next to him and patted his hair. It was oily.

"Hey, Chicken," I said quietly.

His eyes were nuts, yellow, blank. Pupils shaking, hands hot and wet. I could smell the stench on him—three, four days without showering.

Then the doorbell rang, and the dog bolted out of the room, barking, and I heard its feet stomping down the stairs loud, and Chick's head jerked. More didn't move.

"Who's that?" he said to me.

"That's Duke," I said. "He's a friend."

"Is he the last one?"

"Yeah," I said. "Sorry."

More nodded.

"Get the door," he said to Jason.

"Man, I just sat down," Jason said.

CROOKED

"Get the door, faggot."

Jason stood up and dragged his feet out of the room. Chick's head sank back down, and his eyes closed again like a sleeping doll.

"How do you know him?" said More.

"We went to high school together," I said.

"Oh, yeah?" he said, like he didn't believe me.

"Yeah."

Chick's mouth was open, eyes twitching under the lids.

Then Duke was in the doorway, and the dog ran in, tongue and tail waving around; it sniffed Duke's knees and then ran to Chick and started growling.

More laughed.

"He doesn't like Mexicans," he said to me.

"Hey, man, I'm Duke," Duke said like an asshole, sticking his hand out to shake More's like we were at a keg party.

More looked at it for a second and then shook it.

"More," he said.

Duke looked around for a seat but there weren't any chairs available, so he leaned against the wall and tried to look casual.

Jason came in behind him with a carton of orange juice and almost tripped over his own feet.

"Shit," he said, dazed, staring at the floor like he'd dropped change.

"What can I do for you, Mel?" said More.

Duke glanced at me and looked confused.

"We came for Chick," I said. "We haven't seen him in a while."

More held his hand out to Chick, presenting him.

"He's fine," he said.

More held his hands in his lap and sat straight up. It looked like he was about to start laughing, nose started to flare, tiny smile started to spread across his face.

"Hey, so what kind of stuff do you guys have here?" Duke said.

More didn't move, didn't look at Duke, just kept staring at me.

"You get stuff from Chick?" More said.

"Yeah, sometimes," said Duke.

"He gets it from me," More said slowly. "I thought you knew that."

Duke scratched the back of his neck.

"Yeah, I figured," he said. "You know, I heard your name a lot."

"Oh yeah?" More said. "What do you hear?"

"No, I mean, I've heard Chick talk about you, coming to see you . . . stuff," he said, trailing off.

More nodded.

"You hear about me, too?" he said to me.

"A couple of times," I said.

Duke pulled out his wallet and opened it, started thumbing through. I thought, please, Duke, don't buy anything.

"What can I get for you?" More said.

"I don't know," said Duke, sniffing loudly. "How much you want for amps?"

I closed my eyes and tightened my fists, thought, No, Duke, let's just get Chick and go.

"Six each," said More.

Duke nodded, looked back in his wallet, mouthed numbers.

"Can I get four?" he said.

"That all you want?" said More. Then he looked back at me. "What about you?"

I shook my head.

CROOKED

"Come on, now," he said. "You came all the way here. Might as well get something."

"No thanks," I said. "I'm good."

"What about you, Diamond Duke?" More asked, and Duke looked surprised. "That's what people call you, right?"

Duke smiled and said, "Yeah, sometimes."

"You want anything else?"

I stared at Duke hard and tried to get him to look at me, see my hands shaking, see how I was holding my breath.

"I'd like to see what else you have," Duke said.

More smiled and said, "Jason, show Duke what we have in the kitchen."

Jason stood up and stretched. His shirt hiked up above his stomach, and he scratched near his belly button, and the sound of it made me feel sick; it sounded like he was scratching canvas.

"Come on," he said to Duke.

Duke followed him out. I heard them walking down the stairs, Duke's heavy steps.

"What do you have in the kitchen?" I asked More.

"Whatever you want," he said.

I looked back at Chick and shook his arm, and his head rolled up slowly like it was full of water, eyes opened halfway.

"Hey, Mel," he said. "What's going on?"

I held his face in my hands and tried to get him to look at me straight on, focus, but he couldn't, eyes kept rolling around.

"You ready to go?" I whispered.

He smiled again and almost looked about to answer, but then his eyes closed and his head dropped down, chin to his chest.

"He's not in any condition to leave," More said.

I didn't look up.

"What did he take?" I asked, staring at the carpet. It was brown.

"A little bit of everything," said More.

My feet and ankles were going numb from being on my haunches, and I pictured myself falling over, falling face down in the dirty brown carpet. I tried to smile and act normal, not scream and crack into a thousand pieces.

"But really, though," I said. "What's he on, anyway?"

"I told you," More said. "He's had a little bit of everything."

He stood up and walked over to me and Chick, and I stood up, too. Didn't want him to stand over me. My feet were asleep.

More stood in front of Chick and kicked him lightly on the shin.

"He's been here since Thursday," he said.

He shook his head at Chick like he was a homeless person asleep on his doorstep. Then he walked to the desk in the corner of the room and grabbed cigarettes off the top.

"Do you want a cigarette?" he asked.

I shook my head. I felt hot under the raincoat, sweat between my shoulder blades.

"You don't smoke?" he said.

"No," I said, and my mouth was dry. I felt for a second like I couldn't get any words out. "Yeah, no, I smoke, I just don't feel like it. Right now."

My voice sounded far away, but More didn't seem to be listening. He leaned against the desk and laughed.

"He's a fucking zombie," he said, pointing his cigarette at Chick.

I felt sweat dripping into my eyes, beading on my lashes. I opened and closed my fists to get the blood going so they wouldn't feel so heavy.

"Your boy, Chick, doesn't have a whole lot of self-control,"

CROOKED

More said, and then he threw a matchbook at Chick like a Frisbee. It hit him in the chest.

Chick flinched; his arms and legs curled up like when you turn a bug on its back and poke it with a twig. I lurched forward and put my hand on Chick's arm.

"Don't," I said quietly, and I tried to say it louder but couldn't; my throat was all clogged up.

More stared at Chick and shook his head.

"Not too smart," he said.

Sweat dripped down my temples, chin, and my breath was shorter, too, my chest tightening, felt like I was being flattened.

Then Duke and Jason came back in, and Duke looked stoned. The dog got to its feet and trotted to them, sniffed Duke's knees and growled.

"Hey, buddy," Duke said, leaning down to pet it.

The dog growled louder, and Duke pulled his hand back. More and Jason laughed.

"He doesn't like you," More said.

"Oh, yeah," said Duke. "I'm not too good with animals."

I kept my hand on Chick's arm and dug my nails in a little; he didn't wake up.

"You all set?" More said to Duke.

"Yeah, man, I'm good," said Duke.

More scratched at the tip of his nose and looked to me.

"Nice to meet you," he said.

"Back at you," Duke said, and then he started giggling.

Jason started giggling, too. Both of them looked like rodeo clowns, Duke weird and overgrown, almost bald, and Jason who didn't weigh much more than a hundred pounds, greasy green hair flopping around.

I looked at More's hands and thick wrists.

"Duke, go get the car, okay?" I said.

"Huh?" Duke said, still giggling. His face was red.

"Get the car."

"Yeah . . . right, cool," said Duke.

He looked around him, like he had brought something, looked down at the floor and then stood back up and waved.

"Thanks for the goods," he said to More.

"No problem, Diamond Duke," said More.

Duke snapped his fingers and pointed at me.

"I'll honk. Come tell me if you, like, need me to carry him," he said.

He looked at Chick and started laughing, and then he rubbed his eyes underneath his glasses.

"Later," he said, and he left.

The dog followed him to the landing of the stairs and barked. I heard the heavy front door open and slam. Felt like it almost shook the walls.

More stamped out his cigarette.

"Chick doesn't have to go," he said.

I stretched my neck out and tried to loosen it up.

"No, really," I said. "I think he's all cashed out."

"He is fucking *cashed*," said Jason, pointing at him, and he started laughing again.

"So what's the problem?" More said to me. "He's an adult."

I looked at Chick's face, small line of drool down the middle of his chin.

"He's all done," I said.

More rubbed his chin with his palm.

"Doesn't look all done to me," he said. "He's just resting."

CROOKED

"He's so cashed out," Jason said, still laughing.

"We are actually going to have to get going," I said, sounding cheery.

"Who are you, honey, his mother?" More said.

I looked down at the carpet. I could see tiny clumps of white fuzz.

"I think he's had enough," I said.

More held out his arms in front of him like he was a preacher.

"There's no problem here," he said.

I shook Chick's arm. He didn't wake up.

"Time to go," I said quietly.

More began walking toward me, slowly.

"You are one stubborn girl," he said.

"Stay where you are, please," I said quietly.

He came toward me, and my eyes fluttered closed for a second, and my hearing seemed to get very good just then. It was like I heard everything in the room at once: More's jeans brushing together, and Jason's feet on the carpet combing it the wrong way, the dog pacing on the landing above the stairs, and Chick's light baby breath. On the street, too, it was like I could hear cars, far away as 19th Avenue, doors opening and closing, pop cans getting crunched under people's feet, kids laughing and clapping, doorbells and phones ringing off the hook, rain and wind blowing so loud it felt like it would bust my eardrums clear through to my brain.

So I opened my eyes, and my hands were still.

CHAPTER

16

Jeannie was two years younger than me and had two kids by two different men. Both kids were living with her grandmother, because her mother was a crackhead. Jeannie'd had the first when she was sixteen, and we had a lot in common because I had an abortion when I was sixteen, so I told her I almost knew. She was a couple months' pregnant with the third when she got to Staley, but it died soon after.

She'd been running around with gangs since she was thirteen and was in for assault this time because she kicked the shit out of some girl who was messing around with her boyfriend, knocked all her teeth out, yanked her shoulder out of the socket, and gave her a concussion.

This once, though, we were in the yard, bad dry heat out as usual, and the skin on my face and neck was burning pink. We stood by the wall, smoking, leaning against the hot concrete, and then Jeannie turned around, away from me, face to the wall.

"Jean?"

CROOKED

She didn't move.

"What's up with you?"

She turned back to me, and she was crying. Her face was long and brown, with her hair clipped just below her ear, like mine.

"Fucking shit, Green," she whispered, like she was out of breath. "My babies," she said. "They think I'm shit."

I wanted to put my hands on her, rest them on her back, or hug her, but she wouldn't ever have any of that.

"When Silvana's born, she had both hands up," she said, showing me, "Like Superman. Like she's gonna fly right out." She closed her eyes and shook her head. "She's gonna think I'm shit."

"Nah, girl, she'll be so happy to see you—she's gonna love you crazy," I said.

She closed her eyes and pressed her face to the wall, mashed her lips against it and said, "She'll be a stupid little bitch if she does."

I stared out the window at the big green wreath and plastic gold bells stretched across Home Depot, at the lights hanging over the awning of the Rafael Inn. It was sunny.

We stopped at a light, and I looked at my mother in the rearview.

"She just finds every little thing I'm doing wrong, shit that doesn't mean shit," she said to Ken.

She pursed her mouth in the mirror and pulled her glasses to the edge of her nose, rubbed the pink lipstick bulb on her lips and then snapped the cap back on.

"Ignore her," said Ken. "That's what drives people like that crazy, if you ignore them."

My mother made a face.

"Kill her with kindness," Ken said.

Then he reached out and touched her chin, and she started to blush underneath all her foundation. I couldn't ever remember seeing her blush. Not once.

She saw me watching, and it made her embarrassed. I could tell, the way she straightened her glasses so she was sure her eyes were covered.

"Well well well, Miss Mel," she said to me. "What time you get home?"

"Around one, I think," I said, staring out the window. Blue sky. No clouds.

She sighed.

"I don't know how you can be out all night and not get any sleep and still function. I'd be a real wreck if I went in to work after a night out," she said. And then, under her breath: "A real Frankenstein monster."

I laughed, rolled my eyes up and held my palms on them, laughing, thinking of the way my mother said things sometimes. A real Frankenstein monster. It felt good to have a nice laugh like that, good in my stomach, right in the pit.

"You're a regular comedy act back there," she said.

I stared at both of them, at Ken's mustache, at the lines on his face where he stopped shaving his sideburns. Looked at my mother's thigh under her pink knit skirt, at a few of her fake curls stuck to the car seat cover.

She pulled up next to the side door at work and stopped.

"See you, Mel," said Ken.

"Yeah," I said. "Bye."

"Bye-bye," my mother said, sing-songy.

I got out and shut the door, and then turned to look at them again.

CROOKED

"Wait. Wait a second," I said, and I leaned down to Ken in the window.

"What is it?" my mother said.

"What's wrong?" said Ken.

Ken's lip was only a little swollen still. He had blue eyes, and the skin was wrinkled at the edges.

I reached for his hand and held it.

"Nothing," I said, and I shook his hand lightly, and I felt his warm red palm, smooth wet fingers wrap around mine like grape leaves.

My mother took her glasses off and stared at me. She held her hand to her chest, and it reminded me of Nana.

I let go of Ken's hand and hurried around to my mother's side.

"Mel, what is this?"

"Just shut up, Ma," I said to her.

I put my hands on her cheeks and angled her head up to me like I was her lover, and she looked confused and surprised and like I'd just bought something and tried to pay with Canadian money. I closed my eyes and held her warm face, and I leaned in and kissed her on the mouth and stayed there, smelling and tasting her lips, feeling her lipstick smear onto me, her foundation on my chin. She smelled like fresh sheets and pillow cases.

She smiled, and I pulled away and saw she was laughing at me.

"What's wrong with you, girl?" she said softly. "You still drunk?"

She was giggling, but her eyes were starting to fill up, made her eyeliner all gray. She put her glasses on quickly and wiped the corners of her mouth.

"Bye, Mama," I said.

"Bye-bye," she said, facing forward, brushing down her blouse like I spilled crumbs on her. "Don't go around kissing everybody, now," she said. "They'll think you're out of your goddamn head."

Then they took off, and I stretched my arm high as it would go and waved hard back and forth. I saw my mother's lanky arm hanging out the window, waving calmly like a bored beauty queen.

I went through the side door and saw Rick and Tommy John standing right inside and waved to them. Rick said, "Hey," but Tommy John didn't wave, just gave me this dirty-dog smile. I smelled his aftershave as I walked past. I punched in and went to the staff room, saw Tino and Angie at the table, and the coffee smelled so good I thought I might cry. I poured a cup and leaned against the stand.

"You don't want to sit with us, Booth?" said Angie, grinning.

"She doesn't like us anymore," Tino said.

"That's a hundred percent right," I said. "You're both a pain in the ass."

They laughed, and I laughed, and Angie yawned and pointed at me.

"Fight on Friday," he said. "You want to come?"

"I'll try," I said.

"Tino's coming."

"Then I'm definitely not coming," I said, and they busted up again.

"No way she's coming now," said Tino.

I turned to the vending machine and listened to them talk, half in English, half in Spanish, and the coffee tasted really good to me; I knew it was from the same brown powder it always was, but it was better than usual.

I looked at my reflection in the Plexiglas. No bags, and my cheeks looked full, a little chubby even. I looked like a doll baby. I felt really awake, and I could feel the coffee sloshing around in my stomach, and it was like I could feel it in my veins and in my head, too, getting to all the pink little muscles moving under my skin and all the hair budding out of my head, pushing the cool nails out the tips of my fingers.

"El sabueso," Tino said.

I turned around and saw them. Two blues, both women. It made me laugh, how they always send women to get women. Then I saw the detective, talking to Joe, standing by the phone I ripped up.

"Angie," I said, and he looked up. "Sorry I didn't get to see you fight."

He smiled but kept his brows pressed down, confused.

Then Joe pointed at me through the glass. I finished my coffee.

The cops opened the door, and the girls walked up to me. Their uniforms were clean and creased.

"Melody Booth?" said the detective. He wore a tie and a brown sport jacket and a blue button-down shirt.

"Yep."

One of the girls came around behind me, and I stared at the detective's mustache and face, down at his hands, his wedding ring. Thought about how many kids he had at home while the girl put cuffs on me. With the real thing, too, all metal, not the bullshit plastic rings they latched onto kids saving the whales.

The detective was on, "You have the right to an attorney," when Angie interrupted.

"What the fuck is this?" he said, and he crossed his arms and stood in front of us.

"Please step aside," the detective said, and the girls each took one of my forearms and started leading me out.

"Booth, who do I call?" Angie said, him and Tino behind us.

"My P.O.," I said. "Call my P.O."

The detective walked ahead of me, and the girls kept their hands loosely on my arms. Their fingers were cold. Joe stood next to the broken phone holding his clipboard to his chest, looking fairly surprised.

"Bye, Joe," I said.

He just stared. Rick and Tommy John, too. Then Tommy John smiled and ran his tongue over his teeth.

They got me outside, and it was bright and hot for a change, and I felt it on my cheeks and closed my eyes for a second, thought very quickly about whether it was Jason or Colin, figured they probably talked to both. All I could think about was how quiet it was after; only noise was that ugly dog licking the blood off More's chest, sounded like it was lapping up water.

One of the girls opened the door to the prowler, and the other cupped her hand on the back of my neck and guided me in. I slid on the leather seat and leaned back best I could, wrists clamped in the small of my back. I looked at everyone by the side door: Joe, Angie, Tino, Rick, Tommy John, Wanda, and the three kids Joe hired for grunt work. All of them in a line. I watched the red lights flashing and turning across their faces, with no sound.

Like this is the only one . . .

Floating
Robin Troy

The Perks of Being a Wallflower
Stephen Chbosky

The Fuck-up
Arthur Nersesian

Dreamworld
Jane Goldman

Fake Liar Cheat
Tod Goldberg

Pieces
edited by Stephen Chbosky

Dogrun
Arthur Nersesian

Brave New Girl
Louisa Luna

The Foreigner
Meg Castaldo

Tunnel Vision
Keith Lowe

Number Six Fumbles
Rachel Solar-Tuttle

More from the young, the hip,
and the up-and-coming.
Brought to you by MTV Books.

MUSIC TELEVISION®

POCKET
BOOKS

LOUISA LUNA

Louisa Luna grew up in San Francisco and now lives in New York City.
She is also the author of *Brave New Girl*.

Photo: T. Adebimpe

Made in the USA
Lexington, KY
17 February 2019